And So I Roam

A Novel

Kate Bothner

And So I Roam

ISBN 978-1-7782773-0-6 (paperback)
ISBN 978-1-7782773-1-3 (eBook)
First Canadian edition

Content Warning:

This novel contains themes and situations that some readers may find disturbing. Although the scenes are not graphic, they may be upsetting to some people. Please read with caution if you are triggered by reading about mental illness, attempted sexual assault, death of a parent, physical violence, or war flashbacks.

For Eric, my True North

For Chase and Cameron, the lights that guide me through even the darkest of nights

For my dad, who is an awful lot like Papa

For my mom, who is nothing at all like Mother

Table of Contents

Prologue

We left Philadelphia on the 8:40 train, the smell of smoke still heavy in my hair. I wished that I had thought to wash it at the hotel, but there hadn't been time. The smell would be a reminder of what we had lost, an unwelcome companion for the next ten days. I did not look back as the train pulled slowly away from the lights and bustle of the city. The window did not afford me a view of where I was going. Instead, I chose to look across the table at Papa, the landscape sliding steadily by in my periphery. The air in the cabin was full of anticipation, and devoid of the sadness that it should have held. Papa's brow was creased, his eyes tired. He wore a proper hat, a crisp navy suit, and a small smile that I knew was only for my benefit.

Papa had booked a drawing room car for our journey, the most opulent way to travel by train. I found myself wishing that he hadn't, that he had found a middle ground between the grand house that we were leaving, and the stark accommodations that we would soon call home. Our cabin felt too roomy with only two occupants where there should have been three. We sat mostly in silence until I retired to my bed, where the rhythmic clacking of the train on its rails soothed me as we rode north into the night.

Book One

Chapter One

1895

The circumstances surrounding our departure from Philadelphia had been set into motion at the dinner party we hosted on New Year's Eve. I can say with near certainty that ours was the only party in the city that included a proper lady's bared underarms, a $250.00 piece of fruit that was eaten by the hired help, and a string quartet that was paid handsomely to play to an empty room. Had I known the outcome of our party I may have weathered the three months leading up to it with more grace. As it was, I did not.

Mother had insisted that we both have new dresses made for the occasion, and no expense was spared to create gowns that Mother felt were befitting our station. It was made very clear to me that this dinner would be instrumental in securing me a husband, and that I was to be the epitome of grace and good breeding. I did not share Mother's enthusiasm for the dinner or the expected outcome, but I obliged her to avoid her wrath.

In attendance were to be the Willoughbys, the Cooks, and the guests of honor: the Stanleys and their son Conrad. I knew this last family well, as they had lived on our street until they had built a new house nearer to their factory a few years ago. Conrad had been a haughty boy that I hadn't much enjoyed being around. As a man he took after his father in appearance. He was quite tall, and handsome by any standards. He had jet black hair that never quite sat right despite the generous application of pomade. Conrad's teeth were straight and white but gave him a menacing look when he smiled. He walked with the same confident air as his father, afforded to him by means of wealth and social standing. He did not yet have his father's jowls and round belly, but they would surely come.

Conrad's character was wholly his mother's, whether inherited or taught, I wasn't certain. As a child he was needlessly cruel to insects and birds, laughing heartily at others' misfortunes. Adulthood had not changed his spiteful nature, only taught him more sophisticated ways with which to exert it. His mother, Perpetua Stanley, was shrewd and sanctimonious, her pinched features reminiscent of a rodent's. I had never heard her speak a kind word unless it was to elevate her family's standing. She was fundamentally unlikeable, and I sensed that she was not to be trusted.

Papa and Frank Stanley had met as neighbors, but had grown to be close friends over the years through endless games of chess and whist. They would retreat to Papa's study where they would reminisce about their mutual childhoods in England. Mr. Stanley lacked his wife's aloofness, and his and Papa's friendship was easy and genuine. As a young child I had often sat outside of the doors to Papa's study and listened to them as they talked. Papa would come alive recounting the time he spent on his uncle's farm outside of Ipswich. He would speak of the lush green farmland and the crisp air that was free of both factory smoke and the smell of sewage. He would tell Mr. Stanley about running the fields on horseback, fishing, and reenacting great battles with swords of branches. I had wished that I could peek around the corner, so that I might see on Papa's face the pure joy that was so clear in his voice. He would fall quiet after each story, a heavy ache present in the silence.

Papa had recently secured several large business loans for Mr. Stanley as his banker. This new facet of their relationship led to many conversations about finance and eventually the business of family. Mr. Stanley suggested that Conrad would be a favorable match for me, and they began orchestrating our courtship. The possibility of me finding someone that I fancied was never discussed.

The next three months had been filled with awkward teas and stuffy parties, during which Conrad and I were to become better acquainted. I liked Conrad less with each meeting; even his name tasted oily in my mouth. The dinner party on New Year's Eve was to be the culmination of these efforts, with the Willoughby's and Cooks' acceptance of me into the upper echelons of Philadelphia society. I felt as if I were a show pony being paraded and critiqued, all to win a prize that I did not want.

***

I was considered to be among the upper class, but only by virtue of my address and Papa's income. I had not participated in the social events that are required to groom a true lady. I was expected to be well-dressed, but the eyes of society rarely fell on me. Mother's contributions to my upbringing ended after my birth and naming. She was an addled woman, tormented by the memories of her time spent as a nurse in the Civil War. She was only sixteen when she volunteered to care for wounded soldiers and prisoners at Saterlee Military Hospital, the largest in the country. The things she saw there broke her and continued to torment her even now. I had never known the sane, sound version of Mother; her fear consumed her bite by bite. If asked to describe Mother's appearance I would have struggled to conjure up her image in my mind, for she was never still, always fleeing her fear. Instead, I would see the lace cuff of her dressing gown that had yellowed with time, the dust-covered cosmetics on her vanity. She had a single tear that always sat at the corner of her eye, threatening to fall at the slightest provocation, or with none at all. Without a mother able to introduce me to society and teach me its rules, I fumbled through the few teas and dinners that we hosted for Papa's banking associates.

My childhood was not lonely or without love, despite Mother's emotional absence. I had been raised largely by our housekeeper Mrs. O'Malley. She had worked for my family for years before I was born, and had a daughter named Fiona who was two months my senior. Mrs. O'Malley's husband had left in the night shortly before Fiona was born, and Papa had insisted that she move into our house and take the large nursery as her own. She had loved and tended to Fiona and me, raising us as if we were sisters. Mrs. O'Malley was a squat Irish woman, her copper hair gone mostly to gray. Her laugh bellowed through the halls of our home, and her arms were quick to offer comfort. She wouldn't stand for rudeness or dishonesty, but silliness was always encouraged. Fiona and I spent our days draping blankets over furniture to make castles, arranging cakes and squares on the sideboard to create a shop, and brewing undrinkable tea from the leaves and pinecones that we found in the garden. Although Mrs. O'Malley had many duties in our home, she was never too busy to play with us. She would carefully fasten old draperies around our necks as royal capes and sing for us as we twirled around the drawing room. She would pack a lunch of fancy sandwiches and fruit for us to eat on an old tablecloth under a tree or help us build a nest of blankets for a bird that had flown into the kitchen window. She taught us how to weave crowns out of flowers and long grass and encouraged us to explore the garden as fairies might.

Mrs. O'Malley died from pneumonia when we were eighteen, taking with her so much of the light in my life. Thankfully Papa had assured Fiona that she would always have a place in our home and offered her the position of housekeeper. Fiona and I had been gutted by her mother's death. We leaned heavily on each other as we grieved, as neither of us could have borne that loss alone.

***

Fiona had been working feverishly to prepare for the dinner party, and Mother had hired Marie, a girl from the market, to assist her. The kitchen had become a hub of frenzied activity. Sauces simmered and geese stuffed with sausage, apples and sage roasted. Cakes cooled and pastries baked. Handsome centerpieces were arranged from chrysanthemums and fern fronds. My skills in the kitchen were rudimentary, but I helped where I could. I chopped vegetables and assisted with laying out the elaborate table setting. I was seated at the small kitchen table on the day of the dinner, polishing silver when Mother entered to check on Fiona's progress. She gasped at the sight of me, ripping the polishing cloth from my hand.

"I've hired help to do this work. Your efforts would be better spent on preparing yourself for tonight," she spat.

"I was just taking my tea in here and visiting with Fiona. She was telling me the funniest thing she saw…" I said before Mother cut in.

"A lady does not fraternize with the help. Your station is above these tasks and these people, and you had best learn that very quickly." Mother clenched her teeth, her head tilted haughtily. I flushed with embarrassment, glancing at Fiona and Maria, apologizing with my eyes as Mother ushered me out of the kitchen.

As I dressed for dinner, I mulled over which version of Mother was more awful. The Mother that I'd known my whole life had paced and fretted, and often retreated into her own troubled mind. She would stare off into the distance, haunted by things only she could see. She had never paid me any mind and was my mother only in title. It was her rejection that had led me to seek comfort and connection from Mrs. O'Malley and Fiona. The love that I found in the kitchen had sustained me all these years, and I was infuriated by Mother's disdain for those who had raised me when she could not.

When Papa had suggested that I should marry Conrad, Mother roused from her stupor to become consumed by planning to ensure my marital success. She berated me for not knowing the myriad of social rules that she had never taught me. I was polite and well-read, but not versed in the subtle nuances that must be observed to survive in high society. My hair would not hold a curl, my crinolines laid too flat, my face was too revealing of my thoughts. I felt my spirit break under Mother's scrutiny, but it was adequate preparation for the judgment of the ladies that I would need to befriend.

In the autumn I had been invited to join several couples on a picnic in the Lemon Hill section of Fairmount park. The invitation had come from Rose Willegar, a woman my age that was well respected within society. I struggled to remember all the rules that Mother had recited about how to sit, how to eat, how to introduce a new topic of conversation. There had been a few small gaffes, but my behavior was passable as that of a lady. The day was warm, and the autumn foliage was incredible. I loved the changing of seasons, but I typically witnessed it from my window or in my own garden. I was grateful for the opportunity to walk among the majesty of the trees as their leaves turned. I was less grateful for my company. The conversation of the group had revolved solely around people and possessions all afternoon. There was no talk of brilliant thinkers, or art, or current events, or anything of any substance at all.

Rose was regaling the group with a tale of a man who had rented a pineapple and had taken it to a party, simply carrying it in the crook of his arm all night. Pineapples were shipped from South America, and few escaped the journey without rotting. As a result, a single pineapple would fetch the equivalent of a man's room and board for a month. Pineapples had become the ultimate show of wealth, and the shape had found its way into decor in the form of silk wallpapers and embroidered towels. I laughed at the image of a man escorting a pineapple to a party and thought that it must have led to some very interesting conversation. The others roared with laughter, and I quickly realized that we were laughing at different things.

"Can you imagine?!" Conrad said loudly. "Renting a pineapple? Not serving it or giving it as a gift, but renting it just to appear wealthy? What a sorry fool. You can't rent your way into the right circles. I hope his pathetic attempt to fool the other guests was seen for what it was." The others scoffed at the man who had been desperate to climb into their midst. They continued, berating all who were deemed below them. These people should not have been revered. They were ugly souls in beautiful wrappings.

I needed to breathe air that was not filled with ridicule, so I excused myself and walked to a nearby pond. I sat on a bench and closed my parasol, laying it across my lap. Mother had insisted that I buy a new one for the outing. She had wanted it to be white, as was the fashion, but I had chosen a deep blue that reminded me of water. The sun felt lovely on my face and was well worth the risk of getting some color. I watched the geese and ducks float lazily around the pond, one with its head tucked under its wing as it slept, and I longed to feel the same freedom. Everything in my world felt too bright, too fast, too loud. I swung my feet back and forth in the fallen leaves, enjoying their papery rustle. The large leaves of the red maple were so saturated in color that they were difficult to look at. The delicate, fan-shaped leaves of the ginkgo tree fluttered with each breath of the wind. These leaves, these trees made sense to me; the company that I had did not. Conrad and another of the men had wandered onto the path surrounding the pond. They both strolled arrogantly, hands clasped behind their backs. The wind shifted and suddenly I could hear their words.

"... doesn't even fill her bodice and is as plain as the days are long. I suppose you don't have to worry about her purity, there's not likely to be any men lusting after her!" The other man said nastily, eliciting raucous laughter from both of them.

"The girls at Rosie's will keep me happy but staring at her face across the dinner table every night will require a lot of Scotch!" Conrad replied with a sneer. He looked my way, realizing that I'd heard them. He smiled at me smugly as if he were above reproach. My face flushed hot with shame. I reluctantly reconvened with the group, and we made our way towards home. Conrad made no attempt to apologize or explain the cruel things that he had said. The others' sideways glances and their whispers from behind their hands did not go unnoticed by me, but they held no weight.

Mother was pacing the entry hall when I returned home, desperate to know every detail of my afternoon. I told her about our picnic with sandwiches of watercress and beef tongue, soft cheeses and fruit, followed by sour cream and raisin pie for dessert. I told her who had redecorated their salon, and who had fired their housekeeper for stealing a diamond bracelet and bronze candlesticks. I told her who was having their carriage seats upholstered in the finest burgundy leather, and who had slipped on the smelly ginkgo berries while walking with her beau and had made a frightful mess of her dress. Mother took in all of these details hungrily. I then told her the story of the man and his pineapple. She laughed and scoffed, much as the others had done.

"What a fantastic idea, Dahlia! We'll host a dinner party and serve pineapple! We'll be the talk of the town. We'll show them," Mother said excitedly.

"We'll show them what, Mother?" I asked, disgust creeping up in me.

"Well, that we can afford it, and that we belong among them," she said indignantly. "I can think of nothing that I desire less than the acceptance of those horrible people. They are all malevolent, predatory and small. I will not marry Conrad, and I will not become like them."

Mother's eyes widened in shock, and then narrowed to slits as she grasped my arm painfully.

"It is far too late for you to decide what kind of life you want. You will not bring shame to this family by failing to accept the opportunity that has been offered to you. You are not pretty, your manners are crude, and your head is filled with ridiculous ideas. You have attracted no suitors, and likely never will. You should be grateful that Conrad is even considering a marriage to you, and you will act as such, regardless of how you feel," she spat, her face reddened and voice full of vitriol. Hot tears stung my eyes, but I refused to give Mother the satisfaction of seeing them fall. I pulled my arm from her grasp and ran upstairs to my rooms. I dreaded the future that I was being propelled towards, but I felt powerless to avoid it.

***

My thoughts returned to the present and I finished dressing for dinner. Each article of clothing and piece of jewelry that I donned felt as if it were a thousand pounds, threatening to drown me in the weight of the expectations imposed on me by my family and society. The expensive gown that the modiste had crafted in the latest style was like a charlatan's costume, the flashy silks and lace intended to distract our guests from seeing the imposter who wore it. I splashed water on my face and looked at myself in the mirror. Dahlia Day. Mother had named me after her favorite flower, perhaps hoping that I would be beautiful, as she was. If you heard my name before meeting me, you might assume that I was beautiful. I am not. Mother was right; I was plain. Taken on their own I have some beautiful features, but together their effect is underwhelming. My right eye tooth is just crooked enough that my lip catches on it if I grin too widely. My eyebrows are unruly, reminiscent of Papa's, their bulk overshadowing the gentle green of my eyes. I am too tall and lack the feminine curves that draw a man's eye. My beautiful name was incongruent with the face that I saw in the mirror. Each time that I heard my name it was a painful reminder of all the things that I was not. I blotted my face dry and stood tall, shoulders back, steeling myself for what was to come.

Papa, Mother and I waited in the drawing room for our guests to arrive. Fiona busied herself with adjusting flower arrangements as she awaited each knock at the door. I had seen the briefest glimpse of envy on her face when she had seen me in my new gown. I'd have happily traded places with her. Mother was gracious and lucid, even lively as she greeted each guest. The smell of cherry cordial wafted heavily from her, betraying the source of her newfound warmth. I smoothed my dress nervously as Papa caught my eye.

"You look beautiful, Dolly. This is going to be a wonderful night," he said, using his pet name for me. Papa announced that dinner would be served, and we all made our way to the dining room. The Willoughbys were seated across from me, Papa was to my left, and Conrad on my right. I was relieved that I would not have to look at Conrad much during dinner. The Willoughbys were at least forty years my senior and were firmly established in Philadelphian society. Mrs. Willoughby had a tremor that kept her head bobbing rhythmically. If the motion were slowed down it may appear as if she were unsure of something, and tilting her head this way and that. Mr. Willoughby was proper and rigid, his stillness drawing a stark contrast to his wife's dizzying wobble. Mother was at the far end of the table, with the Cooks to her right. They were near in age to my parents and had seemed bored and unimpressed since their arrival. Across from them were the Stanleys, who dominated most of the dinner conversation. Mr. Stanley spoke of recent business acquisitions during the soup course, and city and state politics as we ate our fish. Mrs. Stanley took over as the stuffed goose and veal were served, detailing all her work with various charitable causes. The other guests fawned over her philanthropy until a smug smile settled on her face. The food was cooked to perfection, the service impeccable. The company, however, left much to be desired.

Mother's earlier enthusiasm and grace had slowly faded as her over-consumption of cordial caught up with her. Her cheeks were flushed, her eyes glassy. She suddenly let out a ragged belch, stood from the table, and excused herself to go lie down. Every mouth at the table was agape. It was unacceptable to leave a table mid-meal. For the hostess to do it was unheard of. Conduct demanded that we continue as if nothing had happened, and so we did. Papa cleared his throat and asked Mr. Willoughby about his business, but his face betrayed his embarrassment. After a few minutes I excused myself to go help Fiona with the dessert. I knew doing so would be looked poorly upon, but I did not care. I found Fiona finishing the last few slices on the pineapple, as quiet and focused as a surgeon.

"Your mother told me not to bury the pineapple in a cake, and that I must serve it with the crown attached so that everyone would know what it was. This is the best that I could come up with. What do you think?" Fiona asked, her uncertainty clear on her face. She had cut the pineapple into halves, each with the crown attached. She had carefully sliced the fruit and pushed alternating pieces out to create a shape like the bones of a fish. Fiona had shortcake and whipped cream flavored with anise to serve with it. The dessert looked and smelled delicious, and I assured her that it would be well received.

Fiona carried the platter of pineapple proudly and I followed with the shortcake and cream. We both gasped upon entering the dining room as we caught sight of Mother entering from the other end of the room. She was wearing a thin shift hung lewdly off one shoulder, and no stockings or shoes. She had started to take down one half of her hair and had partially removed her makeup. The result was the appearance of two opposing halves of the same woman: the Matriarch and the Madwoman. Mother's eyes were wild, her mouth pulled into a macabre grin smeared in lipstick. She was flailing her arms and said, "don't forget to serve the pineapple! We've bought a whole pineapple for dessert!" in a childish, sing-song voice. The scene would have been comical if the results had not been so socially devastating.

Fiona dropped the platter onto the table and rushed to cover Mother with her apron. Mother tried to push her away, insisting that she was fine and wanted to try the pineapple. Another large belch escaped her lips, followed immediately by the lavish meal she had just eaten, in a broth of cherry cordial. Fiona dragged Mother from the dining room, both slipping in the vomit as they went.

The only sound that I could hear was my heart pounding. No one moved. The syrupy sweet smell of the pineapple blended with that of the vomit, creating a nauseating stench. My stomach turned, and I struggled to keep my own dinner down. Conrad was shaking his head from the corner of my eye, and I heard him mutter, "as expected." Mr. Stanley slowly wiped his mouth with his napkin and then slid his chair away from the table and stood.

"Thank you both for the wonderful meal, but we must be going. We'll see ourselves out," he said in an even tone. The rest of the guests quickly stood to follow him, avoiding the smears of vomit on the floor. Mrs. Stanley's lips were drawn, her head held high. Conrad took her arm and they both made a great show of stepping around the mess on the floor. Papa stood, resignation clear in his slumped shoulders and downcast eyes.

"Thank you for coming. I'm sorry that our evening has been ruined," he said. We heard our guests gather their coats from the foyer closet and leave quietly through the front door. A moment later there was a knock at the door. I opened it to find four men in coattails and top hats, large instrument cases in their arms. It was the string quartet that Mother had hired to play for us in the drawing room. I led the men inside and showed them where they were to set up. Then I returned to the dining room and retrieved Mother's favorite tablecloth from the sideboard. I unfurled it with a satisfying snap and spread it on the floor to cover the mess.

"I've cleaned Mrs. Day up and settled her to bed," Fiona said as she entered the dining room. Her eyebrows were raised in question, perhaps hoping for some direction on how to react to the situation. I looked from Papa to Fiona, unsure of what to say. I could feel laughter bubbling up in me, and my efforts to contain it resulted in a large snort. The sound startled all of us, and we fell into fits of laughter. Maria entered from the kitchen to see what the commotion was. The shock on her face was only there for a moment; she was trained to turn a blind eye to the private matters of rich folks, and so she began clearing the table.

"Sit with us Maria," I said between giggles. "Have some pineapple." Papa wiped tears from his eyes with a handkerchief, bursts of deep laughter rolling from him. A man from the quartet stuck his head into the room and his eyes panned the scene. An expensive tablecloth lying in vomit, the remains of an elaborate feast on the table, two servants and the residents of the house sharing a pineapple, and the smell of sick and cordial in the air.

"Shall we play?" he asked politely.

"Oh, yes. Something lively, I think. And please, try some pineapple," Papa said to the man, his voiced strained as he fought off the next wave of laughter. Fiona opened a window to let the fresh winter air in and propped the door to the drawing room open with a chair so that we could hear the music. We ate and laughed for hours, ringing in the New Year as we sat amongst the wreckage of our lives.

Chapter Two

1896

After New Year's Eve, Mother reverted to her former self, pacing and rocking and fretting. The spectacle of the dinner party was never mentioned; there was no sense in discussing something that could not be undone. No callers came, no invitations were received. I felt nothing but relief. In mere moments Mother had rid my life of all that I disliked: the impending wedding to the man that I loathed, the crushing social pressures, the petty people. I was free. The odd thing about my freedom was that it had teeth. As a lady of society, I knew exactly what was expected of me, even if it did not please me. There was an ease that came with never having to make decisions or strike out on my own. There were no risks to take, and I knew the exact path of my life far in advance. A part of me craved that certainty, but a much larger part of me relished the thought of a new and different life.

Papa called me into his study the following week and showed me an advertisement in his newspaper. It showed rolling hills backed by mountains, fields of grain in the foreground and read "Life in the West is Best." The fine print described large plots of farmland for $10, or ready-made farms available for purchase.

"Have you ever filled your hands with rich soil, Dolly? Breathed the scent of the earth?" Papa asked wistfully.

"No, Papa..." I began, before he continued with his reverie.

"The happiest times of my life were spent on my uncle Edward's farm. Perhaps we're not meant to live in stone cities, gray as far as the eye can see. It's a shame that you've lived twenty years without once touching the earth." He looked at me then, the hope clear in his teary eyes.

"Shall we go?" he said quietly.

"Yes, Papa. Let's." My mind was already reeling with excitement.

***

The next four months were a whirlwind of preparations. Papa arranged to buy a farm near Calgary, on Canada's Prairies. It had two houses, outbuildings, a well and fences already built. The land agent told Papa that the owners were homesteaders who had decided to try their luck in the Yukon gold rush. Papa booked train passage to take us and our belongings to our new home. We would leave in April to arrive on the Prairies as spring did. Papa had also arranged for the sale of our house in Philadelphia, along with most of our furniture. We knew that our new home would be very small, and that only the most necessary items should be packed.

I found deep satisfaction in the process of clearing my rooms. The pure excess in which I had lived my life thus far suddenly disgusted me. I had found trunks filled with my childhood dresses in the attic; I could feel the itch of the frilly lace collars even as I looked at them. I packed them into our carriage and brought them to the large orphanage nearby, along with all my old porcelain dolls and toys. During my foray into high society, I had not felt like myself, almost as if my skin did not quite fit. As I rid myself of the trappings of wealth and status, I felt that foreign skin shed away.

My only sadness as I prepared for our move was that Fiona would not be joining us. I had assumed that she would come with us, as a member of the family, not our housekeeper. The arrogance of assuming that I knew what was right for someone else seemed to be the only trait of the wealthy that I had successfully adopted. She had arranged for employment with another Philadelphia family with a glowing reference from Papa. Fiona had another reason to stay: her new beau Vincent. He had swept her clear off her feet, and the passion between them was evident to anyone who saw them. Vincent would run all the way to our house on his lunch hour just to give Fiona a wildflower and a kiss. After he left, she would stand with her back to the door, hand to heart, eyes closed and her fair Irish skin flushed red. They would stay out until all hours at a dance pavilion, or simply walking about the city. There was no concern for propriety, only thoughts of their next meeting. I envied the passion and excitement that consumed Fiona, as well as the freedoms that she enjoyed, and wondered if I would ever find the same for myself.

Mother behaved exactly as I expected she would. She moped and hid in her rooms on the third floor, refusing to pack anything. When Papa told her of our plans to move to the farm, she refused to come with us, saying that Papa was punishing her for her behavior. Papa patiently described the simple, cozy life that he had envisioned for us, trying to ease her worries. His words fell on deaf ears. I tried several times to help Mother sort through her many dresses and choose which ones she would pack. She would scream and wail, throwing herself on the piles of silk as if I were trying to take her child from her, though I doubt that she would have reacted so strongly if I had been taken from her.

Mother began refusing to come out of her rooms, even taking her meals there. I decided that we could have dresses made for her when we arrived on the farm and gave up attempting to pack anything aside from her jewelry. Mother had a large velvet bag and several boxes filled with expensive jewelry that she had collected over the years, which I retrieved from her room one afternoon as she slept. I carefully tore the stitches from the lining of one of my travel trunks, placed the valuables inside and sewed it shut. I hoped that having these irreplaceable heirlooms and gifts from Papa would bring her some comfort in our new home.

Papa packed his chess set and his grandfather's mantle clock, as well as the book that Mr. Stanley had given him that detailed the flora and fauna of the Prairies. Papa had resigned from his job as a banker and spent his free time visiting with Mr. Stanley. I suspected that Mrs. Stanley wasn't aware of Mr. Stanley's visits to our house. We had become social pariahs, but Papa's friendship must have been worth the risk for Mr. Stanley. I both admired and appreciated his loyalty.

I put our China, crystal and candelabra into crates, packed with delicately embroidered napkins. We would take the smaller sideboard from the kitchen, so I reluctantly removed Mrs. O'Malley's canning supplies from it, as Fiona would be taking them with her to her new home. I lingered over each jar for a moment, relishing the memories that they held. I filled the empty space with pans for loaves, a large pot and frying pan, and the knitting basket and skeins of yarn that Fiona had given me. I also added the large sewing tin that contained all manner of pins and thread, and heavy shears; I would need to learn how to sew on the farm. I had only ever produced needlepoint, the pastime of wealthy ladies who needed only ways in which to spend their time. I looked forward to using my time to sew useful items that would make our lives easier or more comfortable.

I visited the modiste that had made all of my dresses since I was a child. Angelique greeted me happily, remembering the small fortune that Mother and I had spent there a few months ago. Her demeanor changed once I told her that I wanted farm dresses made.

"You'll need to find a simple seamstress to sew your farm frocks," she said haughtily. "I have neither the plain fabrics nor the time for such garments." I nodded my understanding and left the shop. My carriage driver recommended that I inquire at the shop that his wife used. I was met there by a kind woman, her face curious when I arrived. After I described what I wanted made she readily agreed.

I chose simple calico in four different patterns and felt far more excitement about these dresses than I had any others in my life. The fit was comfortable, and they had no lace or frills, no crinolines filling out the skirts. The bottom hem was three inches shorter than I was used to. The seamstress explained that farm dresses were made shorter to avoid dragging through mud. I had her make me four simple aprons, and four country bonnets, and I ordered seven pairs of thick cotton stockings, two shifts, and four new pairs of bloomers. I couldn't contain my excitement when I picked up my new wardrobe, nor when I packed the garments in my trunk. Most of my preparations were complete. Now I just had to wait.

***

Mother continued her downward spiral. One evening upon collecting Mother's dinner dishes from outside of her room, Fiona found Mother's long, golden tresses laid across the plate. Her hair had always been a source of pride for Mother, thick, shiny and the exact color of honey. Mother would not admit anyone into her room, and so we sent for a doctor. Papa finally resorted to breaking the door down, in an odd physical display driven by desperation. Once inside, the doctor found Mother to be nearly bald and suffering from hysteria. He left a supply of sedatives for us to administer and suggested that a home for the mentally infirm might be the best place for her. Papa felt that what Mother needed was fresh air and new scenery, and that she would settle nicely on the farm. I felt that a private home with staff trained to care for people like Mother would be the best place for her. Papa decided that we would delay our train passage by one week to get

Mother's hysteria settled, as it would have been impossible to manage her on a train in her current state.

Within days Mother responded well to the sedatives and was much calmer. She would sit and rock in her chair, content with her own company. I convinced Papa to take a tour of a private mental facility just across the Delaware river from us. His head had fallen in defeat when he agreed. "I suppose we should at least take a look," he said softly. Fiona had gone to oversee the delivery of our trunks and small furniture to the train station in anticipation of our departure in three days. She fed Mother her lunch, gave her a sedative and settled her for an afternoon nap. Fiona offered to stay with Mother while Papa and I went on our tour, but we assured her that Mother would sleep for the entire three hours that we would be away. Fiona took the opportunity to begin setting up her new room before her employment began in a few days. She promised to visit once more before we left.

Papa and I dropped our traveling cases off at the hotel that we would stay at until our departure and ordered a full dinner for three to be delivered to our room at 6:00. We took our coach to the private home for the mentally infirm that was built on sprawling, manicured grounds. The doctor who operated the home was kind and soft-spoken, the staff all wore gentle smiles. After the tour we thanked the doctor for his time and made our way to the coach.

We headed towards home, where we would retrieve Mother and her traveling case. I had already decided to walk through each of the twenty-two rooms in our house before we left. I needed to say goodbye to the only home I had known. I needed to feel the ghosts of Mrs. O'Malley's songs in the kitchen, hear my childhood laughter in the nursery. I needed to feel the ease of Saturdays with Papa in his study and walk the groomed lawns one last time. I regretted not doing this days ago, before the furniture was draped in ghostly sheets and the rooms were stripped of personal belongings, the things that made a house a home. I would have to settle for a tour of our home with all its ghosts on display. My thoughts returned to the present, and the dilemma of whether Mother should accompany us west or not.

"I think the home was very nice, and that Mother would receive the help that she needs there." I said to Papa as our carriage made its way into our quarter of the city.

"I can't bear to abandon her there, and then move two thousand miles away, never to see her again. When we were wed, I promised to care for her. This feels more like an unburdening," Papa said, looking out the window of the carriage instead of at me. "I can't do it, Dolly. It's just not right. She'll come to the farm with us. The country air will do her wonders. You'll see," Papa said, his voice full of resolve.

We needn't have debated Mother's future. We saw the great plume of smoke, followed closely by the frantic ringing of the bells of the Fire Brigades. Our driver told us that he could not take the carriage any further, as the streets were clogged with water pump carriages and onlookers. Papa and I leapt from the carriage and ran towards the fire. My heart knew what I would see before my eyes confirmed it. Our three-storey home was engulfed in flames. Black smoke rolled out from the eaves like the steam from under the lid of a boiling pot. There were dozens of men running every which way with their leather buckets full of water. The pump carriage was being operated by four men, with two more holding the long, canvas hose. They were not spraying our house, instead they were aiming their spray at the trees and neighboring houses.

"Elizabeth!" Papa yelled frantically, searching the crowd for Mother. His yells caught the attention of the Fire Brigade Chief, who stopped Papa's movement towards the house. The heat emanating from the fire was intense as we neared it, and it seemed as if all the air had been sucked out of this place.

"Sir, Sir! You cannot go any further, it's not safe."

"My wife is inside! Oh Lord, she must be so scared." Papa's face crumpled as he spoke.

"I'm sorry, Sir. We could not save her. We couldn't get inside, all the doors were barred from within," the Chief said, his hand on Papa's shoulder to steady him.

Tears streaming down his face, Papa said, "Then break the door down! I'll go if you won't!"

"She's gone, Sir. The screaming stopped when the floor collapsed. We're just trying to prevent the fire from spreading to the other houses now. I'm so sorry, there was nothing we could do."

Papa slumped in the Chief's arms at this, a tortured wail escaping from his lips. My mouth hung open in shock, my eyes darting across the scene, trying to make sense of it. Numbness spread through me. Mother was gone. Another fireman helped us to a bench a ways down the street, and a kind neighbor brought us each a cup of water. Papa and I stared at the fire, not talking, for there were no words that could change what we were seeing. The ringing of the bells became less frequent and the crowds dispersed. A small group of firemen were charged with monitoring the fire and preventing its spread. Papa and I sat on that bench, waves of shock rolling over us. The sky grew dark, the embers of our home glowing softly. Papa and I made our way back down the street to our waiting carriage. We rode in silence to the hotel and found our suite of rooms, where we were greeted by a table laid out with a full dinner for three.

***

"The doors were barred from within." The Chief's words echoed in my head over the next few days. Mother had always been her own jailer, locking herself away in her mind full of horrors. She must not have been able to bear it any longer and had become her own executioner as well.

Fiona stayed with us at the hotel and helped us make arrangements. Mother's remains did not require a full casket. Instead, we were given a decorative crate the size of a hat box to bury. We did not have a wake, as we lacked both a home to hold it in, and people wishing to pay their respects. Only Fiona, Papa and I attended the burial. The service was short; only the Reverend spoke. I didn't know how to grieve a person that I had barely known; I felt only pity where sadness should have sat.

Papa and I decided to leave as planned. There was nothing left for us here now. Papa realized that he had canceled the insurance policy on our house to reflect the date that we had originally planned to leave. In the chaos of Mother's hysteria he had not revised it when we delayed our departure date. The policy may not have covered the fire regardless, as it had been intentionally set. As a result we had lost the proceeds from the sale of our house, leaving us with much less money than Papa had planned. We would need to make do. Fiona accompanied us to the train station to see us off. We embraced for a long time, unable to let go. I didn't know how I would manage without Fiona in my life.

"I'm sorry that you're leaving like this, your mother gone and plans turned upside down. There's a beautiful life waiting for you on the Prairies, I just know it," she said with tears in her eyes and an encouraging smile on her face. I stepped away reluctantly, wishing Fiona good luck in her new job, and a happy future with Vincent. I promised to write and tell her all about our new home, and she promised the same.

Papa and I boarded the train that would take us away from this gray city and its heartaches. We left our ghosts in Philadelphia. I hoped that they would stay there.

Chapter Three

It's a disconcerting thing to travel long distances by train, to wake to scenery so different from that which you closed your eyes to the night before. I felt as a baby must when they drift off to sleep in the warmth of the sun at a park, and wake at home in their nursery. It was jarring, really, that each morning I would wake in this unfamiliar bed, my mind struggling initially to identify the strange sounds and smells, the steady rumble of train on track. It was always Papa's gentle snores from across the cabin that anchored me, brought sense back to my surroundings. Each morning brought new views from our window. We saw herds of cattle grazing, rivers churning at the bottom of deep valleys, trees and towns off in the distance.

Our meals were brought to us at different times each day, as they were prepared in towns along the route rather than on the train. Our food was served on fine China with proper place settings. We also had tea served twice a day by a man in a starched white shirt, a fresh flower in his lapel. Papa told me that the passengers in the common cars were having a much different experience than we were. They slept sitting upright in their seats, were responsible for supplying their own meals, and shared one latrine between forty people. As our train stopped at each town swarms of people would alight from the train to stretch their legs and mill about on the platform, breathing air not scented with the smells of bodies unwashed for too long.

When we reached Montreal, we switched to a Canadian Pacific Railway train. All of our trunks and furniture were transferred by the station workers, leaving us three hours before our departure. Papa and I wandered around the beautiful city, older even than Philadelphia. We enjoyed the warm spring sunshine and delighted in the sounds of French being spoken all around us. It was a beautiful language, melodious and lacking any hard edges. Because I did not understand the words, my ear heard only the cadence and intonation, the emotion of what was being said. My governess had taught me some French, but only as far as basic vocabulary and the written conjugation of verbs. She had spoken in the loud, broken manner that one does with someone unfamiliar with a language, as if my understanding would increase with the volume of her voice.

Papa and I visited several small shops and patisseries as we roamed the cobbled streets. We couldn't resist buying two slices of tourtiere, a veal pie with a flaky, golden crust. Papa spotted an empty wrought iron bench in Place d'Armes, a public square filled with people. We sat on the bench and ate our pie straight from the paper that it was wrapped in, both of us delighting in eating without the formality of silverware and tablecloths. I had never seen Papa so relaxed, a smile fixed firmly on his face. A man in full dinner dress played a lively tune on his violin, his hat upturned next to him should anyone like to leave some coins. Another man walked with jerky, sweeping steps on tall stilts. He wore a suit that was striped red and white, with pants that covered the stilts perfectly. His face was painted as a clown's in white, with red diamonds around his eyes. He did not speak as he lurched around the square, his knees bending too near his body, as a spider's do. The predatory appearance of the stilted man made me shudder and I turned my head, my gaze falling on the Notre-Dame Basilica. I stood and pulled Papa by the hand towards the building.

I had spent very little time inside of a church. As a family we had attended only enough to not draw attention to our absence. I felt no pull to religion, but I felt drawn towards this majestic structure. I opened the heavy wooden door and stepped into a dream. The ceiling curved beautifully into soaring arches, and light poured through the stained glass of the domes. Everywhere my eye fell there were intricate carvings and statues. I felt overwhelmed by all that my eyes were trying to process. At the place of honor behind the altar was an enormous pipe organ. Thousands of pipes rose from the floor, the metal glinting gold. I didn't think that I could bear to hear it played. I imagined that its resonance would be felt rather than heard, its timbres rending me into a million pieces. Papa and I stood and gazed around the nave, speechless. After a time, we looked toward each other, nodded slightly, and turned to leave. I imagined that my face looked much like Papa's: soft around the eyes and jaw, mouth open in wonder, eyes bright. A peace that ran bone deep had come over me, settling into the darkest of my corners, and it was not broken even by the harsh sunlight as we exited to the noisy square. We walked in silence, ambling slowly towards the train station. The air in the Basilica had left us altered, its effects fading slowly.

Just before boarding our new train, we bought two golden doughnuts rolled in sugar and still warm from the pan. They were sold by a man carrying several dozen on a long wooden dowel, a small platform at the base. It had the appearance of a sword sheathed in pastry, brandished rather wildly by the vendor as he called out in French.

We made our way to our platform and found our assigned car; this one as lavishly decorated as the last. The walls were paneled in dark wood on the lower half and papered in silk at the top. The table was covered with a crisp, white tablecloth, its benches upholstered in royal blue velvet. There were four wall sconces rather than candlesticks, as everything must be secured on a moving train. Banking the table was a double sleeping berth on the right, and narrow beds stacked one on the other on the left. The pillowcases were scalloped at the edges, with a delicate diamond pattern embroidered on them. Each bed had a royal blue coverlet, as well as a thick wool blanket folded at the foot.

Across from the narrow beds was a comfortable settee and a small table with an oil lamp. Our car had its own latrine, as well as a separate room for the wash basin and pitcher. The windows had bulky drapes that could be drawn to darken the car. They were tied with golden ropes, though one was unsecured, the only flaw in this exquisite cabin.

Our attendant entered before we had even departed, bringing our dinner. He removed the silver lids from our plates with a flourish… revealing tourtiere. Papa and I laughed, confusing the attendant. Papa explained that we had just eaten some but would love another slice. The pie was just as delicious this second time and was followed by a baked apple pudding with a maple glaze. Papa and I were full to bursting after eating two full meals in as many hours. He stretched out on the settee while I curled up on the banquette. I leaned my head against the glass and watched the world roll past as we pulled from the station. We had six more days left in our journey and my excitement was building with each mile that we traveled.

***

The landscape grew more wild as our train met the Prairies. There were dense green forests banking the tracks in places, miles of unbroken plains in others, and deep snow still covering the ground. Just before we entered Manitoba, I witnessed a huge bull moose burst from the trees in a spray of snow and run alongside the tracks. It had heavy antlers that spread five feet or more and was taller than a horse. Its gait was steady and somehow graceful despite its ungainly appearance. The moose kept pace with the train for a minute or more and I was able to watch it in profile as it ran. It had a beard where its neck met its body, which bounced as the moose ran. Papa and I both watched it intently, mouths agape in wonder. The moose ran back into the trees, gone as fast as it had come. I marveled at how the last six days had brought me more wonder and awe than the previous twenty years.

The towns became further and further apart, as not many settlers had braved these parts. I had lived my whole life in a city of nearly a million people. The sparseness of settlements made me feel nervous for the first time. Papa, on the other hand, seemed to grow more relaxed with each mile we traveled, staring out the window and saying things like "look at all the trees", or "imagine all of the animals that live in the depths of that forest." Only a few passengers would leave or board the train at each stop, and they all wore heavy furs and high boots. The meals grew simpler as we trekked on, which suited me just fine. Papa and I had enjoyed the venison stew with root vegetables and biscuits as much as the tourtiere.

As we neared our new home I was struck by the sky. It seemed that the Prairies had been given much more of it than other places. It stretched further than the sky that I had seen every other day of my life. I couldn't wait to stand on our farm and take in all of its vivid blue expanse. Our train stopped in Calgary, a small but bustling new city sprung up at the curve of the Bow river. No snow covered the ground, just dust and the faint beginnings of spring grass. Papa and I would need to board another train heading north, while this one continued west all the way to the ocean. We sat in the seats with the rest of the travelers, no posh car for this last hour of our journey. The other travelers appeared to be farm folk, the women in simple dresses and the men in denim pants and wide-brimmed hats. I suddenly felt ostentatious in my traveling dress and feathered hat. The adults were polite enough not to stare, but I was drawing the eye of many children. I was glad that I had had dresses made back in Philadelphia and wished that I had thought to pack one in my travel case. Papa sat at the edge of his seat, tapping his foot impatiently. He checked his pocket watch, folded and refolded his newspaper, retied his shoes.

"We're almost there, Dolly. I hope it's as good as we've imagined all these months." Papa shifted nervously in his seat. It wasn't. It was much, much better.

Chapter Four

The train slowed as we approached the station; the brakes screeched, and a cloud of dust rose and then fell slowly as we came to a stop. The train tracks ran parallel to the town rather than through it. I sat on a bench on the platform while Papa saw about the unloading of our things. It felt lovely to sit out in the fresh air after ten days on a train. I could see the backsides of the buildings that lined the main street of town. Some were one-storey, with a false front above, others appeared to have living quarters on the second storey. Only one other person had gotten off at this stop. A man about my age wearing a cowboy hat slung a large rucksack onto his back, bent to pick a spear of wild grass, and tucked it into the corner of his mouth as he walked slowly to the east. He had an easy gait, as if he were in no hurry to be anywhere. This made me feel at ease. Gone were the pushy crowds on busy streets, everyone rushing to this place or that.

Papa emerged from the train station with a stout man in a brown suit and matching hat. I could tell that Papa had explained Mother's absence to him by the tilt of his head and the slight tension in his brow.

"Welcome, Miss Dahlia. I'm Jack Porter, your land agent." He wore the half-smile reserved for people whom you pity. "How was your journey?"

I curtsied slightly, unsure of the level of formality expected in this new town. Mr. Porter's eyebrows raised ever so slightly, making me regret the curtsy. I extended my hand, face flushed.

"It's a pleasure to meet you, Mr. Porter. Our trip was wonderful, but I'm glad to have finally arrived," I said with a smile. We walked toward the horses and wagon already loaded with all that we owned, arranged ahead of time by Mr. Porter. He explained to Papa how to get to our new home, the directions peppered with east and west instead of left and right. These country lanes had no names, and so rivers and gnarled trees were given as landmarks rather than buildings and intersections, as they would have been in Philadelphia.

"James, Miss Dahlia." Mr. Porter tipped his hat. Papa thanked him and we climbed up onto our wagon. He handled the horses with surprising ease and led us to the mercantile. Though I had only ever seen Papa as a busy, successful banker, he seemed right at home here, as if this were where he was meant to be.

We were greeted with smiles and curious looks from the townspeople, not the suspicion that we might have faced in a large city. The door to the store creaked as we entered, a small bell also announcing our arrival. My boots echoed conspicuously on the floorboards, drawing unwanted attention my way. I wandered down each aisle of the store admiring the items for sale; some were familiar, but some were so foreign that I couldn't possibly guess their purpose, metal farming implements I supposed. The left side of the store was dedicated to farming supplies, and it had a large door that was propped open. A man stood just inside the door, rolling an enormous spool of barbed wire towards a waiting wagon. He smiled and tipped his hat to me before returning to his work.

Further down the left side, one-hundred-pound sacks of flour were stacked six tall, and pallets with sacks of sugar were piled in neat pyramids. A carefully lettered sign said "*Small dry goods available at the counter.*" I walked towards the counter at the rear of the store, where Papa was introducing himself to the shopkeeper. The man was wearing a striped shirt and a vest, with red sleeve garters encircling his upper arms. My modiste Angelique had once explained to me that most men wore them to make their sleeves the proper length and prevent their cuffs from getting dirty while working. Men's shirts all came with extra-long sleeves when ordered, so as to fit any frame. I had never seen Papa wear them because he had all of his clothing made by a tailor, instead of ordered from a catalog. I looked forward to a time when Papa's tailored shirts wore out, and he would also wear charming sleeve garters.

The shopkeeper was warm and welcoming, and asked where we had come from and where we were headed. Papa answered his questions with evident excitement, nodding and gesturing with his hands, then asked for sacks of flour, oats, and sugar, a pound of butter, some salt and a small bag of tea. After some thought he added an axe and two newspapers to his order. Papa paid for his things and the shopkeeper went to speak with the man who loaded the goods.

"Are you missing the city already? Or wondering what has happened in the world during our trip?" I asked.

"I am eager to learn about our new home, but the newspapers are for the latrine," Papa said with a wink. We brought the wagon around to the side door to have our supplies loaded. As we pulled away from the store he handed me the reins. My shock must have shown on my face because Papa laughed.

"We don't have a coach and driver, a groom, or a housekeeper anymore. We are now all of those things. You need to learn how to live out here, and you might as well start now," he said, encouraging me. Papa showed me how to click my tongue and flick the reins gently to set the horses to moving, and how to use the reins to make them turn, slow, or stop. I sat at full attention as we drove northwest out of town. As we traveled, Papa explained that he had met our neighbor, Willy Southern, inside of the train station. Mr. Porter had arranged for him to greet Papa and talk about livestock. He would be delivering our dairy cow later that afternoon.

We bounced wildly on the wooden bench of the wagon as we made our way down the dusty, rutted lane. Someone had been kind enough to place a folded woven blanket on the seat to cushion it, but it was still uncomfortable. Farms fenced with barbed wire lined our route and some modest houses could be seen from the road. They looked as though they held only a few small rooms, built for utility rather than social posturing. We made a few turns as Mr. Porter had directed, and after nearly an hour we came to a gate that had a piece of white cloth tied to the post.

I turned the wagon onto our farm. The lane rose gently, obscuring our view at first. We crested the small hill and gasped in unison. We were atop a hill, our land rolling gently away from us. The grasses in the fields were just beginning to turn green, and we could see for miles and miles. Our view was to the east, and I could see a large wood, its trees still bare of leaves. Far to the right I could see the glint of sun on water, and Papa told me that there was a lake there. A small wooden house sat to our left, with a thick stand of trees behind it. The latrine and a well were further ahead on the same side. On the other side of the lane was a large barn, its wood grayed with time. Despite the weathered appearance, it stood straight and sturdy. There was a small shed that Papa said was a chicken coop, as well as a large outdoor pen with a short fence. Farther to the right was a large, fenced pasture.

We climbed down from the wagon and continued to stare. Gone were the streets and their crowds, the factories and their smoke. Clean air filled my lungs, and a gentle breeze blew across this wide-open space. I felt tears wet my cheeks. Papa came to one knee and placed his palm flat on the earth. He collected a small pile of dirt and rubbed it slowly between his hands as he surveyed the land before him, eyes squinting from the sun. He brought his hands to his face and inhaled deeply, as if he could come to know this land, or measure its value simply by its smell. Papa closed his eyes and exhaled loudly through his open mouth, as one does after slaking a deep thirst. It was a pleasant, satisfied sound that implied that something had been taken from him and had been returned at long last.

We walked towards our new home, both grinning widely. The house was a single storey and had two large windows flanking the door. A simple porch led to the house and was covered by an overhang. A barrel had been cut in two to create the flowerpots beside the door. Even though they were bare of flowers they felt like a homey touch. A wooden bench sat on the porch, facing towards the east. I couldn't imagine growing tired of the view that it afforded.

I took a big breath in before Papa opened the door. The door slid open smoothly, as though its hinges were recently oiled. We were in the kitchen, with the living area visible at the back of the house. There were sturdy cupboards lining the wall to my right and underneath them was a work surface with a deep basin sunk into it. I noticed a door of around two feet square set into the floor, which Papa explained was the cellar access. Beside it was a free-standing tall table with thick legs and a shiny, oiled wood surface. We'd had something similar in our Philadelphia kitchen that was used for rolling out dough.

The previous residents had left a beautiful kitchen table with six chairs. It was clear to see that it had been lovingly made by someone with exceptional woodworking skills. We ventured further into our home and found a wood stove with a large cooking surface, and to its right was the fireplace. The surround and chimney were made of smooth river rocks, and flat flagstones were laid in front of the fireplace and under the stove. A heavy beam acted as the mantle; fine craftsmanship again evident in the seamless joints of its supports. To either side of the living area was a large bedroom with a window. Each room contained a double bed, a large wardrobe, and a wooden washstand with a basin and pitcher.

Papa chose the room to the left, which was drenched in morning sun. The window in my room looked up into the trees near our house, and I was sure that when the leaves appeared I'd be able to hear the wind in them at night. I returned to the living area and noticed a wooden folding screen tucked into the corner near my bedroom. Each panel was the size of a door, and tiny hinges allowed it to be folded flat or opened to be used for privacy. The panels consisted of three blocks of wood, all beautifully carved with scenes of families, animals, or plants. I could not imagine anyone leaving something like this behind but was grateful that they had. Tucked behind the screen was a half barrel like the ones on the porch. We did not have a bathroom, so I surmised that this was our new tub. The wooden screen would provide privacy for the bather if anyone else was in the house. Three pegs were set into the wall behind the tub to hang clothing and bath sheets.

I went to Papa's bedroom to tell him about the screen and found him sitting on his bed grinning ear to ear.

"Can you believe this place, Dolly?" he said with a laugh. "I'm struggling to remember why I ever thought that we needed more than this." He continued to shake his head in disbelief. I told Papa about the screen, and he rose to see it. We ran our hands over the carvings, appreciating its beauty.

"Let's go settle the horses in the barn and then we can unload the wagon," Papa said. We unhitched the horses and led them to the barn. There were four stalls on either side of the doors. At the back was a storage area, a small workbench and the hayloft. I was confused by the fresh straw laid in two of the stalls and small bales of hay stacked near them.

"Willy told me at the station that he had gotten the barn ready for us. He lives just down the road and will bring our cow over later today,"

Papa explained. He showed me how to brush the horses and clean out their hooves. I had never been so close to a horse before and had a healthy fear of being kicked. He showed me how to run a hand along their rump and walk closely behind them to always let them know where I was. This seemed counter-intuitive, and I would have preferred to make a wide arc behind them each time.

The previous owners had left two shoulder poles with notches in each end to hang a bucket. Papa told me that as a child on his uncle Edward's farm they had been called milkmaid's yokes, because fresh milk was carried in them. We made our way to the well near the house and filled four buckets. The water we drew was as cold as ice and had a freshness that I'd never tasted before, and we drank deeply from our cupped hands. We carried the water back to the barn for the horses, much of mine sloshing from the wobbling buckets. I was unaccustomed to work, and felt fatigued after this small task.

Willy Southern ambled slowly down our lane leading a fat dairy cow by a rough, homemade stretch of rope. He wore a faded blue shirt, three buttons left unfastened. The cuffs were rolled to his elbows, and the fraying at the collar revealed the shirt's age. Willy's denim pants were also rolled at the cuffs. The denim was work-worn but not filthy. At the right front pocket there was a faded spot about one inch wide and three inches long. It suggested that he regularly carried something in that pocket, a small, foldable knife perhaps. Willy's face wore several days of gray stubble, and the finest hint of dirt could be seen in the lines of his face. I was not put off by his rough appearance, for he had a wide smile and deep crinkles at the corners of his kind eyes.

"Hello there, Miss Dahlia! I'm Willy Southern. I've got yer dairy cow here, and I was hoping to do some fishing," he said, gesturing to the fishing pole propped on his left shoulder. Willy's voice had an unmistakable southern drawl. Each word was as long and sweet as pulled taffy.

"It's a pleasure to meet you, Mr. Southern," I said, remembering not to curtsy.

"Please, call me Willy," he said before continuing. "The river runs wide and flat through my land, rocky and terrible for fishing. Yer oxbows slow it to a trickle and its prit near impossible to catch anything worth cooking," Willy said, stroking the cow's head as he spoke. I had no idea what an oxbow was or how it slowed a river, but I nodded politely. Papa emerged from the barn then and greeted Willy with a firm handshake.

"Is it the fish you're after, or the fishing?" Papa said knowingly as we walked back to the barn with the cow in tow. Papa and Willy began talking about the barrow pig that would be ready for us in a few weeks, and they walked over to inspect the pig pen while I settled the cow in her new stall.

I had seen cows in pictures of course, and in the fields as our train carried us west, but never this closely. She stood about four feet at the shoulder and had a bony, squared-off rump. Her tufted tail swung in wide arcs to keep the flies at bay. Her coat was a deep red with patches and dots of white, like a map of the world. Willy had told us that she was an Ayrshire cow. They originated from Scotland and were hardy and resistant to the cold winters, their milk high in butterfat.

I made my way to the head of this large animal to find gentle eyes framed by impossibly long lashes. Her ears were huge, the size of my hand at least, and they swiveled lazily. Her jaw worked steadily on some grass that she had found. I laid some straw for bedding and fetched water for her trough, spilling a little less from my buckets this time. I gave her some feed to tide her over until she could graze in the pasture and ran my hand slowly down her neck over and over, soothing us both.

Willy had left for the river while I was in the barn, and a few hours later he walked back through the yard, a line with three fish in one hand and his fishing rod in the other. He gave us one of the fish for our supper and offered to help us unload the wagon. We were grateful for his help. Papa and I had unloaded the smaller crates, but the heft and dimensions of the sideboard and trunks made them impossible for me to move. Willy suggested that I remove the items in the sideboard to make it lighter. I unwound the twine that had secured the doors during our journey. The contents were not as I had packed them. I ran my hands over the smooth glass of the canning jars that I had reluctantly removed from the sideboard before we left. The large, black canning pot contained the jar lids, tongs and sturdy wire rack that were needed for canning. Tucked into the handle of the pot's lid was a single sheet of rolled paper. It read:

Dearest Dahlia,

These will be of more use to you than me. Ma would have wanted you to have them. I know that by the time you read this I will already be missing you terribly.

Love always,

Fiona

Tears streamed down my face as I clutched the note to my chest. I had underestimated the pain that I would feel when we left Fiona. I had spent every single day of my life with her. Her laugh and spirit were infectious, her love without rules or conditions. I removed the canning supplies from the sideboard and found Mrs. O'Malley's thick recipe book tucked behind them. I opened the book at random and ran my finger along each line of the recipe, taking comfort in touching something that Mrs. O'Malley had once touched. A dried pansy fell from between the pages, pressed there long ago. There was hope inherent in the saving of something beautiful for another day. I felt Fiona and Mrs. O'Malley here with me, bolstering me as they always had.

Papa and Willy managed the furniture and trunks with a strength that surprised me. They were both thin and of average height, their frames not suggestive of might. After the wagon was unloaded, we sat at the beautiful kitchen table and drank ladles full of water fresh from the well. I asked Willy about his accent, and where he had been before here. He told us that he was born in Texas and had spent most of his life atop a horse as a ranch hand. He leaned back in his chair, his left foot resting on his right knee. He lit a hand-rolled cigarette as he told us about falling madly in love with the daughter of the rancher. They had planned to marry and start their own ranch, but her father had forbidden it and had sent Willy packing. Willy had a far-away look in his eyes as he continued. He had heard about the opportunity for homesteading in Canada and had made his way north with nothing but his horse, a saddlebag containing his few belongings, and a broken heart. Willy looked around the table for an ashtray, and then tapped the ash of his cigarette into the rolled cuff of his pants.

"And I've been here ever since," Willy said, forcing a smile. We invited him to stay for dinner, but he declined, saying he needed to get home to tend to his animals. He gathered his fish and his rod, tipped his hat and bade us a nice evening as he left the house.

***

Papa showed me how to gut the rainbow trout and remove its scales, and then we pan-fried it in butter. Papa had shown me how to light a fire in the wood stove, a task that I would need to do several times a day. The fish's skin crackled and popped as it fried, and the red flesh softened to pink. Papa and I were accustomed to having our meals prepared for us, and as such hadn't thought to make anything to accompany the fish. It was of no matter. The trout was so much more flavorful than the halibut and cod that I had eaten my whole life, and we each had a full filet to enjoy. I apologized to Papa for not preparing anything to eat alongside the fish.

"We're just learning, Dolly. We need to see what's before us instead of looking for what's not there," he said, raising a forkful of trout in toast.

"What's an oxbow, Papa?" I asked as we ate.

"It's the u-shaped collar that attaches oxen to their yoke."

"Oh. Willy said that we had oxbows in our stretch of river, and that they slowed its flow through his land," I said, confusion clear on my face. Papa laughed.

"Oh, yes. Oxbows are also the name for u-shaped bends in a river as it changes course. They look much like ribbon candy. Over time they can be cut off from the river and they form little lakes the shape of crescent moons. Oxbows are a wonderful place for livestock to drink, and we've got three just through those jack pines. We'll walk down tomorrow so you can see them."

After we tended the horses and cow, Papa and I moved the two comfortable chairs near the fire, his red tufted one and the green one that was now mine. I made a pot of tea and we sat in companionable silence. As I looked around our new home, I noticed a horseshoe nailed above the front door. I pointed it out to Papa.

"Yes, I noticed it earlier. It's an old superstition that a horseshoe over your door will hold your luck. It must always be hung with the curve at the bottom, so that your luck doesn't run out of it. I think it started in Ireland, but the tradition has been adopted by people all over the world".

"How is it that you seem to know something about everything?" I was amazed at the sheer volume of his knowledge.

"Well, I suppose it's because I listen when people talk. I met many people in my years as a banker, and they all had something interesting to say when I made time to hear it," he said, before taking a sip of his tea. I think that Papa's keen interest in the words of others was one of his most endearing qualities. He was never dismissive, and his attention to those around him made them feel valued.

We sat by the fire for a while longer, enjoying the comfort of our new home, our new life. My body was unaccustomed to the heavy work of a farm, or any work at all really. My limbs and eyelids grew heavy, and I excused myself to bed. I crawled between the cool sheets of my new bed and fell into the deepest, most restful sleep that I'd had in years.

Chapter Five

SPRING

It was incredible to watch our little piece of the Prairies come to life during the spring. It felt as if the trees showed tiny green buds one day, and a full crown of leaves the next. The animals wandered the pastures all day, never seeming to get their fill of the tender shoots of new grass. We thought ahead to planting our garden and had ordered many packets of seeds from the mercantile. The days on our farm were routine: tend the animals, prepare meals, maintain the house and outbuildings, and split log after endless log for the fire. My sense of security was bolstered by the monotony. I needed to know the shape of my days.

Our first week on the farm was largely spent unpacking our trunks and familiarizing ourselves with our land. Papa placed his chess set on a side table near his chair, his clock on the mantle, and a rifle that I had never seen before on the wall by the door. I decided to unpack things only as I needed them, rather than filling our home with unnecessary clutter. I hung my new farm dresses in the wardrobe and packed my traveling dress away without even washing it. I unpacked the simple kitchen dishes and left the fine China buried under linen in a trunk. It was remarkable how little we actually needed here.

We moved the still-full trunks into the sod house, which was hidden from view from the main house. Papa had discovered it while returning from the latrine on our first day here. It was built into a hill, only one wooden wall visible from outside. It was a single room, less than a quarter the size of our wood house. We used the space for storage of extra supplies, and it seemed that the previous residents had done the same. The sod house had a large cellar with sturdy shelves lining each wall. In it we found a wooden butter churn, two metal and two wooden pails, empty flour and sugar sacks, and a broom. I was once again grateful for the things that had been left for us, things we had not even known that we might need.

***

One afternoon a few days after our arrival I was surprised by a knock on the door. When I opened the door, I was greeted by chaos. A woman was bent away from me, the seat of her dress all that I could see of her. She was speaking loudly in another language and trying to separate two little boys wrestling in her skirts. Two larger boys ran wildly around the yard, one carrying a pie and one waving a stick. The woman finally succeeded in separating the little boys and shooed them out to play.

"Bring the pie!" she yelled in English as she straightened the kerchief that she wore on her head instead of a bonnet. Turning towards the house, she gasped to find me standing there.

"Hello, Miss. I'm Inga Chornyk, I live just down the road. I heard in town that we had new neighbors, and I came to welcome you," Inga said breathlessly.

"Hello Inga, I'm Dahlia Day. It's a pleasure to meet you," I said just as the oldest boy delivered the pie to his mother without slowing from a run. The dish wobbled in Inga's hands, and she sighed loudly, a sound she must make often given her present company. I invited her in, and she yelled a warning to her boys to behave as she sank into a chair at the table.

"Would you like a cup of tea?" I offered.

"Oh, I'd love one if it's no trouble. I've made an egg pie for you and your father," she said, telling me that she already knew about Mother's death. "Where did you come from?" she asked.

"We're from Philadelphia. We lost my Mother and our home in a fire, and felt that a change of scenery would be best."

"Oh, dear. I'm sorry for your loss. There's nothing so hard as losing your mother," Inga said softly. I grunted, noncommittal, before continuing.

"Papa spent some time on a farm as a child, and wanted us to have the type of simple life that he remembered. I'm so glad that we've come."

"Well, I'm glad that you've come as well. There aren't many neighbors out this way, and I could use the company of another woman."

"Where did your family come from?"

"Ukraine. The chance to own land and live in freedom was too strong to resist. Life can be hard here, but it was much harder there. We came five years ago, with three boys in tow. Our youngest was born in the back of the covered wagon on the night we arrived on our plot of land," Inga said with a laugh.

"That must have been a long, difficult journey," I said as I poured our tea.

"It was, but worth it, and we had help. We travelled with my sister Olena and her husband; they continued on further west. We also traveled with a woman that taught us English. Our journey lasted almost a year, so by the time the wagon train arrived on the Prairies we could all speak it pretty well."

"Yes, I should say so! What are your boys' names?" I asked.

"The oldest is Marko, then Artem, Borys and Petro. My husband is named Olek. I'm sure that you'll meet him soon." Inga carried the conversation from there, reminding me of Mrs. O'Malley as she filled every pause with words. She stuck her head out of the door and yelled to her boys to stay out of the pig pen. I watched Inga as she spoke. She was five or ten years older than me, and short in stature. Soft curls of dark hair escaped the kerchief around her face, giving her an angelic look. Her large eyes were as black as coal, plump cheeks flushed pink. Her smile was wide and genuine, and rarely left her face. Inga had the sturdy build of a woman who worked hard. She was stunning.

"Not one girl to rub my feet and help with the wash," Inga lamented, eyes looking heavenward. I laughed, imagining what her life must be like. Inga drank her tea quickly and stood to leave.

"I better round up my boys before they knock the barn down." She seemed only half-joking, thanking me for the tea, giving me directions to her house and inviting me to come by any time at all. I thanked her and made the same offer. Inga corralled her children, dragging one by the ear as they made their way down the lane. I measured their progress by the cloud of dust that followed them as the boys ran and jumped the whole way.

***

Papa showed me how to milk the cow, and it quickly became one of my duties. It was a chore that needed doing very early each morning, long before the sun rose most days. If I slept too late, I would be woken by the increasingly frantic lows of the cow, the sound carrying easily from the barn. I was used to sleeping until midmorning, wasting much of the morning in bed, for lack of anything to do. Now I rose early, and loved my mornings with the cow. That first hour of each day held magic, possibility. I would make my way to the barn, retrieve my milking stool and buckets, and sit with this sweet animal. The only sounds would be the gentle, rhythmic stream of milk hitting the bucket, and the occasional sigh from the horses as they slept. I often emerged from the barn just as the sun began to rise, the skies lit up with pink or orange.

I began making butter in the old wooden churn that we had found in the sod house. It required a great deal of time and energy, but little thought. My mind would wander, and I would begin to recite the list of tasks that I needed to complete, or items that I needed from the mercantile, as Mrs. O'Malley used to do. Papa came into the house one morning as I churned, nattering away to myself.

"Who are you talking to, Dolly?"

"Myself, I suppose. I'm trying to remember a list of things that we need to pick up next time we go to town," I laughed.

"You reminded me of Mrs. O'Malley just then," he said with a soft smile, "and you've given me an idea for your birthday gift."

My twenty-first birthday was on June first, but the day was so hot that it felt more like August. Papa had arranged for Willy, Inga, Olek and the boys to come for a picnic. We spread a few blankets by the lake at the far end of our land and watched the birds dive for plants to eat. The boys splashed around in the shallows in their undershorts, and emerged screeching, covered in leeches. After Inga had settled the boys and dealt with the leeches, we ate the food that everyone had brought. Inga made a potato salad with dill, bacon, and vinegar dressing. Willy brought roast beef shaved thin to pile on fresh rolls. We filled out our plates with sweet pickles. I baked a cake that dipped sadly at the center, my first solo attempt at a cake. I tried to hide the flaw with extra chocolate frosting, and our guests ate every last bite.

Papa presented me with a gift wrapped in plain brown paper and tied with twine. Inside I found a small schoolhouse slate, ten pieces of chalk, and a small bottle of maple syrup. He explained that the slate was to write my chore lists on, and the maple syrup had reminded him of our train from Montreal. Inga gave me a snow-white kerchief that she had embroidered with tiny flowers of blue and yellow.

"I thought you'd like that for the summer. It will keep your hair from your face, and won't be as hot as a bonnet," she said as I admired the stitching.

"It is beautiful," I said, as I fastened it under my hair. Willy gave me riding gloves that he had made from buttery-soft leather.

"I imagine you'll need those before long. I'm not used to making gloves for women. I hope they're all right," Willy said humbly, his drawl adding even more charm to his words.

"They are perfect, Willy. Thank you." Tears filled my eyes at the generosity and kindness of these people that I had known less than two months. I hugged everyone and thanked them for my presents. I said a silent word of thanks to the Universe for bringing me here, where every moment felt like a gift.

***

Dearest Dahlia,

Happy birthday! I hope that you have found some way to celebrate on the farm. I loved reading all about your new home. It sounds beautiful, but lonely. I would go mad staring at the same few people every day! My new job is keeping me busy, the two little boys are a lot of fun, but they get into all sorts of trouble. The lady of the house is kind, the man rarely home. Vincent has been working long hours, so I have not seen him as much as I would like. He still has not proposed marriage, but I hope that he will soon. I miss you every day.

Sincerely,

Fiona

I wished that I could have spoken with Fiona, as I felt that there was much more that she hadn't said. I did not enjoy communicating through letters. They provided only the writer's choice of words and robbed me of the knowledge that could be gleaned from their delivery.

I could feel something from people when I spoke to them. The mystics referred to it as aura, others simply calling it connection. For me it was a sense deep in the pit of my stomach. The tilt of a head or the set of a jaw, where a person's gaze fell and what they did with their hands; these things told me more about a person's nature and intentions than a thousand written words could.

I replied to Fiona's letter, and told her about my birthday picnic, my friendship with Inga, and planting my first garden. I thanked her for the thoughtful gift of her Ma's canning supplies and recipe book and assured her that I would use them a great deal. I did not tell her that I wanted nothing more than for her to come live here with us. I needed to let her find her own way, as I was finding mine.

***

I had not mentioned Mother to Papa since we had watched the strange hatbox containing her remains being lowered into the ground. This quiet omission grew until it was uncomfortable for me. I chose a day of fruitless fishing to talk to Papa about her. He sat in the deep grass, me on a log stump, our fishing lines slack in the fast-moving river.

"Mother would have hated it here," I blurted out, instantly relieving the burden I'd felt as the words had sat on my tongue for weeks. Papa cleared his throat and shifted uncomfortably. "She would have worn clear through the floorboards with her pacing."

"I know. I think you were right that the private home would have been the best place for her."

"Am I awful for not missing her? I keep expecting to feel sadness, but there's only pity. I don't know how to miss someone that I barely knew, who existed only on the periphery of my life until the autumn before she died." The confession brought even more relief.

"You're not awful, Dolly. I suspect that she intentionally withdrew from us in order to protect us from her madness. Perhaps that's how she showed her love." The words hung between, both of us watching our fishing lines. "The truth is, I never really knew Elizabeth either. Her time as a nurse in the war had broken something inside of her before we ever met. Our parents arranged our wedding, and we both allowed it to happen. I mourned her loss many years ago, along with the loss of my dream for a wonderful marriage." We sat in silence for a few minutes, listening to the river bubble over the rocks on its banks.

"I deserved a mother. She didn't care one fig about me until last year, when she woke up and terrorized me for being so inadequate. She gave me no guidance, and then berated me when I became lost," I said through choked sobs. Papa put his rod down, came over to me and pulled me to my feet. He held my head against his shoulder and stroked my hair gently as I wailed and shook. We stood like that for a long time, until the last tears had fallen, leaving hiccups in their stead. Papa held my face in his hands and looked into my eyes.

"You did deserve a mother, and I'm sorry that you didn't have one. We can't ask someone for more than they can give, and Elizabeth had nothing at all." Papa wiped the tears from my cheeks. I nodded and looked down at my feet, suddenly embarrassed by my outburst.

"Let's head home. I don't think we're going to catch anything today," Papa said softly as he gathered his rod and the empty bucket that ought to have held a few fish. My catharsis had left me feeling lighter, my perspective shifting ever so slightly from a place of anger to one of understanding. I shook my head a few times, as if to rid my mind of thoughts of Mother. Over the next few months my perspective continued to evolve from ire to understanding, and eventually from tenderness to forgiveness. Mother had suffered for most of her life, her doors barred from within. I refused to do the same.

Chapter Six

SUMMER

Willy and Papa's friendship continued to thrive. He became as excited as a child whenever Willy asked him for help, as if he were about to embark on an adventure. I saw Papa shed the suit and serious nature of the banker he had once been. He had always been kind and reliable in his affections, but never effusive. His eyes and brow had seemed committed to an unspoken worry, and though he smiled often, those smiles had never reached his eyes. Papa's smiles now took over his entire face, eyebrows raised and mouth slightly open, as if he were surprised. He had found deep satisfaction in farming and living close to nature, and his friendship with Willy provided the connection that he craved.

Papa could invent any number of excuses to go over to Willy's, but never required one. Willy was always glad to see him and happy for the help he offered. We headed to Willy's one afternoon on a mission to pick up our barrow pig. Willy had told us that the piglet had been castrated to prevent its meat from taking on the musky flavor of an intact boar, as well as to avoid the pig terrorizing the countryside in search of a mate. We stopped the wagon near the farrowing barn that doubled as a nursery for the piglets as they grew.

I was unprepared for both the smell and the noise that assaulted me as I entered the barn. The piglets shrieked and squealed, their noise reverberating off the barn's walls. The smell was so overpowering that I could taste it, each breath choking me. Willy noticed our arrival and made his way through the sea of piglets with agonizing slowness. He told us to choose any piglet that we wanted. Papa told him that any one would do, and we hurried to the door, desperate for air. We burst from the barn, gasping as if we had spent several minutes under water. I wondered how Willy didn't carry this smell with him on his hair and clothing. I could smell it clinging to me after only a few minutes inside of the barn.

Willy emerged from the barn carrying a twenty-five-pound piglet wriggling and squealing. The piglet settled once he was placed in the back of the wagon, finally still enough for me to see him clearly. He was the exact pink of scalded skin and was covered in bristly white hairs. Some brown spots could be seen dotting his sides. The end of his snout was flat and wet, and sniffed continuously. His eyes were small and shifty, and his large ears glowed red when backlit by the midday sun.

"What shall we name him, Papa?" I asked excitedly, already taken with this tiny piglet. Papa and Willy exchanged a knowing glance.

"If I may, Miss Dahlia, it's best not to name an animal that yer fixing to eat." Willy said.

"Oh, I see." I blushed at my own naivete. "What does he eat?"

"He'll eat prit near anything, though you'll need to start him on cornmeal feed. Scraps from the kitchen and weeds from the garden can go right into his trough. Best be careful in that pen though, he's likely to eat you if given the chance." I started to laugh, but my laughter turned to a shiver once I realized that Willy wasn't joking. We paid Willy for the piglet and headed towards home, our winter's supply of ham oinking and scratching in the wagon the whole way.

The pig quickly established himself as a thorn in my side. He immediately discovered how to escape from his pen and did so numerous times a day. He was smart, but not sly, and would scream with glee upon each escape as he tore at full speed past the house or into the fields. No matter how many times we patched and reinforced the fence, he would find a way out. I eventually gave up trying to contain him and only closed the gate to his pen at nighttime.

The pig would follow us around the farm and into the barn as we went about our chores. He joined the other animals as they grazed in the pasture and watched intently as I fed the chickens. He never once broke into the fence that Papa erected around the garden, and never grew tired of rooting and snorting around the other 160 acres.

***

Each morning after I had milked the cow and led the animals out to the pasture, I would spend some time in my garden. It's a wondrous thing to plant tiny seeds and then watch them turn into tender green shoots that reach for the sun. When I had finally dug my hands into the soil for the first time I understood what Papa had meant all those months ago. The earth was damp and cool, and I loved the sensation of patting soil down over a newly planted seed. I hadn't thought to place markers in my garden so that I could identify the plants in their infancy. In truth, I likely couldn't identify most of these plants until they bore fruit. All of our vegetables in Philadelphia had come from the market or were cultivated by Mrs. O'Malley with no effort on my part. I knew the importance of producing a great deal of food to see us through the winter, and I was committed to growing the best garden that I could. Papa understood that this was a project that I wanted to do alone, and after he helped me till the soil, he'd given the garden a wide berth.

Inga had given me advice on how to plant: which plants grew well next to each other, which ones needed full sun or partial shade, and how to water each plant. I followed her advice on planting and walked the rows each day, plucking any weed that took root. I would gather up the weeds that I had pulled and take them to the pig's trough along with the eggshells from that morning's breakfast.

As yet, the garden showed only the most tentative signs of growth. That is, except for the peas. They had grown in a large cluster near one corner rather than in a row as I remembered planting them. I was so pleased that they were growing that I didn't care how or where they grew. I had staked the plants with long branches, anchoring the stalks with loosely-tied twine. They stood three feet tall already, and so early in the season! I envisioned tender peas straight from the pod or boiled and served with butter and salt. Impatiently, I inspected my pea plants each day, looking for the first pods to appear among the flowers.

Inga dropped in one day, unexpectedly. It was rare for Inga to come to the farm. We usually spent time at her house on account of her needing to mind her children, so this visit was a welcome surprise.

"My boys are driving me 'round the bend. I usually go into town when I need a break from the boys pulling on my skirts, but thought I'd come see you instead."

"Well, I'm glad that you did, I could use some company."

"You don't go into town much, do you? I never see you at church, and it doesn't seem that anyone else there knows you," Inga said, eyebrows raised.

"No, I don't. I have no desire to do any social climbing, and church has never been for me. I'm content with the company of the friends that I have. We were treated very poorly by those that we considered friends in Philadelphia, and I'm not eager to see that happen again," I said, more sharply than I had intended. "I have something to show you," I said as I set water to boil for tea, and excitedly led Inga out to the garden to see my incredible peas.

She stopped walking when she caught sight of the peas. Pride welled up in me, and then she began to laugh. A giggle at first, and then a deep, hearty roar that shook her considerable belly. She tried to speak but her laughter took over each time she tried to begin. I stood there in my confusion, laughing a little despite myself. Inga finally managed a single shrill sentence through her laughter:

"It's Creeping Bellflower, you've staked weeds!" she squeaked out. My face flushed hot with embarrassment. I felt incredibly foolish for a moment before I saw the humor in my situation. I joined in Inga's laughter. We shrieked and howled, tears running down our faces. We would begin to compose ourselves, make a squeaky attempt at speech, and be overcome with a new fit of laughter. Inga stomped her feet and stooped over, snorting in between bouts of silent laughter. When we finally made our way back into the kitchen, wiping our tears on our aprons, we found that the tea pot had nearly boiled dry as we had carried on in the garden. The pig ate well that night, feasting on a bumper crop of Creeping Bellflower.

***

Summer brought a heavy heat that could not be escaped. It settled into our little valley and smothered all who lived there. The horses and cow would graze in the pasture early in the morning and gather at the fence before the sun hit high noon, desperate for the relative coolness of the barn. The birds flew lazily, if at all, their songs infrequent and subdued. Even the bugs seemed to wilt under the heat, flying at half-speed. The ground had not felt rain in three weeks, and it cracked under the heat of the sun.

The farm had been overtaken by grasshoppers, who thrived in this hot, dry weather. Each step in the fields would send a new horde leaping in every direction. Most days I would feel the tickle of one that had found its way under my skirts, sending me into a fit of slapping and wriggling. The farmers around us were affected as well, watching their harvests dwindle with each day. We seemed to have fewer of the pests than farms to the south, but there were enough of them that I worried about our pastures and vegetables. I was desperate to save my garden, spending hours picking the awful insects off my plants. Inga suggested using water that had been boiled with garlic, or a light dusting of flour to keep the grasshoppers at bay. I tried both with limited success and watched helplessly as many of my vegetables were eaten before they had ripened enough to be picked.

Papa and I moved about the farm like we were walking in deep mud, the sun sapping our energy. The perspiration left a salty film on my skin, which quickly attracted the dust that was everywhere. No amount of bathing with a cloth could rid me of this feeling, and I couldn't muster the energy that hauling water for a tub bath required. I sought shade in the tall trees beside our house one evening and walked slowly towards the river. I cupped my hands to splash water on my face, surprised to find that it was very cool. I moved quickly to the deepest stretch of river and removed my dress as I went. I stripped off every stitch of clothing that I wore and walked straight into the river. Some rocks were slippery with moss, others rolled under the pressure of my feet. I slid awkwardly on the slimy rocks, struggling to stay upright. The water was so cold that my breath caught in my chest, and I was forced to enter slowly, rather than all at once as I had planned. A tree had fallen into the river, its roots still anchored to the bank. I floated towards the tree and caught a hold of it, my arms draped over the tree and my body floating in the river beneath it. I let my head fall back and savored the delicious chill of the water. I had no sense of how long I stayed there. My breathing was shallow and rapid at first but returned to a normal rhythm as I grew used to the icy flow. I loved the sound of the water flowing rapidly over the rocks; it was the only thing that moved quickly in this heat. The river seemed to be the only thing alive at all, and it lent me its vitality as I bathed. When I felt clean and cool, I slowly pulled myself along the tree towards the bank. I laid on the grass for a few minutes to dry off, and then donned my clothing, my fingers numb with cold.

The first thunderstorm that I witnessed on the Prairies is something that I'll never forget. It rained often during the spring, but never with the ferocity of a summer storm. Papa and I had taken to sleeping in the old sod house during the height of summer in an attempt to escape the relentless heat. It had two beds, and we needed only to bring a sheet for each in order to be comfortable. Its two small windows let in very little sun, and the coolness of the earth seeped through the walls.

One evening after settling the animals in the barn I stood on our hill and looked to the east. The air was heavy and still, and the humidity made my dress stick to my back. The thunder rumbled. It was low and far off but approaching surely. It was impossible to tell from which direction the storm was coming. The sky had an eerie green hue, though no lightning was visible yet. The frogs had fallen silent, waiting, waiting. The trees had a strange look to them, their green color muted and their leaves turned towards the sky; the leaves' silver underbellies visible in anticipation of the rain.

I sat in the dirt and watched tall clouds gather to the north. They were pure white at the soft peaks, and an angry, bruised purple at the bases, looking very much like mountains in the sky. The stillness held. The air was thick with the promise of rain. There was no sound, no wind. I leaned slightly forward, every muscle in my body tense as I waited for this monster's arrival. The first clap of thunder tore through the air, startling me and setting every hair on my neck on end. On its heels came the wind, gusting and angry. The first few drops of rain fell, fat and slow, and oddly warm. More thunder boomed, drawing Papa outside. We stood in silence as the storm drew nearer.

The skies opened, unleashing a hard, driving rain. We ran for the house, narrowly missing the hail that fell large as crabapples from the summer sky. We stood in the open doorway, watching the wind ripple across the fields, as thunder rolled and echoed in the valley. The hail bounced six feet or more when it hit the ground, creating mayhem as it rose to meet the hail that fell after it. When the clouds were spent of hail, a heavy rain took its place. The wind lashed at the trees, scattering the leaves that had been spared by the grasshoppers, now shredded by hail.

The storm departed as quickly as it had arrived, rolling south along the mountains. The clouds cleared before the sun set behind us, its orange glare reflected by the countless drops of water that clung to every leaf and blade of grass. The air was wonderfully cool and smelled of earth that night as it drifted through my bedroom window. It carried on it the symphony of frogs that had been reanimated by the rain after so many weeks of unbearable heat, their wait finally over.

***

Papa asked Willy to give me lessons on how to ride a horse. I had stuck to walking or using the wagon thus far and was nervous about climbing onto the back of a huge animal. My first lesson was a disaster of tangled skirts and spine-jarring bouncing in the saddle. I dressed differently for my second lesson, ready to learn. I wore one of Papa's shirts and a pair of his denim trousers, the waist cinched tight with thin rope, my high laced boots, and my kerchief. Papa and Willy took several minutes to compose themselves after seeing me in my "riding costume." Without the distraction of bunching skirts and bare legs I was able to focus on the ride. Willy had seen that I was sitting with my weight in my saddle rather than on the stirrups, which had been causing me to bounce every which way.

"Put yer weight on yer feet, Dahlia, not the saddle. You won't bounce so much

that way." I did as Willy suggested, and found the ride was already more comfortable. He also noticed that I was squeezing my thighs tight to the mare's chest to stabilize myself, making her snort uncomfortably.

"Ease up with yer legs now, when you squeeze like that it makes her skittish. She can feel yer fear, and she feels it too." I did so, and the mare stopped snorting and shuffling nervously. I learned that a horse was very attuned to the emotions of its rider, and Willy had me dismount and spend time with my mare, stroking her velvety nose and feeding her beets from my hand. Being near her face and looking into her wide eyes helped me to feel more at ease. I inhaled the sweet smell unique to horses, as she sniffed my hands and body in search of more beets. I climbed back into the saddle with new confidence, trusting that she would take me safely anywhere that I wanted to go. I learned how to saddle her, and then how to read her mood from her snorts and nickers. Riding her became much easier as we came to know each other, and I enjoyed each ride more than the last.

***

I continued to see Inga regularly; her lively spirit was irresistible to me. I made my way to her farm in the dying days of summer to learn how to make borscht. Inga had served it for lunch one day, and I had thought about it every day since. She made her soup from heart as she had since she was a girl and offered to teach me how to make it. I scrambled around my house looking for paper to write the recipe on, settling for a crumpled bag that our tea had come in. I needn't have bothered; Inga told me there was no recipe.

I entered Inga's kitchen to find her cleaning up the lunch dishes. The house was bright with the afternoon sun, and spotless as it always was. It was beyond me how Inga could keep her house so clean with four farm boys running about. Cheery half drapes graced each window, adorned with embroidery in blues, yellows, and reds. Neatly stacked dishes and small cannisters for tea and coffee lined the cupboard. Two China serving dishes sat on the highest shelf, safe from the clumsy hands of her boys.

The four boys were gathered around the door that led to their bedroom, jostling for position at the jamb. They were arguing in both English and Ukrainian, making the conversation hard for me to follow. Inga rolled her eyes, sighed deeply, and grabbed a knife from the block. I followed her into the living area, curious to see what she would do.

"I measure the boys on the last day of each season, and carve their height into the jamb," she explained. "They get so excited to see who has grown the most. I swear, they eat like horses just to be the winner each season," Inga finished, rolling her eyes and laughing. Each boy's name was carefully carved into the corner of the jamb that belonged to them. Inga started with the youngest boy and made her way through all four. Each boy stood as tall as possible, chest puffed out and hope clear on their face. As each new mark was revealed the boys would whoop and cheer, proud of their growth. Olek was a large man and his boys seemed to be following suit. After all four boys had a new notch in their jamb Inga shooed them outside to play. I ran my hands along the jamb, admiring this clever way to document growth. I could tell which years had seen bountiful harvests; their notches spaced much farther apart.

I joined Inga in the kitchen, ready to make the soup. Inga whirled around the kitchen, chopping and washing as she chattered about all manner of things. I tended to be still, my busyness confined to my head. Inga was the opposite: never still, always doing several things at one time. This discrepancy in our natures made me anxious, as I struggled to follow Inga's vague instructions.

"Next we'll add a handful of chopped dill, and some salt and pepper."

"How much of each?" I asked, feeling lost.

"Oh, as much as it needs," she replied. "We'll simmer the soup until it looks right, and then it will be done," Inga finished. I looked helplessly at my crumpled paper bag. I had no measurements to write down, and settled instead for a list of ingredients. I left her house full of doubt that I could recreate her incredible soup. My fears were in vain; my borscht came out beautifully. Papa had sat at the table and watched me as I prepared it.

"You're sure learning a lot, Dolly. It makes me so happy to see you thrive here."

"Thanks, Papa. It feels good to care of myself for once. Inga's a great teacher too, I can't take all of the credit," I replied, blushing a little at the praise. I kneaded the sourdough that Inga had sent home with me, and popped it into the woodstove to bake while the soup simmered. When both were ready I ladled the borscht into large bowls.

The silky beets, crunchy cabbage and fresh dill combined perfectly, and I served it with swirls of heavy cream. Papa and I sopped up the delicious broth with thick wedges of crusty sourdough. We enjoyed it so much that we had eaten nothing else for three straight days. I added the recipe in all its vague glory to Mrs. O'Malley's recipe book. I knew that if she could have seen me, she would have been so proud of how much I was learning on this prairie farm.

Chapter Seven

Autumn came on a sea of reds and yellows. This had always been my favorite time of year and experiencing it on the farm was so much better than it had been in Philadelphia. The relative idleness of summer was replaced by the frenzy of preparation for winter. We harvested the vegetables that had been spared by the grasshoppers, Inga helping me make use of every bit of our meager produce. I allowed myself one small bowl of the boiled, buttered peas that I had dreamt of as I had mistakenly tended the patch of Creeping Bellflower. The rest were dried and stored in jars to use in winter soups. My carrot plants had grown tall stems and I had expected to find huge carrots when I pulled them. Instead, I found tiny carrots, the longest measuring only four inches. They fit easily into the jars when I pickled them, filling far fewer than I had hoped. I dried the greens to be used for stock, hoping that the suggestion of flavor would satisfy our bellies when we ate winter soup with little body.

Papa picked up my order from the mercantile, large jugs of vinegar and several sacks of salt, and I set to pickling eggs to prepare for the hens' decreased production in the cold, dark winter. I retrieved Mrs. O'Malley's recipe book from the cupboard and leafed through it, searching for the section on canning. I came across the pressed pansy again and smiled. I struggled with getting the right amount of brine for each batch of vegetables, leaving me with jars that had too much headroom. In a few months I would learn that this extra air led to spoilage. I salted the fourteen trout that Papa had caught, and dried and stored all the beans we had grown. Papa had bought enough alfalfa, hay and straw to fill the hayloft and lean-tos to avoid running out if the snow made the roads impassable by wagon.

I decided to use tin milk cans to store our dry goods after I found a mouse's nest near our sacks of flour. The babies were pink and hairless, and somehow terrifying despite their diminutive size. I gathered up the nest in a cloth and placed it behind the barn, hoping that the mother would somehow find her babies, and raise them away from our food. The mice were preparing for winter as well, seeking any warm place to build homes. They took up residence under the bench in the latrine. Their scratching was unnerving, but I preferred them to the spiders that had lived there in summer. Both were better than the large, scabby rats that had run unchecked on the streets of Philadelphia.

Papa slaughtered the pig while I was visiting Inga one day. I had known the day would come but was devastated all the same. Papa initially hung the carcass in the barn to gut it before taking it to Willy's for butchering. The smell had driven the horses and cow wild, and they had been skittish for days even after we scrubbed the barn floor clean. I missed my companion as I went about my daily chores. I was sad that I hadn't had a chance to say goodbye to the pig, though I'm not sure that I could have looked him in the eyes knowing his fate. Papa could see that I was distressed and suggested that next year we take our pig to Willy's when it was time for butchering. It turned out that not naming the pig hadn't saved me from the heartache of having him butchered. I never again enjoyed the taste of bacon or ham. Each bite required much effort on my part. It was difficult to swallow the shame of my betrayal.

***

We'd never known want or discomfort in Philadelphia. Mrs. O'Malley, and then Fiona, had kept the larders well-stocked and the fires stoked. Every night we dined on tender roast beef with thick gravy, or roasted chickens with golden, crackling skin. Scones speckled with currants, with an array of preserves and clotted cream; or a lemon chiffon cake as light as air were served to our visitors with piping hot tea. Our bed linens were crisp and pure white, and our clothing was meticulously washed and rehung by Mrs. O'Malley. The necessary tasks that had once occurred without any effort or knowledge on my part now consumed my every waking hour.

I struggled to remember how I had filled my days in Philadelphia. I had often been struck with an overwhelming ennui, remedied only briefly by reading or a long walk. This lack of purpose and resulting listlessness had prompted me to spend a lot of time in the kitchen, where conversation and tea were always served.

My one duty every day was to sit with Mother between the hours of one and four. If left unoccupied, she would sleep until dinner and then keep the household awake by pacing the halls all night. At first, I had tried to engage Mother in a card game, needlepoint, or a walk. It quickly became clear that she lacked both the attention and motivation to do much of anything. Mother wiled away her years rocking in her chair, the creak of which threatened to drive me slowly insane, something I often worried on.

Each time Mother relived a horror from her past she left a small part of herself there, until she became a specter of frenzied activity, with no more substance than moth-eaten cloth. I had often watched Mother in profile, looking for hints of her former self. Occasionally her creased brow would soften, and her hands would fall still in her lap. She would relax into her chair and exhale fully for the first time in weeks. A soft smile would play at the corner of her lips, and once she let free a joyous laugh, so uncharacteristic and sudden that it startled the needlepoint right out of my hands. These memories were a gift, as they seemed to be the only respite from her suffering. I had learned not to break Mother's reverie by asking her what she was thinking of, for when I did, her smile would fade, and the tension would return.

When Mother became very agitated it was nearly impossible to calm her. I would sit with her when the fear had churned and frothed into something that could no longer be contained. To me it felt as if I were watching helplessly as she drowned, as I had been for twenty years. One afternoon Mother was unusually lucid, her speech eloquent and her voice strong.

"I was not prepared for the atrocities of war," she began. "I had wanted to help in the war effort, but I was naive to the realities outside of my sphere of existence. I went to the battlefields to help, but the soldiers were beyond helping. Men missing limbs, shreds of flesh where a hand or foot once was. Men slowly driven mad by the deafening ringing in their ears from a cannon's boom; digging in their own ears with any implement they could find in an attempt to quiet it. The smells of blood and gunpowder, the final release of the bowels, and bodies long dead." I shuddered, eyes wide and heart pounding. I dared not speak for fear that Mother would stop talking and this rare glimpse into her mind would come to an end.

"I dressed wounds and gave medicine to relieve the soldiers' pain. These wounds of the body could be treated. It was man's vile nature that could not be cured." Mother grimaced and paused briefly. "Men who, only weeks before had donned vests and tailed coats and sat for dinner surrounded by family, became animals. Screaming maniacally while they hacked at each other with bayonets. Fighting other men to the death for a heel of bread or a soft winter potato when hunger drove them to it. Raping women and even men in the villages they overtook, hatred in their eyes instead of lust." Her head hung low, tears wetting her cheeks. I realized that Mother was not speaking to me anymore.

She was categorizing the horrors that had taken up residence in her mind. I had drawn further away from her as she spoke.

"And the fire. Fire everywhere, taking men's flesh with abandon. It took hours to change each burn dressing, and each second was an eternity of agony for the patient. Many men succumbed to their burns: they were the fortunate ones." Mother's teary gaze fell on me, her mouth turned down at the corners. "I'm sorry. I'm very tired and I'd like to go lie down now," she said in a voice barely above a whisper. Standing from the settee, she drew her robe tightly around her. Her shoulders curved inwards, trying to protect a heart that had already been broken.

Time had blunted the pain that I'd once felt, and I began to feel my heart soften to her memory. I thought about her horrible treatment of me during Conrad's pitiful courtship, and realized that while she hadn't much to give, Mother had tried to prepare me for my future. Perhaps she had felt that the ends would justify her means and had focused solely on seeing me married, as her mother had done for her. Mother now lay buried in a hatbox two thousand miles away, with no one to visit her grave. The anger that I had stored in my jaw and my shoulders began to loosen and were replaced by pity and compassion. Things could not be undone, but I needn't carry this hurt with me through the rest of my days.

***

I loved our new home more with the passing of each day, despite it being rustic and remote. In truth, I was relieved to rarely see others. I hadn't enjoyed my brief sojourn into Philadelphian society, and wasn't eager to repeat it. Inside the house the rough-hewn wall planks were chinked with mud and straw, the simple floors were bare of polish and always in need of sweeping. Water was drawn with effort from the well instead of pumped quickly from a spigot outside of our door. We bathed in a half barrel behind the beautiful wooden screen in the living area, instead of in one of many private baths. The walls in Papa's study had been lined with shelves, housing hundreds of books. We now each had a small collection of our favorite titles sitting atop the mantle. Our home was cozy and comfortable, and contained just what we needed. While the stark differences required some getting used to, nothing in this world could have convinced me to return to my former life.

Our modest home was devoid of silk-papered walls, instruments, and fine China, but the axe and rifle mounted by the door felt like the biggest departure from civilized society. They hung there for ease of use. Papa took the axe down each day to split wood and brought it in each night to keep it dry and prevent it from rusting. The rifle was taken down only when we heard the high-pitched yips and barks of coyotes, or the deep, sorrowful howls of wolves. If you were near the barn when these calls came you could hear them echoed by our animals. The horses would shift and snort in their stalls, the cow would low anxiously. We were fortunate not to lose any of our animals to these predators, but their presence was a constant reminder that we were not alone out here.

Papa decided that I had best learn to shoot the rifle in case I ever needed to protect myself. He cared for it meticulously, despite its lack of use. Each week he would take it down from the wall and clean it with kerosene. He would then carefully rub neat's-foot oil into the metal to prevent the rifle from rusting. Papa explained that the oil could become gummy in cold weather, or too thin when it was warm. As such, it needed regular care to remain functional. Papa and I had laid on our bellies in the long grass and he taught me how to set my sights and aim for a scrap of cloth that he had nailed to a tree.

"Take your time, Dolly. Line it up in your sights, and breath out as you pull the trigger," Papa said in hushed tones, as if we were hunting moose, not scraps of cloth.

The kick from my first shot nearly tore my arm from my shoulder, and the bang startled me something awful. After composing myself I tried again. I missed the tree entirely again, but kept trying until I got a feel for the sights.

"It takes some getting used to, Dolly. Keep trying. You'll get better with each shot," Papa encouraged. Within a month I could hit that scrap of cloth nine times out of ten. I left it hanging on the tree, full of holes, as a sort of trophy. I'd likely never have to shoot the rifle, but I enjoyed the knowledge that I could if the need ever arose.

***

We didn't have many friends on the Prairies, but the ones we had were loyal and true. Inga and I spent as much time together as we could before the snow and cold prevented us from making the two-mile trek to one another's farm. She continued to remind me of Mrs. O'Malley, her excitement contagious and her laugh filling the room. I had never heard Inga complain about her hardships, and her positive outlook had quickly colored my own.

Inga had come over early on the day of Papa's birthday celebration to help me bake a cake. I had wanted to make Papa the lemon chiffon cake from Mrs. O'Malley's recipe book, but had been unable to find a lemon at the mercantile. I decided on a simple butter cake topped with a jar of peaches in their syrup. Inga retrieved the cake from the woodstove, its sweet aroma filling the kitchen. I had steeped several pots of tea, sweetened it, and poured it into jars. Then I placed the jars in a flour sack and anchored them to a tree, letting them cool in the flowing water of the river. The weather was warm for late autumn, and I thought that cool drinks would be welcome.

Willy had brought me some veal the previous day, and I had attempted to recreate the tourtiere that we'd had in Montreal. The pies sat cooling in the kitchen as we continued to prepare for our party. Inga helped me set the outdoor table with our food, and we found stumps and rain barrels for extra seating. Willy and Papa emerged from the barn just as Olek made his way down our lane with his four boys in tow. He was a huge man, tall and broad in the shoulders. He had very masculine, chiseled features, and an unruly mop of light brown hair. His large physical presence contrasted sharply with his gentle demeanor. Olek spoke little, but was always whistling a lively tune.

We sent the boys to the river to retrieve the jars of tea, and then the nine of us settled around the table to eat our tourtiere. I hadn't gotten the seasoning quite right, but the veal, potatoes and onions were delicious. The crust had come out perfectly, golden and flaky. The cool jars of sweetened tea washed down our tourtiere, and I served the cake with peaches and syrup, wonderful despite its simplicity. I noticed Papa looking around the table at our friends as we ate, content plain on his face.

Willy presented Papa with a folding knife just like his own, the handle of which was carved from wood and sanded and polished to a beautiful shine. "Yer always using mine, so I figured you could use a knife of yer own. Mighty handy to have," Willy said humbly. Olek had made Papa a belt of stamped leather.

"You live on a farm, you need a farmer's belt," Olek said with a shrug. It had a small leather pouch that slid onto the belt, the perfect size for Papa's new knife. "Day" was stamped onto the back of the belt, and was flanked with three diamonds on each side.

I had knitted Papa thick winter slipper socks to wear as he sat by the fire at night. I had bought the spun wool months ago and dyed it with beets. My first attempt at dyeing it was not successful, yielding wool that was the color of flesh instead of the ruby red that I had envisioned. I had asked Inga about where I had gone wrong. She told me that I needed to mordant the wool by soaking it in vinegar before dyeing it so that the color would bind. I tried again and produced a wool of pinky-orange. Out of wool and pressed for time, I had settled for this strange hue.

Though I knew only the most basic of stitches and had only ever made flat washcloths, I traced Papa's boot on a piece of paper and used it as a pattern for the sock. The two socks came out very differently, despite my use of the same pattern for each one. The left sock was wider at the toe, and larger than the right. I had miscounted my rows of stitches on the foot and did not know how to fix it. Compensating for my error, I made the leg shorter, ending up with a pair that were the same length but did not match. It was too late to unravel the wool and start anew, so I presented them to Papa in hopes that he would appreciate the thought and effort that had gone into them.

"They're a bit uneven," I said, apologizing before he had even gotten the socks out of the wrapping. Papa's eyes lit up as he held the socks in the air.

"Dolly! Did you knit these yourself?" he asked, already slipping one foot out of his boot to try a sock on.

"Yes, and dyed them that strange color too," I said with a laugh.

"They'll be perfect to wear at night when we sit by the fire. Thank you, they're perfect," Papa said, kissing me on the forehead. The men lit their pipes and cigarettes, and Inga and I began clearing the table. The boys ran around the yard, thumping each other on the heads and hooting with abandon. Inga's youngest son Petro approached me shyly, wrapped his arms around my waist and buried his face in my skirts. He looked up at me with his mother's black eyes, a spattering of freckles across his nose.

"Miss Dahlia, that was the best pie that I ever tasted," he said earnestly. I felt a twinge of yearning to be a mother for the first time in my life.

"I'm glad you liked it, Petro. It's a French pie that I had on a train once. Would you like to take the last slice home with you?" I asked, hugging him to me.

"Yes, please miss Dahlia. I might even eat it on the way home!" he exclaimed, slipping out of my arms to join his brothers in the field.

"He is my sweetest boy. I dread the day that he stops climbing into my lap," Inga said wistfully as Petro ran off.

***

During my childhood, from late autumn to early spring Papa would wear what I had come to think of as his "Saturday sweater." It was knit of thick wool by Mrs. O'Malley some time before my birth. It had horizontal sections of cream and dark brown, alternating solid and patterned blocks. Large wooden buttons ran down the front but were never fastened. Papa would work until lunchtime on Saturdays and would arrive home in time to eat with us before my nap. He would shrug off his suit coat at the foyer closet and don the sweater.

After lunch Mrs. O'Malley would put Fiona and me down for our nap. Though I had my own bedroom, afternoon naps were taken in the nursery, where Fiona still slept at night. Fiona and I would nestle under the down duvet in winter, or a light sheet in summer. Mrs. O'Malley would read from a book of fairy tales or fables, or tell us a story from her childhood. Once she stopped talking, the slow, steady creak of her rocking chair and the gentle clicking of her knitting needles would lull us to sleep.

Eventually Mrs. O'Malley would leave the nursery to tend to something in another part of the house. On Saturdays I would feign sleep, lying as still as could be until I heard her pad off down the hallway. I would creep furtively down to Papa's study, and find him in his deep red, tufted armchair. The weekend issue of the newspaper would be spread in his lap, a lit pipe tucked into the corner of his mouth.

I would crawl slowly under the pages of the newspaper, a wide grin on my tiny face. Papa would act surprised each time and pull me up onto his lap. I'd burrow between Papa in his sweater and the velvet upholstery of the chair. Even then I knew that this was a time for quiet, Papa's reward for a long week of work. I breathed the sweet smell of pipe smoke and heard the quiet rustle of newsprint as Papa turned the pages.

Our Saturday naps carried on for several years, until I was too grown to crawl into Papa's lap. I don't remember our last Saturday in the tufted chair. I hadn't known that it would be our last, and so I hadn't given it the consideration that it deserved. For me home had never been a city or house, but rather a feeling. It was wherever I felt safest, seen, and deeply loved. For me, those Saturdays with Papa in his sweater were home.

Chapter Eight

As winter fell on the Prairies it brought with it a nagging sense of scarcity. I had made errors in my canning, resulting in many wasted jars. They exploded in the cellar, leaving a gray, foul-smelling slime on everything that they sat near. With our preserves largely inedible, Papa and I had been forced to subsist on our ham and bacon, eggs, milk and dry goods. Porridge of oats or cornmeal and bread or rice made up a large part of our diet. When the last of the pig was eaten, I added butter liberally to every meal to provide us with energy. Even still, we both grew pale and thin, and our hair became dull and sparse on our heads. I found myself questioning the wisdom of coming here. We had been fools to think that we could tame this land, or even live among its wildness. We were ill-suited and woefully unprepared for a life on the farm.

I did not tell Papa that I still had several thousand dollars' worth of Mother's jewelry sewn into the lining of my trunk. There were brooches of gold and ivory cameos, strings of pearls and ruby encrusted hair combs, and more diamonds than I could count were set into hat pins, earrings, and necklaces. I might have told Papa about the jewelry, or sold some of it to ease his worries, but I did not. I knew that we could manage on our own and I wanted to prove to myself that I was more than a failed debutante. The large velvet purse full of jewels stayed tucked into the trunk where its presence brought me comfort.

When Papa's socks had grown so holey that they could no longer be darned, I would carefully unravel the wool and knit new ones. Our flour came in 100-pound bags made of sturdy fabric, and I carefully tore the seams and used the cloth for nightshirts and dish towels. Each side of the sacks had a Royal Flour emblem painted on it in red and yellow. Stripping this paint was a long process of soaking and scrubbing, often with limited success. Papa's nightshirts still faintly showed the Royal Flour lettering across his middle, the sight of which never failed to amuse us. We thinned our porridge, and donned extra layers to preserve wood. Our stores were carefully rationed, and I began seeing measures of food not as pounds or jars, but as weeks that they would sustain us. Papa seemed worried too, but remained positive. We worked hard, and made do.

These worries weighed heavily on me, and at times they would grow so large that my head could no longer contain them. Anxiety crept into my body, slowly at first, and then it became a constant companion. It started with a vague unease, or a dull pressure behind my eyes. I became overly vigilant, scanning my surroundings for threats. There were no outside threats, they all came from within. I turned my worries over and over in my head, trying to find a vantage point that made them less menacing, much like Papa counting coins late into the night. Worries about food somehow evolved into fears that I had carried for years, or those I might face in the future. There were some memories that I could not bear even to look at, and these I slunk past carefully, for fear of waking them. As the worries spilled over into other parts of my body, I became restless, or "full of bees," as Mrs. O'Malley used to say. I had lived most of my life with these bees, and I knew how to quiet them. I must move my body, lull them to sleep like a babe in my arms. And so, I would roam. I walked along the river and fence lines, past each copse of trees. I walked clear across our land to the lake where the loons nested, and then back again. I saw my roaming for what it was: I was not walking, rather running from the weight of my situation.

Papa dealt with his worries differently than I did. He was much stiller. He would read or play chess, allowing himself a half pipe of tobacco every night. Papa's chess set was one of the few luxuries that had been lovingly crated and brought with us to the farm. The polished board was inlaid with alternating squares of boxwood and ebony. It sat upon a wooden base four inches tall that was ornately carved with royal scenes: kings on thrones, knights jousting, solemn bishops. Two sides contained deep drawers in which to store the pieces. The men were beautifully carved from ivory and gray marble. In one drawer there was a soft cloth with which to polish the pieces, and the other held Papa's pipe and pouch of tobacco. Chess and the smell of pipe smoke were wed in my mind, I could not think of one without the other.

Papa had begun having chess matches with Mr. Stanley shortly after our arrival here. Each man would make their move and then send a letter containing the coordinates to the other. It would take around two weeks for a reply to arrive, longer in the winter months. Initially it seemed silly to me, and hardly worth the cost of a stamp and paper. My view changed as I saw Papa's excitement at receiving a response and moving the corresponding piece on his board. Papa would spend an evening or two deciding on his next move. The men played through one full game and had started another before the letters grew shorter and less frequent. The stark contrast between the two men's lives became more apparent as time wore on. Mr. Stanley would write of business, finance, and politics. His letters were peppered with bits of societal news: marriages and lively parties, who was climbing in favor, and whose conduct had the ladies' chins wagging. Papa wrote of things of importance to him: the price of feed and supplies, the weather, the latest calamity to befall us or a neighbor.

The tone of these letters went from jovial and familiar, to terse and obligatory over the course of their correspondence. The last letter that Papa had received was still stored in the drawer. It said simply:

> *James,*
> *Rook: F4 to F1.*
> *Regards, Frank Stanley.*

It had pained me to see the excitement that receiving the letter had caused, only to be replaced with disappointment when it was read. Papa had made his next move and sent a reply but had never received one in return. The set had sat untouched since, a painful reminder of the final snub by the society that we had once lived among. I had asked him to teach me to play, but he hadn't felt like playing. Papa's king was still tucked safely between his queen, two pawns and a rook. He had often said that "how a man does one thing is how he does everything." This held true for him, he was as cautious and measured in chess as he was in life.

Winter brought much shorter days, full dark upon us before supper. This forced us to squeeze twelve hours of work into eight hours each day. Everything was more difficult as well. We had to trudge through deep snow to fetch water from the river when the well froze. A pickaxe sat ready for us to break the ice each day. On a rare trip into town I had picked up some lanolin salve made from the oil of sheep's wool. It was our only defense against the cracking of our skin, which had grown dry and raw from the cold. We took turns splitting wood each day to feed the woodstove and keep the cold at bay. Each night, we sat in our chairs, exhausted from hard work and inadequate meals. We did not light the lamps in order to conserve kerosene, and the firelight was too dim to read by. Often retiring by 7:00 pm, we woke early the next day to do it all again. It began to feel less like living and more like merely surviving.

Papa woke me very early one morning. "Dolly, wake up! Come see the sky!" he said excitedly. I rubbed the sleep from my eyes and pulled on my boots and coat. I followed Papa outside and looked up.

"What is that Papa? I asked in wonder.

"The Northern Lights. Aren't they beautiful?" The sky was lit up with bands of green and yellow. The lights danced and swirled as if pushed by the wind, changing from green to purple. The sky was filled with rolls of light that gathered into the shape of a huge storm cloud, and then dispersed into wisps of red and pink. New ribbons of light formed, and the process began anew, the pattern ever-changing while the inky-blue, star-filled backdrop remained the same.

"I read about them in my prairie flora book. The Blackfoot People who have called this land home for thousands of years believe that these displays are glimpses of their loved ones dancing in the afterlife." I could hear the smile in his voice, though I wasn't looking at him. "I'd like to believe that the Blackfoot are right," Papa said. I smiled as I thought of Mother up there, free at last from the grips of her madness and fear. Mrs. O'Malley would be singing as she danced, laughing and twirling, her head thrown back in delight.

"I think they must be right. Something so strange and beautiful as this couldn't possibly be of this world," I whispered. Papa and I sat outside until the first light of dawn broke in the Eastern skies. I saw the northern lights three more times that winter, each occurrence a gift, a reprieve from the drudgery of winter life.

***

Christmas looked much different than it had in previous years. In Philadelphia our house had been decked with bows and garland, and our tree was decorated with delicate glass ornaments. Mrs. O'Malley had always prepared more food than we could ever have eaten, and the gifts were store-bought and expensive. This year we had chosen a small tree to chop down, and Papa had built a simple stand for it. I tatted twenty small lace snowflakes, and we hung them from the boughs. Papa and I had promised each other not to spend any money on gifts, and we would not exchange any gifts with our friends. It had been a difficult winter for everyone, and we agreed to celebrate the season by gathering instead of gifting. I had knit Papa a warm cap, and he had built me a boot scraper to mount outside the door. I had been driven crazy by the mud and snow that clung to our boots and made a mess of the kitchen. It was the perfect gift. I remembered the gowns and gloves, vase and watercolor painting, and jewelry box inlaid with mother of pearl that I had received last year. They were generous gifts, but held no real value to me. Not a single one of those things had made the trip to the farm.

I made a large pan of cinnamon rolls topped with a gooey glaze, and we mounted our horses and headed towards Inga's. We met Willy at the main road, and he accompanied us to our Christmas celebration. Papa had carved each of the four boys a small wooden figurine with his birthday knife. There were two cowboys, a horse, and a cow. The boys were delighted with their toys and played excitedly with them. Inga prepared a huge pot of soup that was enjoyed with fresh, soft bread. We warmed the cinnamon rolls in the wood stove and enjoyed them with piping hot tea.

As we sat around the fire Olek played his bandura, a flat, lute-like instrument. It had a sound much like a harp, and Inga's sweet voice was the perfect accompaniment. They performed traditional folk songs from Ukraine, nostalgia for home clear on both of their faces. The boys clapped and danced wildly, enjoying this rare opportunity to perform. Later that night I had told Papa that it had been the best Christmas that I'd ever had, and he had agreed.

***

A few weeks later Willy took Papa out hunting, in hopes of getting meat for us to eat. They left before dawn on a warm morning, their rifles slung across their backs. They returned that afternoon, each carrying four pheasants strung together. We roasted pheasant for supper that night, its flavor richer and more wild than that of chicken. We had kept the tail feathers, and when bundled together they had the look of a tropical plant. They'd have fetched a nice price from the milliners in Philadelphia, but they were commonplace here. Over supper Papa confessed that he'd seen a deer while hunting.

"Willy was further back in the dense forest and didn't see it. The deer stood just at the tree line surrounding a frozen lake. I watched it for a few minutes, and then set it in my rifle's sights." Papa paused and closed his eyes for a moment, shaking his head. "It looked so peaceful there among the snow and sunshine, I just couldn't bring myself to shoot it. I'm sorry, Dolly, I don't think hunting is in my nature."

"It's alright Papa, we'll manage," I said with a smile. I loved him more for his kindness to animals and was happy to forego some venison if it meant that Papa's morals were preserved.

"I didn't like killing the pheasants, but it was better than taking the deer. They are not smart birds. They walk around oblivious to their surroundings, bobbing and pecking like chickens. We didn't even need our rifles, we just walked up and bashed them about the head," Papa said, shaking his head.

***

I approached Willy about doing washing or mending for him in exchange for food. He happily handed over shirts, work denim and socks for me to repair. Once all his clothing was mended, I asked about the possibility of making butter for him. He had several dairy cows and sold the milk to the mercantile. Whatever the shopkeeper didn't buy was added to his pigs' troughs. Butter fetched a much higher price than milk and was sought by those who hadn't the time to churn it themselves. Willy agreed to my plan and brought fresh milk over in his wagon every few days. The milk cans weighed over eighty pounds when full, so Willy and Papa would carry them into the house, thumping and crashing as they went.

I made three batches the usual way, churning it by hand. It was exhausting, and so I found a better way. I had once heard that butter was discovered by accident thousands of years ago when a bag of milk carried on the back of a camel had been churned into butter. I filled earthen pots with butterfat and covered them with waxed canvas, then strapped them to the horses and cow when I led them to the river to drink twice a day. The animals' movements agitated the cream along the way, and upon returning home I would have half-churned butter, with much of the buttermilk drained off. I would finish the butter in the churn, salt and knead it, cut it into one-pound bricks and wrap it in parchment, ready for sale. Willy would pick up the butter and the skimmed milk to give to his pigs. In return I would receive bags of oats, sugar, or flour, and occasionally a ham hock or beef chuck roast. I would often find extra things like matches, thread, pipe tobacco or tea in the packages from Willy. I suspect he was trying to help us without hurting our pride. These extra rations saw our bodies through the winter, the knowledge that spring would soon come did the same for our minds.

***

Those of us who lived in the foothills below the eastern slopes of the Rocky Mountains experienced something incredible every winter: chinook winds. Aptly named "snow-eater" by the Blackfoot People, these warm, dry winds could raise the temperature by forty degrees in one day. The telltale chinook arch could be seen to the west, a clear blue sky beneath a bank of gray clouds. Powerful, gusty winds would rush down the slopes of the Rockies, over the foothills and across the Prairies. They would blow at speeds twice that of a train at full steam, rattling our windows in their frames and blowing the door wide open if we had left it unlatched. The deep drifts of snow would wither and melt down substantially, leaving mud in their wake. The chinooks brought us the smallest bit of relief from the biting cold. As newcomers to the Prairies, we were fooled by the first few chinooks, thinking that spring must be near. After three or four days the Arctic winds would return, bringing with them the deep cold of winter. The coldest days were often the clearest, and several times we saw sun dogs: a perfect ring around the sun with a rainbow starburst at the nine and three o'clock positions. As beautiful as they were to behold, they warned of coming snow and air that could freeze your skin in minutes.

Even during the harsh winter, there was so much beauty in this land. The muted, muffled sounds on a clean white blanket of fresh fallen snow, the satisfying crunch of each footstep, the childlike glee of Papa whooping as he slid down our big hill with his bottom on the blade of a shovel. Winter was beautiful, but I felt only one thing as it came to an end: relief.

Chapter Nine

1897

My meager diet during the winter had led me to dream about food each night. Hunger pangs were my constant, unwelcome companion, relieved only briefly by bread and porridge. As spring arrived, I still dreamt of food, but not of roasted meat as I used to. I yearned to feel the crisp pop of biting into an apple just picked, or the satisfying crunch of a new carrot, not yet washed, simply rubbed free of soil by my apron. The colors of canned goods were muted and unappealing, as if I were viewing the jar's contents through a dusty spring windowpane. The two flavors available from canned goods were sickly sweet jams and fruits, or biting, vinegary vegetables. Those jars that I stored helped sustain us through the winter, of which I was grateful. Even so, I was ready for the new growth of spring.

The planting of our garden went much more smoothly this year. Papa expanded the garden, nearly doubling its size. We ordered our seeds early and planted them in the third week of May, as soon as the risk of nighttime frost was gone. Papa built window boxes for me to plant herbs in, and I eagerly anticipated the flavor that they would bring to our meals. The Farmer's Almanac had predicted a growing season of 99 days, and we intended to use every last one of them. Last year's Almanac sat on the cupboard, its cover tattered, and the pages curved, preventing it from lying flat. We had used it to plan our first planting, and to guide the timing of our harvest. This year's edition would be useful as well, but we had learned how to read the clouds to predict the weather and had a better understanding of how to live on the Prairies.

***

Papa suggested that we buy a nannie goat with a kid this year instead of raising a pig as we had last year. He had seen how upsetting it was for me to care for the pig for four months and then eat it for four more. Willy told us that we could buy bacon and ham from him at a good price in the fall, a plan that I was much more comfortable with. Now that we had made it through the winter, I felt ready to tell Papa about Mother's jewelry.

"Papa, we have some money that I didn't tell you about. A lot of money, in fact," I began, holding the large velvet bag of jewelry. "I brought Mother's jewelry, sewed it into the lining of my trunk." I emptied the contents onto the table in front of Papa. He slowly ran his fingers over the pieces, picking some up and turning them over in his hands.

"Twenty-five years of gifts that sat untouched. I'm glad that they will be of some use now." He let out a small chuckle as he shook his head. "Why didn't you tell me about this sooner?"

"I'm sorry, I should have. I wanted us to make it on our own, and we did. We won't have to worry anymore."

"You don't need to keep secrets from me, Dolly. I understand your reasons, though, and admire your determination," Papa said proudly. He took two pieces that were gold, with no precious stones, to town and inquired about how to sell them. The banker bought the pieces from Papa at a discount, as he would have to take them to Calgary to sell to a jeweler. With the money we made we were able to order our garden seeds, pay our mercantile bill in full, replace the canning jars that had exploded in the cellar, and save the rest in my sewing tin.

One morning Papa asked me to ready the pig pen and promised to be back after lunch with our new nannie goat and kid. I patched a few weak areas in the fence and built a threshold inside of the shelter filled with straw for the goats to use for their bed. I gave the water barrels a thorough washing and filled them with fresh water. I cleaned out the feed troughs but left them empty until I knew what goats preferred to eat. Papa came down the lane in the wagon, just after lunch as promised. He leapt from the wagon with a huge grin on his face.

"Dolly! Come see! You're going to love these two!" he yelled to me across the yard. I ran excitedly to the wagon to see our new goats. The nannie was just rising from where she had lain during the ride. She had straight white fur, small horns that curved gently away from her face, and the strangest eyes that I had ever seen. They were the color of honey, with rectangular pupils instead of round. Her face showed little emotion, her gaze disinterested. A tiny white head peeked out from under her udders. The kid stood only about one foot tall and had the softest pink nose. He took a few tentative steps towards me, and then broke into a jerky sideways run, hopping all the while. I burst into laughter at the sight of him. I scooped him into my arms and lowered him to the ground. He ran under the wagon, bleating for his mother. Papa lifted the nannie down to join her kid.

We walked towards the pen and led the goats inside. Papa told me that the farmer he had gotten them from suggested adding a few raised areas to the pen, as goats loved to climb. We retrieved a half barrel from the barn and placed it in the center of the pen. Papa told me that he would build a second house for the goats with raised benches for them to sleep on. He said it was called a "loafing house." He would angle a ramp to the roof so that they could climb up on top of it. I leaned on the fence and watched them happily.

"What are you going to name them?" Papa asked.

"But Willy said…" I began before Papa cut in.

"We're not going to eat these animals, Dolly. We'll sell the nannie's milk to the farmer who makes cheese and sell the kid in the fall. We'll breed the nannie so that she has a new kid each spring. You can love these animals as much as you'd like," Papa said gently.

"I'll need to think about names," I said, choking back happy tears. After a few days I settled on the names Nelly for the nannie, and Buck for the kid. I spent every spare moment watching Buck leap around his pen, his short tail pointed upwards and always wagging. I could just imagine the mayhem of having a whole herd of goats, the kids tearing around continually as they played. I brought Nelly all sorts of twigs and weeds that I found in the trees, trying to decipher her favorites. She seemed to enjoy clover the most, and I picked huge handfuls from the carpet that surrounded the house. When Buck was weaned and big enough, we let the goats graze freely. They did a fantastic job of keeping the long grasses away from the path to the river, and no weeds stood at our fence line. I added the milking of Nellie to my list of morning chores, and Papa and I had a small income from the sale of her milk.

***

Papa had been at Willy's since daybreak, preparing for the branding of his cattle. Every spring the men from the surrounding farms would gather at each farm in turn for the arduous task of roping, sorting, branding, and castrating calves. Each farm had a unique brand that was registered to them, so that cattle that wandered or were stolen could be identified. Most brands contained the owner's initials, as well as bars, diamonds, arcs, or other symbols representing the farmer. The brand was often used as the name for a farm or ranch, leaving the countryside peppered with whimsical places like "Swinging M," "Rocking T," or

"Rafter 9." Willy had told us that his brand was a line above an "S," for Southern, his last name, and it was read as "Bar S."

Olek and all four boys were helping at Willy's, leaving Inga and me to enjoy a rare cup of tea in my kitchen. We offered to prepare supper, but Willy said that he would have a bubbling pot of chili for the men. He kindly asked us to bring biscuits over around 6:00 when they would be finishing up their work. I had finished all of my chores and had nothing left to do but enjoy Inga's company until 5:00 when I started the biscuits. I took two mismatched teacups and saucers down from the cupboard, one patterned with pink roses, the other with blue cornflowers. I had never unpacked the formal set of cups and saucers, preferring instead to use the four odd ones that had come from our kitchen in Philadelphia. I thought of them as Mrs. O'Malley's, and treasured them so. Inga and I sat down with our tea, and I began to tell her about Mrs. O'Malley.

In Philadelphia I took tea in the kitchen with Fiona and Mrs. O'Malley at every opportunity. It was always a relaxed affair filled with laughter and love. I needn't worry about stirring my tea back and forth instead of round and round, nor awkward silences where polite conversation should have sat. There was never a lull when Mrs. O'Malley was present. She talked from the moment she rose until her head hit the pillow at night. If she didn't have anyone to talk to, she would talk to herself. She seemed not to have any internal thoughts; they all found their way through her lips.

Mrs. O'Malley would narrate her actions as she kneaded bread dough or iced a cake and remind herself to pick something up at the market. When she ran out of things to say she would sing in her sweet Irish lilt: church hymns, old Irish folk songs, lullabies. She brought a sorely-needed liveliness to our home. The morning that I passed by the kitchen and heard Mrs. O'Malley panting instead of singing I knew that something was terribly wrong. She had her back to me as she scrubbed clothing on the washboard. Her rattling and wheezing were audible from across the kitchen.

"Are you alright Mrs. O'Malley?" I asked, fearing the answer.

"Aye, child, I just can't seem to catch my breath this morning," she answered with great effort, pausing after each word.

"You'd best sit down. I'll brew you some tea." I smiled with a false cheeriness. She did not draw the wash from the basin, nor dry her hands. She swayed when she stood upright and staggered to the nearest chair. Her lips were pursed, chest heaving. Each breath brought her shoulders nearly to her ears. The terror on her face was familiar to me; I'd seen it on Mother's most days of my life.

It was a Sunday, so Papa was at home. I yelled urgently for him to come. Papa entered the kitchen to find Mrs. O'Malley slumped at the table fighting for breath, and sheer panic on both of our faces. Papa turned on his heel and ran to send for the doctor. I sat by her bedside with Fiona for two days and two nights. The pneumonia was ravaging her body before our very eyes. Her robust frame sunk into the bed; her strong arms now laid limp at her sides. On Monday the very essence of Mrs. O'Malley snuck out unnoticed and fled into the night. She was no longer lit from within. Still, we sat, providing comfort the best we could. We changed the bed linens when she sweat through them, applied cool cloths to her face, moistened her lips with cotton dipped in sweetened tea. Her legs were mottled purple to the knees and her shallow breaths came less and less frequently. Her lips slackened and elongated with each gasp, giving her the appearance of a fish at a pond's surface. Mrs. O'Malley's last breath was not a gasp, but a gentle sigh.

We held the wake in our grand house, packed to standing with all of the people whose lives she had impacted. Papa spared no expense to have the best caterers provide the food, and the house was filled with wreaths and arrangements of lilies. As Mrs. O'Malley's casket was lowered into the ground I felt my sense of security, my surety in life being lowered with her. Each shovelful of dirt hit the casket with a hollow thud, followed by the ringing of the death knell. I looked towards Papa and saw him wince with each thud. His face crumpled; his shoulders sagged in defeat. There was silence after the last of the dirt was replaced. I found myself wishing for something different. Silence was not the way of Mrs. O'Malley.

I heard a sweet, hesitant voice begin to sing "Amazing Grace," and then realized that it was my own. I was joined by over one hundred voices, our song startling a group of crows from the trees overhead. There was a brief pause when the song came to an end before another voice began "Auld Lang Syne." A man accompanied us on his fiddle, and one song led into another, livelier tune. The priest looked about uncertainly, his Bible clutched to his chest, as the mourners began to dance about. We danced and laughed, casting the shadows from the dreary church cemetery. It was the celebration of a kind woman's wonderful life, and it was just the send-off that Mrs. O'Malley deserved.

I leaned my head back in my chair, tears streaming down my face. Inga slid her chair closer to me, and I felt her warm hand in mine. "Mrs. O'Malley seemed like an incredible woman. I can see why you loved her so much," she said softly. I wiped my tears from my face with the hem of my apron.

"She was, and I love her still. You remind me a lot of her," I said with a smile. I thought of Mrs. O'Malley every day, but it felt good to have her story out in the world. I drank my tea that had gone cold as I had told my story and stood to start the biscuits. When I retrieved the biscuits from the oven, they were a mile high, golden, and perfect, just as Mrs. O'Malley's had always been. I cut a small slit in the side of each one and inserted a small pat of butter. I laid clean napkins down in a basket and piled the biscuits inside, wrapping them to keep them warm. Inga and I headed down the lane towards Willy's to join the men for dinner.

Willy had lived on his farm for twenty years, and he'd had the wisdom to transplant saplings in neat rows to act as a windbreak. The trees had grown a foot for each year they'd stood there and formed a tight line around two sides of Willy's home, as well as along the lane. The trees gave the farm an established look, telling visitors that this man was of this land. The harsh smell of burned hair and flesh greeted us, alongside the alarmed cries of a calf as it was branded. I hoped the men would be finished soon, as I didn't think I could bear the sound or smell for long. Papa noticed our arrival and came to meet us near the house.

"That's the last of them," he said, wiping sweat from his brow with the back of his arm. It struck me that Papa had changed a great deal in our year on the farm. His face and arms were browned by the sun, his hair no longer cut by a barber every four weeks. Pocket squares and cufflinks had been replaced by pocket knives and work gloves. It seemed that he had become his true self, and it brought me great joy to see. We watched the men as they walked towards the yard, roping each other with their lassos and laughing boyishly. Olek kissed Inga on the top of her head and placed a hand tenderly on her belly. I wondered if Inga was newly pregnant, and felt the increasingly frequent twinge of desire for a family of my own.

"Willy had Marko and Artem roping like real cowboys!" Olek announced proudly as we dished out supper. Each man had brought a metal bowl from home to hold his chili. No farm around here had twenty bowls in the cupboard, so the men would bring a mess kit with them to each branding. I proudly plopped a tall biscuit onto each bowl of chili, enjoying seeing men's eyes widen with hunger. The men ate with the appetite you might expect from those who had finished twelve hours of hard labor. After the chili was gone, Willy brought out a plate of steaming hot prairie oysters. After the calves were castrated, their parts were thrown into the "nut bucket." They were then rolled in breadcrumbs and fried in lard. It was tradition to eat them after a branding. Inga's boys were eager to try them for the first time. Her second youngest son Borys bit into one with gusto.

"It popped just like a grape!" he exclaimed. I felt my gorge rise in my throat, and politely passed the plate on when it came to me.

"What do you think, Papa?" I asked as he tentatively put a prairie oyster into his mouth.

"I tried one because it's customary, but I don't think I'd eat them of my own volition," he said, a pinched look on his face as he chewed.

***

I sat out on our porch one afternoon listening to the chickadees sing. Chicka-dee-dee-dee rang out their calls, whether announcing their presence or searching for others I couldn't know. Papa came out to join me and cleared his throat nervously as he sat.

"I want to talk to you about marriage," he said nervously. I nodded, grateful that he was sitting beside me so that I could look straight ahead as he spoke.

"I think that Willy might ask for your hand. If he does, I would give him my blessing, but I want you to know that the decision would be yours to make." Papa paused and my eyes widened in shock. Willy had given me no indication that he was interested in me. "I deeply regret promising you to Conrad. I didn't know what kind of man he was when I did, and I won't do that again. I'm sorry for the pain it caused you," he said, remorse showing in the furrow of his brow.

We sat quietly for a few minutes, serenaded by the chickadees as I gathered my thoughts. I looked out over the thick carpet of clover that served as our lawn. Tiny pink and white blossoms stood proudly, releasing their sweet scent into the breeze. I thought about all the changes that I'd seen in the last year. I felt like I was just coming to know myself, and needed more time to decide the direction in which I wanted my life to go. Also, Willy was a kind man, but was ten years older than Papa. I opened my mouth to reply, but Papa spoke.

"I was in love with Angela when I married your mother." It took me a moment to realize that Papa meant Mrs. O'Malley. My eyes widened in shock, but I allowed him to continue.

"She was hired by my parents when she was only eighteen and I was two years her junior. Her warmth and vitality were magnetic. I spent every spare moment in her company, dreaming up countless excuses to do so. I carried on this way for years, despite the knowledge that we could never marry." Papa sighed, and shook his head, as if doing so might free the memories from his head. "My parents arranged my marriage to Elizabeth, and we were wed in a large ceremony. I never found the courage to tell Angela how I felt, and was forced to settle for a different life, with a different woman." Papa fell silent, and I nodded for him to continue. "Elizabeth was haunted by her wartime memories even when I met her. She faded more and more each year, until she became the woman you knew. I loved your mother out of obligation, but never with the fire that I loved Angela." Papa shifted slightly on the bench.

"I had no idea, Papa. I'm so sorry that you couldn't be with Mrs. O'Malley. She would have made a wonderful wife."

"Yes, she would have," Papa said with a wistful smile. "I'm telling you this so that you know never to settle. A marriage of convenience is no marriage at all. I never told Angela that I loved her. If I had, things might have been different. Don't make the same mistakes that I did, Dolly. Someday you'll find the man that sets your heart on fire; tell him, and then never let him go," Papa said, his voice straining. I hugged him tightly, my heart breaking for him. I had never heard Papa speak so frankly, especially about love. He usually kept his emotions close to him, and it was an odd thing to know that he had been pining after Mrs. O'Malley since before I was born.

"Thank you for giving me the freedom to choose my own path. I don't believe that Willy is the right man for me, and so I will wait until I find the one who is. I hope that I choose well."

Chicka-dee-dee-dee the bird's song rang out. I decided that the bird was announcing himself, telling the world what he was made of. I did not yet know what I was made of. I would figure that out while I searched for the man who would set my heart on fire.

Chapter Ten

SUMMER

It seemed that we didn't have Willy's knack for fishing and caught very few that summer. I had planned to salt as much fish as I could to have during the winter months, but I needed to find a way to catch them. One morning as I was fetching a sack of oats from the sod house, I noticed the large trunks we had stored there after our arrival. I was struck by an idea of how to finally catch some fish. I sat before the trunk that had been my hope chest, unsure of what I would feel upon opening it. There was a fine layer of dust on the trunk, and the hot weather had dried out the leather straps of the lid. They creaked as I lifted it, revealing the items that I had once held dear. I was prepared to feel sadness for what I had lost, or nostalgia for a time before this. I felt none of those things.

The first item in the trunk was the cathedral-length bridal veil I had made for a wedding that would never occur. I had spent months of afternoons tatting the lace and stitching it to the tulle. The veil had come out beautifully, but I could no longer imagine myself wearing it. That was of no matter; it would work perfectly as a fishing net.

I looked half-heartedly through a few layers of items in the trunk: embroidered linen napkins, a silk shift trimmed in lace that was meant for my wedding night. Something metallic caught my eye and I rummaged in a tablecloth to retrieve it. I held a silver-plated lobster fork, one of a set of twelve. I began to laugh, wondering how I had ever thought this would be of use on a farm, the nearest ocean a thousand miles away.

"Oooooh, let's eat our lobster." I mocked in a high, squeaky voice. I laughed until I had hiccups, and then tucked the ridiculous fork back into the trunk, to be forgotten for another year. I balled up my bridal veil and walked down to the river. I tied a sturdy rope around each end of the ten-foot veil and anchored it to trees across a narrow section of river. Admiring my handiwork, I left the veil to catch some fish. When I checked it the next day, the veil was rolled up and floating at the surface of the rushing water. I unrolled it and placed heavy rocks on top of the edge that ran along the bottom of the river.

When I returned the following day, there were six trout stuck in my make-shift net. I had thought to bring a bucket, but not gloves to grab the fish, nor a club to hit them with. As a result, I struggled to catch the fish in my hands, chasing them back and forth across the river. Each time I grabbed a fish it would shoot out of my hands, like a well-lathered bar of soap. I was soaked to the waist and managed to capture only two of the fish into my bucket, the rest leaping to freedom over the net. Even still, I walked proudly home with my catch. I tucked a pair of work gloves and a thick stick into my bucket and left it by the path that led to the river to use the next day.

I caught so many fish in the next few days that I had made a giant pot of fish stew and invited Willy and Inga's family over to share it. Willy arrived first and found me near the goat pen.

"Hi, Dolly!" he called as he approached. Papa's name for me sounded foreign on Willy's lips.

"I was hoping to catch you alone." The delivery was gentle, but the words had a predatory ring. Willy's hair had been combed flat with water, and he smelled of pine. As he stepped towards me, his scent reminded me of walking into a deep pine wood. His clothes were freshly washed, his face scrubbed clean of the fine dirt that it usually held in its creases.

"I know that I'm an old man, but we could make a nice life together," Willy began, wringing his hands before he dropped to one knee, seeming to take my stomach with him. "Dolly, will you marry me?" he asked, his pride laid bare as he met my eyes. My throat tightened and I needed to clear it several times before I could speak.

"You are a kind, lovely man, Willy, and I'd be lucky to have you as my husband." Willy's eyes widened and a smile started to appear on his lips, forcing me to hurry in my reply. "... but I am not ready to marry. Coming to this farm has opened a whole new world to me, and I'm still trying to figure out how I fit into it. I'm so sorry," I finished. Willy nodded his understanding and began to stand up. I turned away to conserve his pride, for there is no dignified way to rise from a declined proposal.

"Let's go get some of that fish stew!" Willy said with false cheer, as he turned and walked towards the house. He and Papa talked with Olek on the porch as I checked on the stew with Inga.

"Willy just asked me to marry him," I said, still cringing.

"Did you accept?" she asked in surprise.

"No, I told him that I wasn't ready to marry. He's a good man, but I don't look at him in that way. Am I foolish to wait for the man that takes my breath away? Sets my heart on fire, as Papa advised?"

"No, Dahlia, you're not. My heart still races every time I see Olek, and I can't bear a single day without him. You'll know when you find him, but I doubt he'll find *you* here on the farm." I laughed in response. "Speaking of racing hearts, I have some news of my own. I'm pregnant! The baby will arrive in late fall," she said, grinning widely.

"Oh, Inga! That is wonderful news!" I hugged her close, feeling the sizable swell of her belly under her apron.

"I'm hoping that it will be a girl. Would you check for me?" Inga asked, confusing me. She saw the look on my face and laughed. "You don't need to look inside of me! You use my wedding ring. Get some thread and I'll show you." I fetched a length of string from my sewing tin and brought it to the table. Inga removed her simple gold wedding band and placed it on the table. It was no longer round, the bottom of the ring worn flat by Inga's rolling pin and the handle of her butter churn. She carefully knotted the string around the band, leaned back in her chair and told me to dangle the ring over her growing belly. She said that the direction in which the ring swung would tell us the baby's gender: back and forth for a boy, in a circle for a girl. I did as she directed, and the ring made lazy circles around her belly.

"A girl!" Inga shrieked. We hugged and she hopped from foot-to-foot beaming. We dished up the stew, and Inga called the boys back from the pen where they were chasing the goats. We tucked into our stew, and Inga shared her news with the rest of the table. Congratulations were offered all around, and I saw Olek nod at Inga to continue.

"That's not all. We are moving to the Okanagan Valley to be near my sister Olena and her family." My face fell, my mind reeled. Inga looked at Olek as she spoke. "The winters there are mild, and the soil fertile. There are fruit trees everywhere you look, and blue lakes tucked into each valley. We will leave as soon as we've harvested the garden," she finished.

I could not speak. My mouth hung open, pain clear on my face. I could not imagine life here without Inga and her lively spirit, her gentle guidance. Papa and Willy congratulated Olek, and I fled the table under the guise of clearing dishes. In the kitchen I stood with my hands on the countertop, bracing me against my sobs. Inga entered quietly and stood behind me, arms wrapped around my middle.

"I'm sorry, Dahlia. It's the best choice for us. We had always planned to follow Olena over the mountains, but the time never seemed quite right." I nodded my understanding as she continued. "Marko is already fourteen and will find a wife and settle down in a few more years. If that happens here, then my family will be forever split. I will miss you dearly. We've had some good laughs over the past year."

"Yes, we have. Oh, Inga, I'll miss you so much. Who am I to have tea with now?" The question hung unanswered in the air. We hugged tightly and then began to clean up the dishes. I watched Inga make her way down the dusty lane with her rowdy boys later that night, the last time that they ever did so.

I woke the next morning, still heavy with the emotion of the previous day. Willy had not met my eye all evening. I wished that I had found a way to make him understand that I had not rejected him, but rather the idea of marriage at this young age. I began to doubt the soundness of my decision. A life with Willy would be safe and comfortable, and I was certain that he would treat me well. I thought that I could learn to love Willy in time. Papa's words rang in my head: "a marriage of convenience is no marriage at all." I had chosen to walk this world alone, searching for the man whose love I could not live without, instead of settling for one whose love I could learn to bear.

I stripped the beds of their linens and set to scrubbing them clean, hoping that the heavy work would be an outlet for the anxiety and uncertainty that I felt lurking within me. I hung the bedding on the outdoor line and looked forward to crawling under its freshness with an excitement that most people could not muster for linens. Dried by the sun and wind, in the air thick with pine and clover, fresh bedding was one of the simplest joys in life. I decided to hang the quilts and feather beds as well, to air them of their stuffy, smoky, indoor smell.

I swept out the house and scooped the ashes from the cookstove and the fireplace. I scrubbed the kitchen table and dough board with a stiff-bristled brush and applied fresh oil to their surfaces. I brought a pail of boiling water and vinegar to the latrine and scrubbed that too. I took my broom to the eaves in the house and cleared them of cobwebs. I washed all the windows with vinegar and wiped them clean with newsprint, and then made my way to the barn to scour the water buckets. After all of this was done, I stood at the well and drank one ladleful of crisp water after another. And still, the nagging need to move ran through my body like an evasive itch that you can only locate once it has moved on to a new area.

I changed out of my sweaty dress and washed my face and neck with cool water. I took a saskatoon berry muffin from the kitchen and ate it as I walked down the lane. I went in the direction of Willy's farm, where Papa was helping with the pigs. At his tree-lined lane, I walked right on past, my destination farther along the road. My hand outstretched to the tall grasses that grew along the lane, and I enjoyed the tickle of the spikes on my skin. The vast field of purple-blue alfalfa soon came into sight; I wanted to see it one more time before the farmer who owned this land harvested it. Hiking my skirts and gathering them about me, I slipped through the barbed wire fence, walking a few hundred steps before laying on the ground, the earth warming my back through the thin fabric of my dress.

Directly above me, but high in the azure sky, was an eagle. I watched as it circled slowly, looking for prey. I listened to the rustle of insects, and the erratic breath of a breeze that seemed unable to decide if it wanted to become a wind. A flock of barn swallows flew over me, one of the few birds that I could easily identify due to their sharply forked tails. They swirled and wound around themselves, grouping and then dispersing much like the northern lights had in the winter. I sat upright to look at the alfalfa, but the plants were so tall this near to harvest that I remained lost amid their green stalks. I was heady with the scent of alfalfa, sweet like tea leaves. I stood, dusting off the back of my dress as I peered out across the sea of purple. The wind had pulled the clouds into long, thin rows. Their shape forecasted both a change in weather, and the appearance of the furrows that the fields would have when they were harvested in a few short weeks.

It seemed to me that within society the value of things decreased as their numbers grew. Diamonds, original paintings, and true friends were precious simply because they were rare. A reproduction of a famous painting that could be found in any number of hotel lobbies or drawing rooms paled somehow. It was no longer appreciated for its depth of texture and use of light, the importance of the subject or skill of the artist. It became something that the eyes panned over, almost unseen.

The opposite was true in nature. A stalk of alfalfa was beautiful on its own. A sturdy stem of vibrant green topped with a crown of purple. Each tiny flower that made up the bloom was white near the center, with dark purple lines radiating outwards, the shape of the flower reminiscent of an open clam shell. One could not find fault with the unassuming plant on its own. Taken in large quantities, however, its beauty was immeasurable. The sight of this large field of alfalfa in full bloom left me overcome. The breeze had finally gathered into a wind and blew the alfalfa into waves that rocked like the ocean. The purple of the flowers was mirrored perfectly in the line I saw in the sky along the horizon, and in the places on the mountains where, in the winter, snow and rock meet.

The brisk walk and the view of the alfalfa field had served their intended purpose, settling my bees and freeing me from the anxiety that had been running through me that morning. I took one last look across the fields and rolling hills, storing the memory so that I might look upon it during the darkness of winter.

***

I spent most of the next ten days at Inga's farm, helping her to prepare for their departure. We harvested her garden, which had produced well. Inga told me that they must be mindful of the weight of their wagon, as the trek over the mountains would be very hard on the animals. They planned to take both their horses and oxen, using each team on the terrain they were best suited for, and resting the other. Inga would do no canning this year, choosing instead to bring only her root vegetables and dry goods. The potatoes, beets and onions, and the cabbages wrapped in newsprint were packed into barrels and would provide the family with some food for the winter. They planned on carving a dugout house, much like our little hill home, to house them for the first winter.

We prepared meals almost entirely from the garden to make use of the abundance of produce: salads, soups, roasted root vegetables, and peas fresh from the pod. All that was left had been given to me. I gave Inga the crates that we had brought some fragile items in when we had come to the farm. She packed her empty canning jars, and a few precious items into them. Olek built little crates for the chickens, so they could travel over the mountains strapped to the sides of the wagon. Most of their furniture would be left for the new residents of their farm, as it would not fit into the wagon.

Once all the preparations were complete, I was left alone with my thoughts. That Inga was leaving was devastating, as if she were dying instead of only heading west. I knew that she deserved my encouragement as she set out, rather than my sadness. I made little paper packets and filled them with a variety of seeds from the garden. On the packets of peas, I wrote: "*May the peas in your new garden grow as tall as my Creeping Bellflower.*" From the mercantile I bought one yard of pale pink calico spotted with tiny daisies, one half yard of eyelet lace, and three buttons. I was going to use these things to sew Inga's new baby a dress but knew that Inga would enjoy making precious clothing for her little girl.

On the morning that Inga was leaving, Papa and I rode the horses over to her farm. I had baked two dozen muffins bursting with berries and tied them up in a clean napkin, to feed the hungry Chornyk boys on their journey. Willy had come to see the family off as well. He still avoided meeting my eyes, and our conversations were clipped. I knew that Willy was acting this way out of embarrassment, not rudeness, but it still bothered me a great deal. Willy never came around our farm anymore, preferring instead that Papa go to his. I had mentioned my concern to Papa, who had advised me to give Willy's pride time to heal. This would have to remain a problem for another time, as my focus today was on Inga.

Inga's cheeks were flushed a deep pink, whether from the exertion of packing or her pregnancy, I did not know. I admired her glow and rosy cheeks aloud, causing Inga to laugh heartily. We looked at each other for a long time, our eyes filled with tears. Inga pulled me into a hug, tears falling to freedom on our cheeks.

"Thank you. You've been such a bright light in my life. I will never forget you," she whispered.

"And thank you," I said, "for showing me how to live on the Prairies and for bringing me joy and comfort over many pots of tea."

Inga promised to write with her new address as soon as they arrived in Vernon. The two oldest boys mounted the horses, and the rest of the family climbed into the wagon pulled by a team of oxen. They headed down the lane surrounded by a cloud of dust, as they always were when they departed. Olek turned left onto the main road and stopped the wagon briefly. I imagined that they were taking a moment to look upon their land one last time and bid farewell to what had been their prairie home.

Chapter Eleven

AUTUMN

The end of fall was drawing near, bringing with it a sense of urgency. Papa and I had been tirelessly preparing for what The Farmer's Almanac was predicting to be a long, cold winter. I had canned everything that I could from our garden: sweet pickles, carrots, green beans, stewed tomatoes, pickled beets, asparagus, and a crate of peaches from the Okanagan valley that I'd lucked upon at the mercantile. I had hung bunches of herbs to dry from every rafter in our small house. Strings of garlic bulbs, onions, potatoes, and cabbages wrapped in newsprint were carefully stored in old barrels in the cellar. I had picked blueberries and saskatoons by the basketful and dried what we couldn't eat. I had made sauerkraut and pickled eggs on Inga's urging, remembering to add a few slices of beets to the boiled eggs when canning them. Seeing the bright pink eggs bobbing in their brine, I imagined the eggs bringing a smile to my face when I served them in the dead of winter.

We had enjoyed an Indian summer, with warm days lasting much later than usual. Only the shortening of the days signaled the coming winter. As such, I had canned my jams and jellies a month later than I did last year. My strawberry plants hadn't produced much this year, so I managed only three small jars of jam. I had made half a dozen jars of each blueberry and saskatoon jam, simply because I'd had so many berries.

The task that I enjoyed most was the canning of crabapple jelly. Canning vegetables was an exact science that required the perfect amount of acidity and precise ratios of vegetable to brine, lest your produce spoil as many of my jars had last year. Crabapple jelly on the other hand, was an art. It required patience. You must have one-fourth underripe apples to give the jelly a tartness and high pectin so that it would set. The other three-fourths were fully ripened and ruby red. After boiling the water, sugar and quartered apples for an hour without stirring, you poured the mixture through a sieve. The pulp of the apples was wrapped carefully in cheesecloth and hung on the cupboard to drip ever so slowly into the waiting pot. It was tempting to squeeze the cloth to hurry the juice along, but this would result in a cloudy jelly. The smell inside the house on the day I made crabapple jelly was almost cloying in its sweetness. Once the juice was put into the jars and boiled again the jars were left to sit undisturbed on a sunny windowsill for a full day and night.

I rejoiced in the sound of the gentle pop of the lids as they sealed, on their own time rather than all at once. It was deeply satisfying to hold the jars up to the window and see the crystal-clear jelly of a vibrant red. I knew that Mrs. O'Malley would be so proud of my newfound skills. As a child, I had helped her with the canning each year, but she had always been there to stop me from making errors. I carried this last batch of jelly by the armful to the old sod house. The cellar was the best place for storage, as there were sturdy shelves built around every wall. Lining the jellies up carefully, I marveled at the amount of food that I had been able to put up for the winter. I ran my hand along the glass of the jars and felt the comfort of preparedness.

We made trips into town to gather the items that were small but incredibly important: candlesticks and lamp oil, matches, soap and darning thread. Papa had stacked straw bales clear to the rafters in the barn, and a winter's worth of hay bales were tucked under the lean-to at the side of the barn. He had sold Buck as well. The goodbye was hard, but I felt better about it than I had about the pig. Papa would have the nannie goat bred in the next few weeks so that she would have a new kid in the late spring. We were nearly ready.

Papa was completing the dreaded chore of felling trees to drag home for firewood. I prepared a simple lunch of egg sandwiches and awaited his arrival home. Papa had still not returned home when the clock on the mantle struck 1:00. It was likely that he had chosen very large trees, and I decided to go take a turn wielding the axe. I knew where he'd be, as he sought out birch and poplar because they burned clean and slow. There was a stand of old birch on the far corner of our land, so I set out with our sandwiches carefully wrapped in a clean handkerchief. Papa always did what was right, not what was easy. There were dozens of dead standing jack pine fifty paces from our home. They seemed to me to be an easier choice for firewood, but Papa refused to burn pine inside the house because it was so smoky. Its oily smoke created a flammable creosote buildup inside of the chimney if it wasn't cleaned out regularly. A chimney sweep was a rare find in these parts, so he avoided pine altogether.

I walked leisurely towards the stand of birch, enjoying the warmth of the day. The geese had not yet flown south and flew over our fields daily in search of food or ponds to nest near. A tight wedge flew over me then, the lead bird falling to one end of the V when it tired. To see the geese fly in formation was a graceful thing. To hear them was not. Honking continually and out of sync, they made a terrible racket. They reminded me of the man that had delivered our wood in Philadelphia: lovely to behold but awkward the moment that he opened his mouth.

I glanced west towards the mountains. The rocky peaks were not yet covered in snow, but it was coming as surely as the night. I could see the dark contrast of the trees against the rock and wondered what it might be like to sit up there and look out on this land. I imagined that

I would see for a hundred miles or more. To the east, farms would appear as patches in a quilt, their color determined by what crops were planted there. Shocking yellow for rapeseed, soft purple-blue for alfalfa, golden earthy yellow for wheat. The foothills would roll seamlessly into the vast prairie. To the west I would see deep into the Rocky Mountains and their majestic peaks, perhaps tiny towns tucked into the valleys.

I had wanted to save my sandwich to enjoy with Papa, but reasoned that if I ate it along my walk, I could take over the cutting when I arrived, and Papa would be able to rest. Stopping, I removed my sandwich from the bundle and reknotted the handkerchief. I'd used the first bit of dried green onions to flavor the egg, as the spring onions were used up long ago. The woody texture of the dried onions ruined the creaminess of the egg. I laughed at my distaste for the winter provisions when the snow had yet to fall. As I finished my sandwich, I wished that I'd have thought to bring water. Hopefully Papa had some left in his canteen.

As I crested the last hill on my way to Papa I gasped, hand to heart, at the breath-taking view before me. The stand of birch was nestled into a glen, its crown seemingly ablaze. I had not come here in late autumn before, and had not seen the way the reds, oranges and yellows blended into this incredible sight. I wanted to sit on that hill and allow myself time to process its beauty. To allow my eyes to drink in its magic. To burn these autumn-lit trees forever into my mind, so that I could take the memory out and turn it this way and that anytime that I liked. Instead, I rushed down the hill towards Papa, his axe, and the back-breaking chore at hand.

I couldn't hear the axe striking wood. In fact, I heard nothing at all. No hint of Papa whistling while he worked, no flutter of wind. Even the birds had fallen silent. Panic began to rise in my chest, the place where awe had sat just minutes before. I scanned the woods frantically looking for Papa. I ran wildly down the path carved by wildlife over the years as they made their way to the river. The path curved to the left and there, in the partial clearing I saw Papa. He was lying on his back, a giant birch across his body from right shoulder to left hip, his axe still clasped into his right hand.

"Papa!" I shrieked as I ran to him. I sank to my knees at his side uttering, "no, no, no, no, no". Papa's eyes fluttered and opened slightly, and I was filled with the slightest glimmer of hope that he would survive. "Don't move, I'll fetch Willy to help."

Papa snorted. "Where would I go? There's not time, Dolly."

"Then I'll hitch the horses and pull this tree off you. I can settle you at home and then send for the doctor," I said desperately.

"Just sit with me." So, I sat. Papa closed his eyes and smiled. I rose and stepped over the tree to Papa's left side. I laid down at a right angle to him, our heads touching. The wind began to blow, softly at first, but quickly gathering speed.

"Can you hear that?" Papa whispered with a gurgling cough. "Wind through the leaves of a trembling aspen. There is no sound quite like it."

We laid there looking up into the canopy of autumn leaves together, listening to them flutter.

"You've brought me so much joy Dolly, and I'm glad that you've now held the earth in your hands," Papa whispered, almost inaudible. I squeezed his hand until his last breath passed through his lips. His face softened, pain no longer contorting his mouth and brow. I stood slowly and headed towards home to hitch the horses.

I buried Papa where he laid, so he would forever look up into the leaves of the trembling aspen. The wind was still now, and the fluttering of the leaves had ceased like the beating of Papa's heart. I had thought briefly of burying Papa's sweater and chess set with him, but I could not bear to relinquish any tangible connection to him. The horses had easily pulled the tree from off of Papa. They stood hobbled at the river now, unaware of the weight of their task. Digging steadily, I was oblivious to the rough wood of the shovel's handle. The task rubbed the tender skin on my hands, in spots that had not been toughened by swinging an axe. I tugged Papa's wool cap down to block the blank stare from his open eyes. Then I slid Papa into the hole as gently as I could. The first shovel full of dirt was the hardest to throw. It felt so wrong to cover Papa in dirt and doing so was an admission that he was really gone.

I hoped I had given Papa the burial he deserved. I know that he would have scoffed at the thought of lying for eternity beneath the crushing weight of a marble statue or granite headstone. To sleep forever beneath the aspens felt like just what he would have wanted. Even though I was exhausted and terribly thirsty from digging, I could not tear myself away from this place. I laid down beside the freshly turned earth and looked up towards the sky with Papa one final time.

Dusk was nearing and the setting sun lit up the world with an almost other-worldly glow. Each leaf and blade of grass was brought into intense focus; the leaves were ablaze in the glory of autumn. The sun set and a full Hunter's moon rose high into the sky, and still I stayed. I could smell earth and fallen leaves, hear the first stirs of the night animals, feel the sudden chill of this late autumn night. The sorrowful wail of a loon rang out from the lake at the other side of the farm. The first time I had ever heard a loon's cry, I had mistaken the sound for the howl of a wolf. Papa had told me that it was a loon calling for its mate, saying "I am here, where are you?" Another call carried across the land to me, full of the emptiness of solitude. I wailed my own call of sorrow. I am here Papa, but where are you?

I sat up slowly and faced the head of Papa's grave. Placing my palm flat on the damp, cool earth, I grasped some earth in my fist, rubbing it between my hands as Papa had done on our arrival to this land. Bringing my hands to my face, I inhaled deeply. I did not exhale a contented sigh as Papa had done, rather a choked sob. Letting the earth fall from my hands, I stood slowly, stiffly. I turned towards home and walked reluctantly towards an existence that had suddenly and inexplicably been stripped of Papa.

Chapter Twelve

I did not leave my bed for three days after Papa's death, except to feed the animals, stoke the fire and use the latrine. My thoughts went from self-pity, to incredulity, to despair and back again. I knew the importance of completing Papa's task of gathering wood, so I headed to the trees right outside my door. The jack pines may have been low-hanging fruit, but they were all that I could manage. I looked first for the seasoned deadfall that was ready to burn, and then those that were dead but still anchored in the earth. Jack pines are a curious tree. They are thin with sparse branches, and impossibly tall. When you stand among them and look to the sky, they seem to converge on each other the way train tracks do as they fade into the distance. These pines didn't simply drop their cones to create new trees. Their seeds were found in armored gray pods that resembled a caterpillar's cocoon. They required an inferno to release their seeds and were often the first trees to start growing anew after a forest fire. Time would tell what remained of me after an inferno. The fire of my grief had only started burning; I was not yet ready to drop my seeds.

Chopping the wood provided the outlet that my grief needed. I swung that axe until my arms fell limp at my sides and every muscle I had screamed in protest. Somehow, I found the strength to haul and heat water for a scalding hot bath each night. I would sit in the tub for an hour or more until the water was tepid and no longer soothed me.

After ten days of stockpiling wood, I reverted to walking my panic and sadness away. Not leisurely strolls through the meadows, but determined treks through dense thickets and across shallow rivers. If I could string all these hikes together end-to-end, I might have walked all of the way back to Philadelphia, felling every forest along the way.

Winter was a blur of pain, my days unanchored by the routine of meals or errands. No one else knew that Papa had died, and I made no attempt to tell anyone, even Willy. He had not come to the farm since he had proposed, perhaps still embarrassed by me declining. I was alone in my grief. I did not sit to eat, choosing instead to graze on crackers dipped in jam or my canned produce straight out of the jar while standing in the kitchen. All the food that I had canned seemed tainted by the bitter taste of Papa's death. I ate it anyway, forcing each swallow. I tended the animals half-heartedly, milking the cow and goat simply to ease their discomfort, often dumping the pails of fresh milk straight onto the manure pile. I left the eggs out for the skunks and coyotes to eat, uncaring that it drew predators to my home. Grief felt like a rotting tooth, angry with infection. At times it was searing and hot, others it was a slow, dull ache.

I made a large pot of soup filled with potatoes, onions, cabbage and the last of the bacon; I kept it outside to freeze at night and would heat it to boiling each day. The vegetables developed a strange chewy texture from their repeated change of state, and I found a mouse gnawing at a piece of potato on the frozen surface one morning. I did not care. My little house grew filthy as the months wore on. Floors unswept, clothing and linens rarely washed. Papa had been right, the pine created a great deal of smoke, and its film covered everything. I was overwhelmed and did not know where to start to bring things back to order. And so, I didn't.

The one bright spot in each week was Saturday afternoon. Before the snow grew too deep and the temperatures dropped, I would make my way to the stand of birch and spend a few hours with Papa. I would bring an old quilt to spread by his grave and talk about whatever came into my head. I began wearing Papa's sweater under my coat when winter's true grasp hit in late November. By mid-December the snow had drifted past my waist in most places, and the cold prevented me from staying outside for more than a few minutes. I could no longer visit Papa and so I retreated once more to my bed. Christmas passed without any recognition.

January brought a frigid cold, the likes of which I could not have imagined. My breath caught in my throat, eyelashes froze together, skin became reddened and numb after walking the twenty steps to the barn. Three feet of snow clung to the roof of the house, and I had no means with which to remove it. I hoped it would insulate the house and keep the heat from the wood stove from escaping, as I was burning through my stockpile of pine at an alarming rate. The chill could not be shaken, even though I filled the stove every three hours around the clock. I had taken to sleeping fully dressed, save for the boots.

I dreamt of fire one night, as I often had after Mother's death. Opening my eyes, I felt the acrid burn of smoke at the back of my throat. I sat up and saw the haze filling the house, an ominous red glow visible through my open bedroom door. I dashed from the bed into the living room and saw that the stove pipe was red hot. I opened the door to the wood stove and heard a loud whoosh as the chimney fire hungrily sucked up the air to feed its destruction. The eaves were starting to catch. I hastily threw on a coat and boots and grabbed Papa's sweater and his chess set, using the quilt from my bed to carry my things. I found the sewing tin that contained everything I had of value: Mother's jewelry, the deed to the land, Papa's Will and a bit of paper money and coins. The coins rattled loudly in the tin as I ran from the house. Dropping my makeshift sack, I ran back into the kitchen for Mrs.

O'Malley's recipe book. The smoke choked my every breath, and I emerged from the house gasping.

I took the items to the sod house and hoped that they would be safe there. It was upwind from the fire and constructed of earth on three sides. I sped to the barn and found the animals wild from the smoke. The horse's eyes rolled in their heads, their nostrils flared, and they thrashed in their stalls. Opening all the stall doors, I coaxed the animals to the fenced pasture so they could run off their panic. The chickens didn't seem in danger because their coop was farthest from the house, so I left them where they were. I looked back towards the house to see smoke billowing from the open doorway.

I overturned a rainwater barrel and sat watching my home burn. So many things I wished I could have saved: Papa's chair, Mrs. O'Malley's mismatched tea cups and canning supplies. Suddenly the windows blew out with a magnificent crash and a section of roof fell in on itself. Steam joined the smoke as hundreds of pounds of snow fell into the fire. I was helpless to stop this tragedy that was unfolding before me. So, I sat and watched in the heat of the blaze, truly warm for the first time in months.

I took up residence in the one-room sod house. There was a large bed to one side of the woodstove, and bunks to the other. It reminded me of the cabin on the train that carried me here, though much cruder. The simple home had been carved into the side of a hill by the first settlers here. Thus, three walls were windowless. The interior was lined with rough-hewn planks. The ceiling was low, and the light let in by the two small windows near the door was minimal. It should have felt claustrophobic, but instead it felt sturdy and safe. No drapes were hung at the windows, no rugs covered the floors.

I said a little prayer of thanks that I had decided to store the food, extra clothing and supplies here. Stacked near the door were the two large travel trunks that we had never unpacked, their contents long forgotten. When I was finally able to round up the horses, I made a long-overdue trip into town. I bought only what I needed most: simple fabric and thread for two dresses, flour, sugar, tea and lamp oil. The shopkeeper greeted me with a smile, pulling a stack of old newspapers from under the counter. Papa and I had enjoyed the mystery story that was printed in installments every Saturday. We hadn't always made it into town on Saturdays, but the shopkeeper had always reserved a copy for us so that we might follow the story.

"I figured that the snow must have made your lane impassable, so I kept a newspaper each Saturday for you. I've also got the things that your father ordered." He then laid three neatly folded work shirts and a pair of black ruched sleeve garters on the counter. My knees weakened. This was the first interaction that I'd had in months, and still I was not ready to talk about Papa's death.

"Yes, the snow was awfully deep, and I didn't dare risking the trip. Thank you for saving the newspapers," I said, struggling to keep my voice even. I paid the shopkeeper and hurried from the store. That night I baked three loaves of bread. The heavy work of kneading the dough was a welcome outlet for the anxiety I felt creeping in. I did not even let the bread cool before slicing it and slathering it in butter which melted instantly. It was delicious beyond most anything that I had eaten in my life.

My anxiety continued to grow and replace the sadness that I had known intimately during this long winter. I busied myself with cleaning the sod house and making it livable. When that was done, I walked the short distance to the main house to see what could be salvaged. Only two walls stood, and precariously so. The smell of burnt timber was still strong. I gathered my nerve and stepped into what was once my home. The area at the back of the house where the stove sat was reduced completely to ash. Papa's chair, the old wooden sideboard, the canning supplies, all gone. The corner where the two remaining walls stood held the kitchen table. Its finish had bubbled in the heat, leaving it looking as if it had been left out in the rain. The school slate that Papa had given me was unscathed, as were the rifle and axe hung beside the doorway. There was little else that could be saved. As I walked back outside, I saw the horseshoe still nailed above the door. I laughed as I remembered Papa's superstition about removing it, for fear that bad tidings would find us. Still, it hung, yet my life had been reduced to a wasteland. I climbed up on a chair and pried the horseshoe from its spot. Nailing it above the door in the sod house, I hoped to hold onto any luck that remained.

February brought a string of chinooks. The warmth was welcome, but the winds that brought it were violent. The wind didn't rattle the hill house as it had the wooden one, but its presence could not be ignored. The wooden shakes blew off the barn roof in places, littering the yard. Dirt and loose straw whipped about. The animals didn't care to be out much. Neither did I, but I was desperate to visit Papa. The last two chinooks had reduced the snow on the ground to only a few inches deep and I finally felt that I could make it across the fields.

The walk to Papa's grave was treacherous. The snow in shaded areas had a hard crust that would break as I stepped on it, the rough edges of each hole cutting into my ankles. The snow where the sun hit was soft and slippery. I fell several times but kept going. My right stocking had come loose from its garter and bunched painfully in my boot. I slid and limped awkwardly all the way to the birch stand, to Papa. The trees looked skeletal bare of their leaves. I had forgotten to bring a quilt to sit on, so I crouched instead. I told Papa about the jack pine and the chimney fire. I told him about moving into the hill house and eating green beans straight out of the jar. I told him about the void that his death had left in my life, and how it grew bigger every day. I told him that I was trying not to look for what was missing, and instead see what was left. My legs began to cramp from crouching, so I said goodbye. Taking a different route home, in the hopes that it would be less difficult, I found myself climbing a steep slope to the top of a hill blown clear of snow. I hadn't reattached my stocking to its garter, and it had rolled into a painful lump at the tender part of my foot between heel and toes.

The wind atop the hill was howling and I instinctively turned leeward to protect myself from it. Cowering in my grief, it felt as if it had no bottom. I missed Papa with an urgency and turmoil that wound itself into every moment of every day. It was fluid and changing, forever appearing in new ways. Anxiety began to well up in me. A hot flush began in my feet and crawled up my legs, preparing my body to flee this threat. Fire licked at my heels, searing and scarring as it tore through me. As the flush hit my head, I felt dizzy and disoriented, unable to focus my eyes. My chest tightened and drawing breath was nearly impossible. Swaying, I knelt down to put my bare palms to the ground. The dirt was cool; the rocks and dried grass pressed painfully into my hands. I wanted to curl up on this hill until the crushing wave ebbed. Instead, I stood and turned to face the wind, leaning into it, chest forward and arms trailing behind me. I imagined that I was a figurehead carved into the prow of a ship. A maiden with a steely gaze looking out over the ocean. While figureheads bring luck to a crew and guide the ship safely home, I had been unable to navigate my life in a way that led me to anything but despair.

The wind tore across the prairie and allowed nothing to escape its assault. I stood firm and a deep groan escaped through my clenched teeth. That groan grew into a roar; the deep, guttural sound of complete abandon. I screamed for all the things I had lost, and all the things that I'd never had at all. I screamed for Papa, Mother and Mrs. O'Malley. I screamed for this life that had become nothing more than tragedies strung together by hardships. I screamed for this beautiful land that could hurt me in a hundred different ways and did so without restraint.

I screamed until I was hoarse, and then I screamed some more. I screamed until my anger had turned to resolve.

I did not curl up on that hill and submit to the grief I'd felt since Papa's death or the anxiety I'd carried since childhood. They were heavy and had burdened me for far too long. The wind continued to lash at me, whipping my hair and skirts, but the feelings inside of me no longer mirrored it. Now calm, I was flooded with a clarity that I had not known before. On my way home, my gait was purposeful, my head held high. I did not remove my wet clothing or wash my tear-streaked face, simply fell into my bed and slept until the lowing of the cow woke me the next morning.

Chapter Thirteen

SPRING

I wandered the narrow aisles of the mercantile to pass the time as the men loaded my wagon with bags of livestock feed and pantry staples. This morning, I had felt lonely, craving the sound of voices other than my own. The earliest hints of spring were in the air and there was a palpable excitement as we all emerged from our winter dens. I imagined the townspeople yearned for gulps of air warmed without the aid of a wood stove, and the tenderest touch of sun on bare skin as much as I did. The chinook winds had brought warm air and clear skies, and the shopkeeper had propped the door open. Fresh air found its way into the store and carried on it were the laughter and shrieks of children at play. The sounds of the town mimicked my own mood. I had woken feeling fresh, clear-headed and hopeful.

Making my way to the back of the store where the neat piles of textiles were kept, I fingered bolts of fabric and thought ahead to new dresses once warmer weather settled in. A brown serge in a herringbone weave had been reduced in price. It would do well for fall, but I would swelter in it during summer. My eye landed on a beautiful peacock blue sateen that felt as fluid as water in my hands. I glanced around to ensure I was alone in the aisle and brought the incredible fabric to my face. It felt cool, smooth as river rocks, and deliciously frivolous. Holding the cloth away from my face, I marveled at how the blue had hints of purple or green depending on how the light fell. It brought to mind an art exhibit I had seen at a museum in Philadelphia. The paintings were all of menageries around Europe, the grandest of which was at the palace of Versailles. They depicted animals that had no business being in France, nor any possibility of meeting in the natural world: lions, tigers, monkeys, bears, and more species of birds than I had known existed. I saw many paintings that day, but in each one I found myself looking for the peacocks. If the peahens made any appearance in the paintings at all they were brown and drab, fading into the background. But the peacocks! They were of the most magnificent coloring and strutted and preened in ways that made me envy their confidence.

This delicate fabric would be ruined by lunchtime on the farm if I made a dress of it. It was of no concern to me though. A restrictive dress would have been a terrible waste of the qualities of this weave. I had another purpose in mind. Philadelphia was known for its textile mills, and I laughed out loud at the thought of this fabric being made there, and still finding me here. I asked the shopkeeper to cut me three yards, giddy with the thought of buying something just for me, with no purpose other than to bring joy to my life. He seemed surprised at my choice of fabric, but smiled in response to my excitement. His heavy shears made slow, careful cuts and sounded the way a heavy object does when dragged over a wooden floor. My long winter of sadness lifted slightly with each cut. The fabric was carefully folded, rolled, and bound with a yard of pale green ribbon, the shopkeeper's gift to me for spending a small fortune. I held the bundle in the crook of my arm as one might hold a new babe.

Reluctant to have my outing come to an end, I found the table where the large, heavy Eaton's catalog lay open. These wondrous books could be found in every small town, the only way for those who dwelled outside of the cities to get items too unique or dear to be kept in stock in the mercantile. I had often considered finding an old edition to bring home, to get lost in during the long winter nights. Now, I paged through the catalog of things of all manner that could be ordered from afar: weather instruments and harpsichords, looking glasses and Bibles; kits that contained all that you would need to build a home, including the plans and nails. Save for the Bibles, the pages containing these expensive items of whimsy were pristine, untouched by the fingers of the people of this town. The sections displaying farm implements and fencing supplies, or sturdy work boots and rifles were dog-eared. The print was smudged and faded in spots; these pages well-read. These items were necessary for life on the Prairies. One had no need of a harpsichord after a long day of branding cattle or threshing grain. A hot, hearty meal to fill their bellies and a lively tune on the fiddle to buoy their spirits were all that these settlers dared to ask for.

I made my way to the till, where a counter lined with jars of candy stood. I took my time choosing a sweet. There were pipes of black licorice, Scotch mints, and ribbon candy in many flavors. Decision made, I asked the shopkeeper for ten lemon drops, the train schedule, and a newspaper. I paid for my purchases with a smile and hurried to my wagon with the seeds of several plans sown in my mind and a lemon drop on my tongue.

When I returned to the farm, I unloaded the wagon hastily. I brushed the horses and cleaned their hooves to catch my breath between stacking the sacks of feed and fetching fresh water. Stroking the horses' impossibly soft, velvety noses, I gave each one a large carrot and a winter-softened apple, inhaling the wonderful aroma of their hot, grassy breath. I had not had the nannie goat bred in fall, so she would be without the company of a kid this spring. She slept in a stall with the cow, and they seemed to enjoy each other's presence. I spent a few minutes petting each of them, and scratching behind their ears.

The urgency that I'd had on my way home ebbed as I fell into the routine of my chores. I mucked out the stalls and laid fresh straw for bedding. The manure pile beside the barn had grown quite large, and I reminded myself that I needed to take it by wheelbarrow over to the garden before the ground softened with the warmth of spring. The sun was beginning to dip near the horizon, so I made my way to the chicken coop. I shoveled and re-laid straw, replenished their food and water. Securing the chickens in the coop to roost for the night, I left two cobs of dried corn as a treat. Though it was hard work, I enjoyed caring for these animals who gave me so much yet asked for so little.

Once back in the sod house I found the slate and chalk that Papa had given me to keep track of tasks that needed doing, intending to add the relocation of the manure pile. I hadn't used it in months as I had been listless and uninspired, only able to see as far as the next day, sometimes the next breath. Several lines on the slate were unreadable, the chalk brushed away by some object that had been stacked on top of it. One line remained, biting as I read it: *chop wood for winter*. It was the chore Papa was trying to complete when the tree fell on him, taking him from this world. With Papa gone the task had fallen to me. Now I remembered the urgent need that I'd had to gather wood and walk away my sadness. I looked down at the slate and its ill-fated task before wiping it clean without hesitation and starting a new list of chores.

I wrote "*move manure pile*" as neatly as I could with the awkward stick of chalk. The clumsy scrawl looked right at home on this schoolhouse slate. After some thought I wrote "*sew robe*, *get pup from Willy*, *write to Fiona and Inga*," on the slate before putting it down. A high-pitched, urgent growl from my stomach reminded me that I had not eaten since breakfast. I set two eggs to frying and toasted a thick slice of fresh bread. Toast cut thickly was my favorite, so that it had both a golden crust and the soft chew of fresh bread. I buttered my toast and slid the fried eggs onto my plate before seasoning them and smearing a generous dollop of crabapple jelly onto my toast. I ate ravenously, savoring each bite. After the meal my thirst was so strong that I chose to forego a drinking glass, and instead drank straight from the ladle of the water bucket. With my hunger sated and my thirst slaked, I brewed some tea and brought the whole pot to my chair beside the fire. My knitting and stationery were left alone. I sat with my tea and allowed all the positive emotions of the day to wash over me. Hope. Gratitude. Purpose. I had not accomplished much as far as tasks went today, but I'd most certainly made progress. Shedding the well-worn shell of my grief, I crawled into bed. I was ready to live again.

The first chore that I chose to begin the next morning was the one that I was most excited about. I swept the floor in front of the wood stove clean and laid the quilt from my bed onto the floor. Carefully I unrolled the beautiful blue sateen just enough that it filled the length of the quilt. I brushed off the back of my dress and laid carefully atop the fabric, my arms spread wide to get a sense of its dimensions. I cut two pieces with the utmost of care. They created a large T when laid beside each other. I needed no complicated pattern for what I was making. There would be no stiff collar, button holes or darted waist. Taking the pieces of fabric to the table, I began to sew.

Prior to my arrival on the farm I had never sewn an article of clothing. I would visit the modiste and milliners on Chestnut Street, the hub of Philadelphia fashion. These shops would carry the newest styles out of Europe and could produce them to order. The process was long and arduous, and I would be required to stand atop a short platform to have the dresses altered. My whalebone corset cinched as tightly as possible, the modiste would dart the waist to create the desired silhouette. The physical discomfort of these fittings was considerable, but it was the critical, scrutinizing eye of the dressmaker that I dreaded the most.

She would make use of the sunlight pouring through the front windows to afford a better view of the fine stitching. As such, the altering platform stood in full view of any passersby on the street. Young girls or women without the means to own such dresses would stand and watch the process, faces pressed to the glass without shame. The shame was all mine, on display. I would sigh with relief when the dressmaker asked me to turn so that she could stitch the back. The back of the store was easier to face, with its racks of clothing in various stages of completion, and large bolts of rolled fabric waiting to become dresses for Philadelphia's social elite. I would have been content with only new bonnets, shawls and gloves, but Mother had insisted that I always be dressed impeccably in the latest styles.

My attention returned to the blue sateen before me. I did not own a sewing machine, so all my stitching was done by hand. The long, unbroken hems and slippery fabric made the process of sewing this simple garment painstaking. The fine weave would have shown any errant stitches or hems that were torn out and redone. I was meticulous in my efforts, as I knew that the final result would be magnificent. When I grew hungry for lunch, I carefully rolled the fabric and laid it aside. I would work on it each morning when the sunlight found its way through the two small windows of the sod house, just as the modiste of Chestnut Street had done.

That afternoon I fastened my bonnet, retrieved an 8-foot length of rope from the barn, and made my way up the lane. Arriving at Willy's farm, I found him tearing down the field atop his horse. I was startled at first, fearing bad news. I saw the smile on his face, hair blowing back from his forehead, eyes wide with excitement and knew that all was okay. Willy had told me once that he loved to take this horse to a full gallop. The horse had a racing lineage and needed to satisfy his urge to run. When he was denied this opportunity, he would become agitated, nipping at the other horses, and bucking wildly around the pasture. I saw now that it was not only the horse's desires that were satisfied by these runs at an alarming speed. Willy's face laid bare a deep contentment. When they tore across that field, both horse and rider were free.

"Well hello, Miss Dahlia!" Willy called from across the yard. "I bet you've come for yer pup. The litter is in the stable with the horses, follow me." We made our way to a quiet stall at the back of the stable. There sat a black dog that appeared to be a herder. She was medium-sized, with a shock of white at her chest. Her eyes and ears were alert, but she did not seem bothered by our presence near her pups. The pups were not calm. They tore around the stall, diving into the straw and nipping at each other's tails. Shrill yips and tiny, comical growls could be heard from the four pups. Three were mostly black like their mother, and one was a shocking orange. Willy had joked that her father had been a fox, and the combination of her appearance and her temperament made me stop to consider whether he might just be right.

When I had finally gathered the nerve to call at Willy's a few weeks ago to tell him the news of Papa's death and the chimney fire, I was met by a man that showed the weight of a long, cold winter. Willy had spent his days much as I had, holed up in the house except to care for his many animals. He alluded to his own winter of melancholy and loneliness but did it in the roundabout way that men had when speaking of their feelings. We did not mention his proposal, nor my declining of it. Time had taken the sting from things, it seemed.

Willy had felt awful that he hadn't checked in on Papa and me, and that he hadn't been there to help when I had needed it. I assured him that I had made it through, and that I wouldn't have been great company as I wallowed in my grief. Attempting to lift my spirits, Willy had shown me the pups. I had sunk to my knees in the stable and the pups had crawled all over my lap, grunting and squeaking as their proud mother sat watchfully nearby. I held each one to my face and inhaled their sweet, hot breath. Immediately I was drawn to the orange pup, favoring her above the others. She seemed feisty and fearless. Willy had told me that the pups would be weaned in three weeks, and that I could have my pick of the litter. I had claimed the orange pup for my own, and then waited very impatiently for today to arrive.

Willy and I caught each other up on our news and plans for spring planting. He helped me fasten the rope to my orange pup and I made my way down the lane. The walk home took four times as long as it should have. The pup leapt into the ditches in search of mice, and ran back and forth across the lane, stumbling often on her still-clumsy legs. She ran under the fence that lined the road and became helplessly tangled in her rope. Lurching continually, she soon turned what I had intended as a leash into a noose. For fear that she would strangle herself in her excitement, I removed the rope from her neck. We made our way home by fits and starts, me questioning the wisdom of bringing this much chaos into my life. When we arrived home, I gave her a bowl of water before she collapsed into a heap on the quilt that I had left spread on the floor that morning. I tended to the animals as she slept, my mind already moving to the next task on my list.

When my pup woke from her sleep, she explored her new home. She sniffed every corner, toppled my knitting basket, and dug in the woodpile. I gave her more water and the last of the porridge from breakfast topped with fresh cream. After taking her outside I folded an old blanket for her bed, returning the quilt to mine. The pup sat on my lap and looked up at me. Her ears were perky by turns. Perhaps both would stand in time. They were tufted with black at the tips, just as a fox's were. It was unlikely, even impossible that she was part fox, but her look was very much like that of a fox kit. And so that's what I named her. I laid Kit on her bed when I stood to boil water for tea and she fell instantly and wholly into a deep sleep, as pups do.

I gathered my things as the tea steeped and brought the whole steaming pot to the chair that sat opposite mine near the fire. The wide-armed chair was made of wood from this farm, left here by the original settlers. It had no padding, no velvet upholstery like Papa's chair that had been lost in the fire, but it would have to do. I took Papa's Saturday sweater from where I had draped it over the back and slid my arms into its familiar warmth. I sat erect and uncomfortable at first until I kicked off my house shoes and pulled my feet up onto the chair. Then I spread the newspaper that I had purchased days earlier across my lap. That the news was old now did not matter; the paper was merely a prop, a gateway. I slid open the drawer of Papa's chess set and withdrew his pipe, bringing the bowl to my nose and inhaling deeply. The sweet smell of the tobacco had faded over the months, so I found the pouch of tobacco, filled the bowl, and tamped it down as I had seen Papa do so many times.

I struck a match and held it to the tobacco, puffing vigorously to make it light. The smoke did not feel in my chest the way it smelled in the air. What was sweet and velvety became harsh and burning in my throat and lungs. I coughed a large cloud of smoke out of my mouth and nose, my sinuses burning now as well. Coughing violently, I jostled an ember from the pipe onto my lap. I patted it quickly, but it had already left a small hole in my dress. With the pipe back between my teeth, I puffed ever so gingerly, taking the smallest sips of the smoke. I was heady and tingling from the tobacco. I leaned back against the chair and closed my eyes to stop the spinning inside of my head. Papa. Where was he? Why could I not feel him here as I wore his sweater and smoked his pipe?

A wave of nausea came over me and my mouth began to water. I carefully tapped what remained of the tobacco into the fire. I had been sure that I would feel Papa here with me. I set the newspaper aside and turned sideways in the chair, bringing my knees to my chest. Pulling Papa's sweater tightly around me, I settled instead for the memories of a lifetime of Saturdays.

***

It took me two weeks to turn the three yards of peacock blue sateen into a robe, inspired by the water-like feel of the smooth fabric. It had wide, flowing arms and simple lines that allowed the beauty of the cloth to shine. When I wore it, I felt as if I were submerged to the neck in the ocean, the tides pulling me gently this way and that. I had thought a lot about the Pacific ocean recently, and wanted desperately to see it. The robe made me feel closer to the water. I had trimmed the cuffs and made a sash from the pale green ribbon that the shopkeeper had given me. The robe was not of the latest fashion and did not adhere to the strict rules of decency. I could not have cared less. It was the single most exquisite thing that I had ever worn, and it roused in me a raw, feminine power that I had not known I possessed. When I wore my robe, I was beautiful for the first time in my life.

Chapter Fourteen

A bundle of letters awaited me when I finally went into town to make an official record of Papa's death, several each from Fiona and Inga. I visited the doctor and told him the story of the tree that took Papa from me, my heart in my throat as I spoke the words aloud. He looked down his nose over his half-spectacles at me. "Why did you not report this sooner?" he chided.

"The roads were impassable with all of the snow, and I was lost in my grief," I replied, my head held high. I held his gaze, daring him to scold me further. The doctor looked down and filled out the death certificate with the date that I provided.

"You'll need to take this to the Postmaster so that it can be registered with public records. I'm sorry for your loss," he finished as he handed me the death certificate. I went back into the post office as instructed and was scolded by the Postmaster as well. Finally, I visited Mr. Porter at the land office.

"Well hello, Dahlia! What a nice surprise!" he said as he rose from his seat.

"Hello, Mr. Porter. My Papa died," I blurted out. "I want to sell the farm." He came from behind the desk and placed his hands on my shoulders.

"I'm so sorry. How did it happen?" he asked gently, the pity on his face almost too much for me to bear.

"There was an accident while felling trees," I said, my voice cracking. Tears filled my eyes, blurring my vision. "I've brought Papa's will, and the deed to our land. I lost the main house in a chimney fire, but the sod house is sturdy. I'd like to include the horses and wagon, as well as the other livestock in the sale. I'm ready to leave as soon as it's sold."

"I'll advertise the farm for sale immediately, I have several families looking for established farms in the area. I'll be in touch." I thanked him for his help, and walked to my mare feeling light, a mountain of strain removed from my shoulders with a few simple errands. I stopped into the mercantile to pick up the seeds that I had ordered, and then climbed onto my mare.

We did not walk slowly along the dirt road as we had on our way to town. I led the mare to the soft strip of grass that lined the lane and urged her until we were at a full gallop. Great clods of dirt flew from her hooves as she ran. The sensation of moving at such speed was terrifying, but ripe with freedom; I hoped that she felt it too. We slowed as we approached the farm and walked towards the barn. I let Kit out of the house to join me, dried the mare of her lather, and fetched fresh water. I brought my forehead to her nose in gratitude for the exhilarating ride that had helped me leave my worries somewhere miles away from here.

As soon as I sat at the kitchen table, I tore into my letters, beginning with Inga's. I was eager to hear about her new baby and their new home. Inga wrote that their trek over the mountains had been long and hard, but the boys had enjoyed the adventure. They had seen nimble mountain goats climb sheer rock faces and were sung to sleep every night by the deep howls of wolves. They had begun work on their dugout house as soon as they arrived and had slept six across on the floor in front of her sister's wood stove until it was completed.

Inga's happiness with her new home was evident in her letters. Her tone was elated in the letter announcing the birth of her daughter, Oksana. She was described as a quiet and content baby, with a head of dark curls, and as beautiful as could be. The last letter had a worried tone. Inga asked if we were alright, as I hadn't responded to any of her letters. No, I hadn't been alright, I thought to myself as I folded the letter, but I was now.

I opened Fiona's letters next. It had been six months or more since I had sent her a letter, and I felt a distance between us. She told me that Vincent had finally proposed, and they were to be married in July. Then she described the bridal gown that she was making, and invited me to come to Philadelphia for her wedding. The letter dated one month later told of her discovery that Vincent had been seeing many other girls, and that the wedding had been called off. Fiona sounded sad and defeated, and I wished that I was there to comfort her. Her final letter was full of worries about our well-being, as Inga's had been. She hinted at trouble with the family that employed her, and a desire to start her life anew.

I wrote to each woman explaining my silence and breaking the news of Papa's death. I struggled to find the right words to impart such awful news. I then told them of my plans to head west and invited Fiona to join me on my journey. I missed her terribly and thought that a new life out west might be just what she needed. Tomorrow I would make another trip into town to post the letters.

I called Kit back from where she was playing in the field, retrieved the spade from the barn, and headed to the garden. Kit was thrilled at being allowed through the garden fence; it was the one spot on the farm that she had not yet been able to explore. Now five months old, she had grown both bigger and more curious. She ate several insects, sniffed along each side of the garden, and then began digging. Kit had dug wide holes in the yard and the pasture, much to my dismay. She would paw furiously at the earth, turning her body in a circle until the hole's dimensions were just right. Once the hole was completed, she would lie down inside of it, panting from the exertion, and proud as could be. I only planned to till a small section of the garden, but I was grateful for Kit's help.

As I would not be here in autumn to harvest or eat anything from the garden, I planted only a few vegetables so that the new residents might have something to put up for winter. I planted potatoes, onions, cabbages, and beets; the chore went even more quickly than I had hoped. There were still many hours of daylight left, and so I decided to complete another task. I splashed some water on my face and gathered a small garden trowel, a bucket, and the bulbs that I had special-ordered. I made a quick sandwich of muddled saskatoon berries and thickly spread goat's cheese, filled my canteen, and set off.

My sandwich was a perfect blend of the tart cheese and sweet berries, and as I popped the last bite into my mouth, I wished that I had made two. I drank deeply from the canteen and crested the hill overlooking the stand of birch. Following the old wildlife trail as it wound through the wood, I soon came upon Papa's grave. The mound of dirt had settled over the months, barely noticeable now as new grass took up root. I used the trowel to cut two circles into the grass, one on each side of Papa's grave. The roots loosened as I pried at the sod, peeling it back to reveal black earth. The package of bulbs gave six inches as the ideal depth to plant them, and I followed the directions, planting as many as I could inside of each circle. After the planting was done, I filled my bucket at the river, and watered the bulbs.

"I'm going away, Papa," I said aloud. "I'm heading further west to see what I might find. I've planted dahlia bulbs here where you lay, so that I'll always be right beside you." Sitting quietly for a few minutes, I remembered Papa and how much we had both grown once we had planted our feet on this farm.

"I love you so much and miss you every single day. I know that you understand my need to go. This farm was the thing that called to you. There's something calling to me too." I laid my head down near Papa's and looked up into the boughs of the trembling aspen. There was no breeze to rustle the leaves, but I could hear the sound in my mind. The smells of soil and new growth were in the air. I laid there in the warm sun until it felt right to leave. With a final goodbye to Papa, I left with a light heart, assured in my decision to go.

***

Mr. Porter found a buyer for the farm within a week of listing it for sale. I spent the following two weeks preparing for my journey, while I awaited Fiona's arrival. The two large trunks that had been stored in the hill house in our first few days here now laid open before me. They contained nothing that I wanted, nor planned to need. Mrs. O'Malley's recipe book, my sewing tin and the quilt from my bed fit into one travel case. My dresses and undergarments, blue robe and Papa's sweater fit in another. I had decided to leave the chess set. Papa would have preferred that I left it for someone else to enjoy, rather than toting it a thousand miles over the mountains for sentimental reasons. I was excited about my journey and tried to prepare mentally as well. The smoke and fire that I had dreamt of for years were gone, replaced by swirling blue water.

***

Fiona arrived exactly three weeks after I had mailed my letter to her. I had received her reply one week ago, detailing her plans to come here and then accompany me west. The farm had its own rhythms and routines, and as such, I was not used to being governed by the clock. I was mucking out the stalls in the barn when I realized that Fiona was arriving today, and I would need to race to the train station to get her.

Bringing the wagon was necessary because I didn't know if Fiona could ride a horse, and she'd surely have trunks with her. Without even washing my face or straightening my hair, I hitched the horses quickly and set off for town. The horses tore down the road in a cloud of dust, and I slowed them only after I nearly lost the wagon in the ditch. I arrived at the station sweaty and covered in dirt, the smells of my morning chores still clinging to me.

Fiona stood on the platform, a small trunk and two bags piled neatly beside her. She looked even more like Mrs. O'Malley now, with a pleasant plumpness that she hadn't had two years ago. Her eyes were still bright, her coppery hair falling into gentle curls around her face. Crying despite myself, I was relieved to see my dear friend after so long. I ran to her, and we embraced.

"You smell like a goat, Dahlia," Fiona said with a laugh.

"I likely do; I was mucking out the barn and lost track of time. I came without even washing up," I said, joining in her laughter. Fiona held me at arm's length and peered at me.

"You are stunning! This country life must suit you. You've lost your softness, though." A frown had replaced her smile. I nodded around the lump in my throat, not wanting to mar our reunion with talk of heartache. We gathered Fiona's bags and loaded them into the wagon. Fiona told me about her train ride and her excitement about traveling west with me. We talked the whole ride home, trying to make up for two years of missed time.

I showed Fiona around the farm quickly, and then set water to boil for tea before changing into a clean dress and standing at the washbasin to comb my hair and clean my face. Every morning, I had stood there, but had never really peered at myself in the mirror. Fiona had called me stunning, and I looked closely now to see if I could see what she had meant. Hard work had rid my body of fleshy curves, leaving long, lean muscles in their wake. My cheekbones were high and well-defined. My lips were full, cheeks flushed. My eyes were the same pale green that they had always been, but somehow their unusual color was more apparent now. I had lived through more than I had ever thought possible, and those victories showed in the confidence that I now carried.

The pot rattled on the stove as it came to a full boil, and I filled the teapot and left it to steep.

"I can't believe that you live here," Fiona said, her voice dripping with judgment as she looked around the single room of the sod house.

"I didn't have much choice after the main house burned down. I like it, it's cozy," I replied with a shrug.

"It's smaller than the nursery in your Philadelphia house."

"It's all that I need," I said, feeling defensive. We drank our tea and made small talk. I had foolishly expected things to be the same between us, but they were not. We had both changed over the last two years, and I felt as if I barely knew her anymore. I was hopeful that our trip would offer an opportunity to reconnect. After supper, Fiona joined me outside for the evening chores. Her long city dress dragged in the dirt, and she swatted at the flies that buzzed around her. She watched me milk and muck, brush and water, her incredulity laid bare on her face.

"I never thought I'd live to see this: Dahlia Day ankle-deep in manure, with a smile on her face!" Fiona exclaimed. I smiled and shook my head.

"I love farm life. It suits me much better than a fancy house in the city, and the boredom that came with that life."

***

During my last few days on the farm, Fiona had not wanted to join me on my long walks, so I took them alone. I walked to every corner of the farm, saying goodbye to the trees and the hills, the river, and the birds. I sat in the tall grass by the lake and took in the sounds of the frogs. A loon wailed its familiar call, but it didn't evoke the deep loneliness that it once had. The sound of the water soothed me as it always had, and could hardly wait to see the Pacific Ocean at long last. I spent hours brushing and petting the animals in turn, thanking them silently for taking care of me here. Willy had agreed to tend the animals for the two days between our departure and the arrival of the new residents.

The night before we left I hauled and heated water so that Fiona and I could bathe. All our clothing was washed, and everything was packed and stacked near the door, save for our traveling outfits. I had written a long letter to leave for the new owners, detailing everything about the farm and the best way to do things. Reading through it afterwards, I crumpled it up and fed it to the fire. Leaving instructions would rob the new family of the lessons and satisfaction gained from finding their own way. On a new sheet of paper, I wrote:

> *I hope that you will love this farm as much as we have. I've planted some vegetables and left some jars of preserves in the cellar so that you might have something to eat this winter. I've left two trunks full of things that I could not bring with me, do with them as you wish.*
>
> *Sincerely,*
>
> *Dahlia Day*

***

Willy arrived early the next morning to take us to the train station. I chose to say goodbye on the farm, rather than at the train station. "It's been a pleasure being your neighbor, Willy. Thank you for all the help you gave us, and for being such a great friend for Papa."

"The pleasure has been all mine. You've breathed life back into this old farmer's heart," he said with a small smile. His hand held the back of my head tenderly as I hugged him. He loaded our bags for us, and then he and Fiona waited with Kit for me to join them in the wagon. I filled my hand with dusty soil, and then let it fall as I looked out across our farm. I did not smell the earth as Papa had once done; I knew its scent, and my years here had shown me its value. Here, I had found myself among the hills, the trees, the river. I had learned that my capabilities far exceeded my presumptions of them. Despite all this, I was still plagued by restlessness. I felt compelled to search for something elusive, unnamed. And so, I roamed.

Book Two

Chapter Fifteen

SUMMER

1898

I sat with my face pressed to the window in our train car, Kit curled up in my lap. We had taken a short train south to Calgary, and then boarded The Canadian Pacific Railway train that would take us west. I had watched in anticipation as we neared the Rocky Mountains, and then we were in their midst, unable to see their peaks. Our first stop was in the town of Banff, where a hotel the size and likeness of a castle stood. It had towering turrets and many wings, and was built from stone dug from the mountains that surrounded it. The railway owned the Banff Springs hotel, and travelers could stop off there for a few days if they wished. I had not booked accommodation at the hotel, as we were only a few hours into our journey, but the train would stop there for four hours, nonetheless. The hotel stood commandingly in the valley, bordered on all sides by mountains. One could not lay their eyes on anything ordinary; beauty permeated every view.

We decided to visit the natural hot springs during our stop, leaving Kit inside of the private sleeper car before walking towards the steamy pools. The water was not heated with wood or coal, but rather bubbled up hot from deep below the surface. It smelled of boiled eggs, as it carried sulfur with it to the pools. Bathing costumes were available on loan with the price of admission, and Fiona and I hurried to change into them.

We giggled at the sight of each other in the heavy wool suits. They were dark brown in color, and consisted of a short-sleeved jacket, with a peplum that made up the knee-length skirt. Short pants much like bloomers were worn underneath. There were several pools ranging in temperature from that of a very hot bath, to a comfortable room warmed by a fireplace. I waded into the hottest pool, relishing the heat as it eased my tense muscles. I leaned back against the edge of the pool and stretched my legs out in front of me. Having bathed sitting upright in a half-barrel for over two years, reclining in the soothing water was bliss.

We rinsed off with fresh water after we soaked and put our traveling dresses back on. Then we wandered through the paths that surrounded the grand hotel. Walls of stacked stone surrounded beds of flowers, and a large greenhouse stood near the kitchen entrance. The air in the mountains had a scent unlike anywhere else that I had been. The essence of many varieties of trees and wildflowers, and the crisp smell of glacier-fed rivers found their way into my nose. Reluctantly, we reboarded our train and continued west.

We stopped a short time later to let passengers off at a chalet that stood beside Lake Louise. I sat staring from my window out onto a lake that appeared as if it had been painted by an artist with a very loose grip on the use of color. The lake was nestled between mountains on three sides. The left shore was shaded by peaks, while the lake and other peaks were bathed in sun. Lake Louise was a shade of blue-green that defied description, and surely could not be real. Later that night our attendant had told us that minerals washed down the mountains, giving the water its incredible color, and the coloring could be seen in several lakes in the area.

We dined on roasted chicken, new potatoes, and asparagus that night. It felt strange to eat food that I had not prepared, but I enjoyed it, nonetheless. Our train left the Prairies and entered British Columbia, winding through the mountains via Roger's pass. We crossed a bridge that spanned a deep valley and it felt as if we rode among the clouds. Wild rivers churned great rapids, their water milky white. I sat with my face pressed to the window until the sun set, taking with it my view of these majestic mountains.

Fiona's mood seemed to darken as we rode into the night. I asked if she was alright, but she said that she just needed some rest. We climbed into our respective beds, and I drifted off to sleep. I woke as we chugged through Three Valley Gap, and another lake surrounded by mountains. Only a sliver of blue sky could be seen between the peaks that rose sharply on all sides. The flora had changed sometime during the night. We were now among huge red cedar, moss and ferns covering every patch of ground in an explosion of green. I could feel the moisture in the air, and it was clear that plants thrived here.

We stopped finally in Sicamous, a small logging town on the shores of Shuswap lake. Alighting from the train, we waited for our bags to be unloaded. I looked around at the weeping willows standing near the water, their long strands of leaves dancing in the breeze. People were enjoying the shade that they provided on this hot summer day. A railway employee was telling a small crowd about local history and attractions. As we approached, he described an ancient creature named Shugumu that was rumored to live in the lake. The man told us that tribesmen had been spotting it for thousands of years, but no proof of its existence could be made. I shivered at the thought of a huge beast lurking in the depths of the water.

We wandered down the platform with Kit. I had leashed her for fear that people would mistake her for a fox and harm her. She drew curious looks wherever we went, though people did not seem to fear her. We bought two of the largest peaches that I had ever seen and took them down to the lake to enjoy while we waited for our next train. I let Kit run free and she splashed and dove into the lake to cool off. She tore around the grass where we sat under a thick tree and pounced on the bugs that abounded here. Fiona and I ate our peaches, sticky juice running down our chins.

"You've been awfully quiet," I said to Fiona as we enjoyed our fruit.

"I've been wondering if I made the right choice in coming out here. I had thought that things would be the same between us, but I barely recognize you now."

"We've both changed, but that doesn't mean that we can't still be friends. We'll have lots of time to get reacquainted."

"I was always the girl living in your house, and later, your housekeeper. I don't know how to act now that I'm not your employee," she said, redness flooding her cheeks.

"Act as you would with anyone else. I've invited you on this journey as my friend, Fiona. I no longer have a grand house and hired help, and thank goodness for that. I have no expectations of you; I simply thought that we could use each other's company," I finished. We washed our faces with water from the lake, rounded up Kit, and made our way back to the train platform. We boarded a spur line to Vernon, where Inga would fetch us from the station.

Green, leafy trees and mossy forest floors gave way to rounded hills covered in dusty scrub brush. The heat on the train became unbearable, and we shifted in our seats and fanned ourselves with our hats. Fiona finally felt ready to talk about what was bothering her. "I almost died of shame when I heard that Vincent was cheating on me, seeing loose girls every chance he got. Of course, it was that nasty Shirley who told me, and happily so." Fiona looked down at her lap, and I waited for her to continue. "He didn't even deny it, just told me that he was a passionate man and couldn't help himself. I thought about marrying him anyways. I'm scared that I won't find anyone else."

"You will, and you deserve much better than Vincent would have given you."

"I suppose. I had been making a gown for our wedding. It hung from the drapery rod in my bedroom, mocking me. I should have tried to sell it to get back the money I had spent on the silk. I didn't though. I ripped it to shreds and then burned it in the woodstove in a fit of rage. It smoked something awful, filling the kitchen, and the lady of the house was right angry with me," she said, shaking her head.

"I understand the feeling. I turned my bridal veil into a fishing net," I said with a laugh.

"My troubles didn't end there. The man of the house took notice of me during one of the rare times that he was home. He began visiting my room late at night, and I avoided his advances at first." My eyebrows raised at this, and I tried to keep the judgment from my face. "I was desperate for affection after losing Vincent, and finally relented, inviting him into my bed. We carried on our affair for several weeks before the lady of the house grew suspicious. I got your letter then, and decided to take the chance to get away. Not soon enough, though. The lady discovered us in my bed, and threw me out into the street. I did not get my last pay packet, and had no money. I had already booked and paid for my passage, but slept under bushes in the park for two days until my train departed." She looked up at me then, gauging my expression. Tears rolled slowly down her cheeks. I moved to her side and held her as she cried.

"I'm so sorry that you had to go through that, Fiona. I had no idea. I wish that I had been there to help you." After a time, Fiona stood and washed her face of tears. "Please don't waste another minute worrying about money. I have enough from the sale of my farm to get us anything that we need," I said reassuringly.

"I should not have done what I did with that man. I'm sorry that I hurt a woman who was very kind to me and welcomed me into her home. That said, I'm not sure that I've learned my lesson. It seems that I am a very poor judge of men's characters." She seemed to deflate, sighing deeply. Our train came to a stop in a cloud of dust as she finished speaking. We each finished a glass of water and stepped off the train into the sweltering heat. I had never felt so warm while outside before. In fact, I had only felt this way when sitting too near a roaring fire. That heat had been easy to move away from; this heat was impossible to escape. It felt difficult to draw breath, and I was sapped of all energy almost instantly. My dress clung to my back, and my feet had swollen, making my boots feel as if they were two sizes too small. I looked about for Inga, desperate for shade.

I spotted her beautiful, smiling face at the far end of the platform, and led Fiona towards her. Inga ran the last few steps to us and pulled me into a tight hug. I could feel the heat rolling off her body but bore it for the sake of being near to her once again.

"Look at you! You've grown even more beautiful somehow!" Inga gushed, holding me at arm's length to look at me fully. I laughed off her compliment.

"Inga, please meet Fiona. Fiona, this is Inga." Inga hugged her warmly, Fiona stood rigidly in response.

"Dahlia has told me all about you. I feel that I know you already," Inga said and Fiona smiled weakly, still recovering from her sadness on the train.

"It's nice to finally meet you as well, Inga."

"And this little ball of mischief is Kit," I said, scratching her behind the ears.

"Well, isn't she the sweetest thing!" Inga stooped to pet her, and Kit relished in the attention. We collected our small pile of belongings and followed Inga to her wagon. The horses stood at a hitching post, drinking deeply from the troughs. Inga allowed them to finish before we headed down the road.

"Of course, you had to come when it's hot as Hades out! The only way to escape the heat is in a lake. Luckily for us there is a lake in each valley around here. We'll be at my farm in half of an hour, and we can cool off then." She kept the wagon in the shade when she could, for the benefit of both us and the horses. We rode mostly in silence, save for the quiet panting of Kit and three women wilting in the summer sun.

The road led down into a valley, the hills lined with neat rows of fruit trees visible at every turn. Inga had told us that fruit grew easily here, and that they had an orchard rather than large fields of grain. They grew some crops for animal feed but made a good living off the apples, cherries, pears, and peaches that they grew. Inga told us about how wonderful it was to be near her sister again, and that she was very happy here. She asked me what had made me decide to head further west.

"The farm wasn't the same after Papa died. I was lonely and dreaded trying to survive another bitter winter. I suppose I'm looking for something, though I'm not sure what," I answered, laughing at my cryptic response. Inga looked at me questioningly, but said nothing. We pulled into the yard, stopping under a huge tree. Two of her boys ran out of the house wearing only short pants, their skin golden from the summer sun.

"Miss Dahlia!" they yelled as they approached. I suddenly wished that I had thought to bring them each a little something.

"Hello, boys!" I said as they rushed into my arms.

"We're going down to the pond to swim. See you later!" As quick as they came, they were gone.

"You'll get a better look at them at suppertime. Not a one of them would miss a meal, even in this heat." Inga smiled as she climbed down from the wagon, pride in her children clear in her voice. She unhitched the horses from the wagon and led them to the barn where Olek would dry and water them. We went into Inga's home, a neat wooden building with two full storeys. Inside it was bright and sunny, embroidered valances atop each window. The windows stood open, but no breeze flowed through them. Inga's sister Olena came into the kitchen with Oksana in her arms.

"Olena, this is Dahlia and Fiona," Inga said, gesturing to us. "And this is my sister Olena." She was tall and thin, but her black eyes, dark curls and beaming smile made her easy to recognize as Inga's sister.

"Hello, Olena. It's so nice to meet you," I said. "And this sweet doll must be Oksana." She was tiny, but hale, with huge round cheeks and wide black eyes. Her hair bobbed as she kicked her legs excitedly. I laughed as I scooped her into my arms, relishing the feel of a babe in my arms. "She's beautiful, Inga. She looks just like you." I kissed the dark curls on her head.

"She's the calmest baby that I've ever known, thank Heavens. I couldn't have handled one more boy in this house," Inga replied, pouring us each a tall glass of fresh apple juice. It was sweet and very refreshing after our hot ride in the wagon. We drank eagerly, and then Inga showed us to the dugout home that they had lived in while they built their wood home. Fiona and I would sleep in here during our stay. It was dark and cool inside, and I was glad that we had somewhere to escape the heat.

"Another farm, and another house made of dirt," Fiona said with a groan when Inga had left us.

"It's nice and cool, and we'll have privacy," I said, annoyed that she was being ungrateful.

"Is it too much to ask for rugs on the floors? An indoor bathroom? Or a person my age within fifty miles?" she asked, flopping onto one of the beds.

"We'll only be here for a few weeks, and then we'll go to Vancouver. I hope the accommodations and company will be more to your liking then," I snapped as I left the sod house. I knew that Fiona had been down, but that didn't give her reason to act snooty and entitled. I resolved to enjoy my time with Inga, and not let Fiona spoil my visit. We gathered around a long table in the shade that night for dinner. I had missed the energy and chaos of the Chornyk family, and the boys' antics had me laughing until my jaw hurt. I caught Inga's eye across the table. We each smiled and nodded slightly, acknowledging how nice it was to reunite.

***

Fiona's mood had remained low, and she rarely wanted to join Inga and me outside. After several failed attempts to include her, I decided to let her be. I wanted to climb to the top of one of the hills nearby to see what I might see. Inga agreed to join Kit and me, and we left early in the morning to avoid being out during the hottest part of the day. We wound our way through an orchard of apple and pear trees, coming out into the short brush that topped the hills. Kit ran and pounced as she always did, eager to explore all the new smells. The landscape was almost uniformly brown, faded by the relentless heat of the sun. Blue lakes could be seen tucked into each valley, just as Inga had said. I could see many homes, their farms filled with fruit trees.

The skies here were hazy, the clouds trapped in the valleys muting the sun. It did nothing to dampen the heat, in fact it seemed to hold it near the ground. Inga told me that forest fires were common in the summer, sparked by lightning. She said that when the smoke settled around the farm and the sun set behind it, the world was lit up with an eerie orange glow. I would have liked to have seen that for myself but was grateful to avoid the choking smoke. As we sat atop the hill, the near constant call of a bird rang out. It sounded very different from the wail of a loon but was just as sorrowful.

"Is that an owl calling in the light of day?" I asked Inga, confused by the unfamiliar call.

"No, that is a mourning dove. They coo all day. It's rather a sad sound, isn't it?" she replied.

"Yes, it is. If people sang as birds did, I think that my song might sound just like that some days." I listened as the dove continued its song. "Have you ever wanted to walk straight up the side of a mountain, and make a new life among the trees? To disappear? Start anew?"

"No, I don't suppose I have. I'd love a moment's peace, but my boys wouldn't live past lunch without me here to feed them," Inga laughed. "I think that this quiet moment right here will have to do."

"I have this overwhelming feeling that I need to find something, go somewhere. I can't for the life of me figure out what it is, but I knew that I needed to leave the farm. It was a wonderful home to Papa and me, and I feel like we were meant to go there, but a lot changed after Papa died, and it no longer felt like home. I wasn't sure what to do, so I thought that I'd head further west, see the ocean. I'm glad that I've been able to see you. You know, I miss you something terrible."

Inga turned to face me. "And I, you. Your heart knows what you need, Dahlia. If you listen to it, you won't be steered wrong." I nodded, and she returned her gaze outward across the valley. We sat until we had drunk our canteens dry, and then made our way back down the dusty hill.

***

We stayed in the Okanagan valley with Inga for two weeks. Fiona was eager to get to Vancouver, and we were both desperate for cooler temperatures. I said a tearful goodbye to Inga and her family, and boarded another train, heading west as I always had. I was in awe of the size and beauty of Canada. Millions of trees covered the mountains, and lakes and rivers were seen at every turn. When we reached the summit of the last mountain before our descent, I could see for miles and miles. I had stopped pointing out all the beauty that I saw, having grown tired of Fiona's sighs and rolling eyes. We spoke very little, and I began to regret my choice of companion for the journey. The train moved steadily down the mountain, onto fertile farmland bursting with produce. The air was much cooler than it had been in the Okanagan Valley, and humid as it had been in Sicamous. After a few more hours we finally reached Vancouver. We were met with fresh sea air and the cries of gulls as we stepped onto the train platform. This was as far as we had planned to come, and we gathered our travel cases to go in search of a room to rent. The city was busy and loud, making me miss the farm. The smell of the salty air stirred something in me, and I felt a sudden, overwhelming urge to see the ocean. We hired a carriage and set out to find a home.

Chapter Sixteen

We were able to find a boarding house that allowed dogs from which to rent a room, on advice from our carriage driver. He waited on the street for us while we went inside to inquire about vacancy. The house sat on a busy cobbled street. I paused a moment to enjoy the clopping of horses' hooves echoing on the stones; it was the sole thing I had missed about Philadelphia. At street level was a Chinese laundry, and a small sign hung above an alcove containing a door, just to the left of the laundry storefront that read: *Ms. Balderson's Proper Boardinghouse for Ladies.* The use of "proper" on the sign should have warned us of what we would encounter upon entering.

The Matron, Ms. Balderson, was the most average looking woman that I had ever seen. Her hair was a flat brown and was pulled severely into a tight knot at her nape. She was of average height and build and lacked any feature of note. I imagined that people's eyes would pan right over her on the street, and they would not recollect ever having seen her at all. She wore a gray dress that buttoned right to her chin, not even a sliver of neck visible. We would come to learn that Ms. Balderson was a dour woman, seeming to live in a state of perpetual vexation. She was both acutely aware of, and bothered by, most everything. Her unhappiness was evident, but the vigor with which she voiced her distaste spoke of a deep-seated anger rather than melancholy.

Neatly printed signs hung in the office, as well as in the rooms, laying out the rules of the boardinghouse. The signs read:

Ms. Balderson's Proper Boarding House Rules:

1. *All ladies must return to their rooms* **no later** *than 8:00 pm on weekdays and 9:00 pm on weekends.*
2. *All ladies will conduct themselves in a proper manner to avoid bringing shame to themselves or this house.*
3. *No male visitors will be permitted inside of the boarding house under any circumstances.*
4. *All undergarments must be hung to dry in the privacy of the rooms, NOT in the communal tub room.*
5. *The use of alcohol and tobacco are strictly forbidden, both within the boarding house and outside of it.*
6. *Tenants will dress modestly at all times.*
7. *Tenants will abstain from speaking or laughing loudly inside of the boardinghouse.*
8. *All dogs will remain quiet while inside the rooms. Any damages incurred will be charged in addition to your weekly rate.*

Failure to adhere to the above rules will result in immediate eviction from the boardinghouse

Fiona and I crept about like mice in the hallways and spoke quietly while in our room. The other tenants seemed to do the same, for we rarely encountered anyone else within the house. There was a sitting area near the reception desk, but it sat empty. It would have been impossible to relax under the Matron's scrutiny. Ms. Balderson was everywhere, seeing and judging everything that occurred under her roof. Despite being in a bustling city, we felt secluded.

Fiona wanted to explore Vancouver and meet new people, and all I wanted was to sit by the ocean. I followed the cries of the gulls and found myself on the shores of English Bay. The sun shone brightly, catching the crest of each gentle wave and following it to the shore. I removed my boots and stockings, digging my toes into the wet sand. A ship was far off at the neck of the bay, making its way towards the port to unload its belly of goods. I wondered where she had sailed from, what she carried. I wondered about the man who stood at her helm, and the ones that swabbed her decks. I walked up and down the beach, looking for shells, watching a small boy play in the surf, and tracing the paths of the gulls overhead. After an hour I walked a short way into the water, clutching my skirts about me.

"I've come," I said softly to the ocean. Looking out to the west across the beauty of the bay, I waited for the rapture or deep insight that I had been expecting. I felt neither. I had expected great, violent waves would crash about me, loosening everything that had become stuck inside of my mind. As the water lapped gently around my ankles, I turned away from the view that was breathtaking, but not quite right. Finding a grassy area, I sat for a while. The warm sun dried my feet so that I could brush the sand easily away. I put my stockings and boots back on and walked back towards the city.

At the boardinghouse, I retrieved the large, velvet bag full of Mother's jewelry. It now also contained all of the money that I had made from the sale of the farm. Worried about the bag being stolen if I walked about the city with it, I chose three pieces of jewelry and put them on. A jeweler was located just up the street from the boardinghouse, and I made my way to the shop. A heavy man with slick hair and an upturned mustache greeted me. He wore a black suit and an emerald green vest. Round spectacles slid continually from where they were perched on his nose, causing him to slide them back into place at intervals.

I explained that I had a large volume of jewelry that I had inherited from my mother and would like to sell it. I removed the brooch, necklace and hatpin and placed them on the pad of black velvet that sat on the display case. The jeweler retrieved his loupe from the end of the chain that was fastened to his vest. He picked up the hat pin and peered intently at it through the loupe, pursing his lips and moving his cheeks in such a way that his mustache danced upon his lip. After he had repeated the process with the other two pieces, he made an offer for their purchase. It was likely less than half of their true value, but I didn't care. They held no value to me. I had rarely seen Mother wear jewelry, and had no memories of any of the pieces. I accepted the offer and told the man that I would bring all of the jewelry to him, a few items at a time.

I began to draw curious looks as I marched up and down the street many times over the next two days, carrying jewelry in one direction and cash in the other. When I had sold all of the jewelry, I added the proceeds to the money from the farm. I counted the bills slowly into many piles on the bed. More than $10 000 lay before me. Enough to buy a grand house and live comfortably if that was my wish. It was not.

Fiona had been spending her days about the city with two other girls that were staying at the boarding house. They had met some men, and Fiona talked of nothing else as she burst through our door each night, minutes before curfew. She was animated and giddy as she told me all about the places they had gone, the things that they had seen. The glint in her eye had returned, reminding me of how she had looked when we were children and she'd had an idea for some trouble that we might get up to. I was happy for her, and the outings had improved the quality of her company.

I spent my days walking about Vancouver. At the wharf I watched rough men unload huge nets of wriggling fish from their boats and strong men haul large crates about the docks. I marveled at the small pockets of the city that were inhabited by people of one culture. Italy, China and Germany were all represented by the lettering on the signs, the dress of the people who went about the streets. I bought food from carts, unsure of what I was ordering. I would simply point at an item and pay with a smile. I happened upon one cart offering borscht, and eagerly ordered a bowl. I burst into tears with the first spoonful, feeling homesick and missing Inga. I was amazed at the flavors that I encountered in the mystery dishes from other vendors: sweet, savory and everything in between. I would stroll slowly as I ate, enjoying the cadence of unfamiliar languages floating in the air.

My time passed pleasantly, but I began to think about traveling to Vancouver Island. I needed to see the ocean as it met land for the first time in thousands of miles. Fiona was in a cheery mood on the night that I chose to broach the subject.

"I'd like to travel to Vancouver Island, so I can see the true western coast, the real ocean," I said excitedly.

"We just arrived here, and I'm having fun with the people that I've met. I don't want to go somewhere else with no people, no excitement. I want to stay in the city," she snapped, her mood darkening in an instant.

"Okay, but I am going. I could leave you some money in order to live comfortably until you find a job," I offered.

"You've dragged me all over the country on a whim, and now threaten to leave as soon as I don't agree to your plans?" she roared, reminding me of her fits of temper as a child.

"I'm not threatening you, Fiona. I'm simply telling you that I'm going, and trying to make sure that you'll be okay when I do. You can come with me or stay, I'm tired of trying to reason with you."

"There's the Dahlia that I remember. You care only about yourself, and when things don't go your way you use money to ensure that they do. I don't work for you anymore. I'll do as I please," she spat as she stormed out of the room. I sat in shock, wondering how I had become a monster in Fiona's eyes.

The next morning Fiona apologized for her outburst and told me that she would come to the island with me, but intended to have a little fun in Vancouver before we left. I was still hurt by her words, but didn't care enough to remain angry. It was Saturday, and I had booked travel for Sunday afternoon. Fiona had been out all day and came home at 5:00 only to eat dinner quickly and freshen up. Rushing back out the door with two other girls, she blew me a kiss and told me she'd return before the 9:00 pm curfew. I knew as she said it that it was untrue.

I took a long bath, and then neatly packed my traveling cases. At 8:30 there was still no sign of Fiona, so I packed all her things too. At exactly 9:00 Ms. Balderson rapped on the door to our room, asking if Fiona had returned. She held a thick register against her chest, which she used to keep track of the comings and goings of the tenants. When I told her that Fiona had not yet returned, she drew a thick line across the page with a flourish. She informed me that she would return to collect payment the minute Fiona returned, and that we were being evicted. I didn't much care about being sent away from this cheerless place but was annoyed at the idea of finding alternate lodging in the middle of the night.

Three very drunk women giggled and stomped up the stairs at 12:38. Ms. Balderson met Fiona at our door and informed her that she must leave. I paid the Matron, and single-handedly lugged our five pieces of luggage down the narrow stairs. I came back to the room to fetch Fiona, who was twirling in the center of our room singing loudly, and Kit, who sat quietly. We made our way down the hallway and through the office to the stairwell, Ms. Balderson's narrowed eyes following us all the while. I slid the handle of a travel case onto each of Fiona's shoulders, did the same with two more bags on my arms, and held the small trunk in front of me, Kit's leash in my hand. I turned to make sure that Fiona was following and saw her as a pack mule, arms hugging large bags as she teetered in heeled boots and a fancy city dress. We made our way down the road to a hotel by fits and starts, stopping often to adjust our precarious hold on the bags.

The doorman at the hotel held the door for us, eyes wide and eyebrows disappearing under the brim of his hat. I deposited Fiona on a settee in the richly decorated lobby hoping that she wouldn't break anything, and paid for a night's stay. A bellhop brought a trolley on which to stack our bags and rolled it ahead of us to our room. When we entered the room Fiona fell face first onto the bed, fully dressed. I removed her boots with a sigh and climbed under the covers on the thin strip of bed that was available. I slept fitfully and rose before the sun with Kit. At 8:00 I ordered tea, eggs and toast to be brought to our room. I woke Fiona, and we ate in silence. Fiona apologized for her behavior as she began to recall the events of the night. I shrugged it off, no longer expecting anything but poor behavior from her.

At 3:00 we hired a carriage to take us to the ship that we had booked passage aboard. The captain looked just as one did in books: neatly-trimmed gray beard, dark blue jacket with tassels on the shoulders, a ruddy complexion, and one eye that was always half-winking, perhaps the result of repeated spyglass use. He welcomed us aboard the ship with a booming voice and a grand swing of his arm. We were shown to our small berth, where we both promptly fell asleep, Kit curled up at the end of my bed. I enjoyed the ship's faint creaks and gentle rocking with the waves; Fiona did not. She spent much of the trip on deck with her head hanging over the rails.

We sailed towards the large island that had broken the great waves before they'd reached my feet in Vancouver. The sky was uniformly gray, as it had been for most of our brief stay on the coast. Bursts of hard rain came and went as we sailed, making it unpleasant to be above board. We finally approached the coal mining town of Nanaimo and slid gently into port. Rain came down in sheets, soaking through my dress in seconds. I slipped and stomped clumsily down the gangplank, and then stood on the wooden pier, drenched by the driving rain. Fiona disembarked with as little grace as I had, and we rushed to the small building that stood just off the pier.

A young man dressed all in brown greeted us half-heartedly as we entered. I explained that we were looking for a carriage and driver to take us over the mountain to the west coast. He looked surprised to hear that two women were traveling alone.

"To meet our husbands," Fiona added.

"We'll need to leave immediately and will pay well," I said. The man gestured to two wooden stools in the corner of the room and asked us to wait while he made arrangements. He donned a hooded rain slicker and dashed out into the downpour. Fiona and I looked at each other and burst into laughter in a moment that reminded me of our childhood. We both looked as if we'd narrowly escaped drowning, puddles forming around our feet on the plank floors. Kit shook vigorously and droplets of water flew from her, wetting the walls and counter. The young man returned with another man in tow. He was very short and slight and wore a tall top hat and tailed coat. He might have stepped just off the streets of New York in his formal attire. I felt unsure of this man's ability to protect us should we be set upon by highway robbers or an animal. He bowed deeply to us and introduced himself as Mr. Tipps in an English accent that brought memories of Papa rushing into my mind. He went behind the counter and emerged holding two long rifles and a small wooden box that I assumed held ammunition.

"I hope to not need these, but I'll be happy to have them if we encounter any unsavory characters on the mountain."

"I'm a fair shot," I said, causing Mr. Tipps to choke in surprise. I was suddenly proud of all the things that I had learned on the farm. Having arrived there as a fairly helpless girl, I had left as a strong woman very capable of handling herself. After he had regained his composure, Mr. Tipps led us to the waiting six-horse carriage. He brought us to a small restaurant that sold hot meals as well as hard tack, jerky and other traveling foods. We bought a few provisions and purchased two canteens which we filled with water.

"We'll ride through the night," Mr. Tipps said through the open hatch in the carriage. "This team has made the trek enough times that they could likely do it on their own. We'll stop in Port Alberni mid-morning to trade the horses out for a fresh team, and me for my brother. He'll take you the rest of the way." Nodding, he slid the hatch closed. We took off with a lurch and headed down the muddy road. The carriage had screens with shutters instead of windows, which we had to keep closed due to the rain. Unable to watch the landscape slide by, I chose instead to sleep. I curled up on the bench at the back of the carriage, our uphill momentum keeping me tucked snugly against the wall. Kit and Fiona followed suit, all three of us exhausted from traveling.

We stopped several times to water the horses and relight the lanterns, and Mr. Tipps took short naps under the carriage on a mat that he rolled out on the mud. Seeing a man dressed as he was crawl out from under a muddy carriage was quite a sight. Our last stop before reaching Port Alberni the next morning was an ancient forest called Cathedral Grove. Mr. Tipps told us about the forest through the hatch as we approached it.

"Some of the trees we'll see are estimated to be 800 years old and stand over 250 feet tall! I bet you've never seen anything like them." I suspected that he was exaggerating; he was not. Stepping from the carriage, the morning light filtered through the canopy 250 feet above us. I walked slowly into the forest of Douglas Fir and Red Cedar, Kit at my side. The ground was covered with moss that silenced our steps, and ferns that brushed against us as we walked. I put my palm flat on the trunk of a cedar and closed my eyes. I could feel its energy, its life. I called Fiona over to do the same.

"Do you feel that? It's as alive as you and me," I whispered after a few moments. Fiona looked at me as if I had been struck about the head, rolled her eyes and walked away. I wound my way through the massive trees, some so large that ten men could have extended their arms around the trunks. Bright beams of light found their way through gaps in the canopy and lit small sections of the forest floor. Papa called these sunbeams fingers of God when they had come from the clouds. I didn't know if they would be called the same here in the forest, but they certainly had the feeling of something Divine.

We arrived in Port Alberni by mid-morning as Mr. Tipps had predicted. Our six- horse team was switched out for one of four, as we would be descending from here onward. Mr. Tipps introduced us to his brother of the same name. If they had not been standing next to each other, I might not have believed that they were two separate people. The latter driver was dressed only slightly less formally than the former, in a tailored suit and fedora. We refilled our canteens, stretched our legs, and bought a few more rations. I walked Kit quickly about a grassy area, and we climbed into the carriage. I grew restless as we departed, anxious to arrive at our destination. Fiona remained quiet, as she had for the entire carriage ride. The new Mr. Tipps led his team deftly down the mountain and towards the ocean.

We arrived on the western coast of Vancouver Island in the late afternoon of the following day. There were trees blocking my view of the ocean from the road, allowing me only brief glimpses of blue. I could not wait any longer, and asked Mr. Tipps to halt the carriage. I burst from the door with Kit on my heels and ran towards the sound, the smell. I dashed through the trees and my boots sunk into sand. I ran, nearly falling at every step until I came to where water met land. The waves pounded the sandy shoreline and erupted into magnificent spouts of water as they crashed into the rocks. I was overcome by the ocean's awesome power and sank to my hands and knees in the wet sand.

"Are you alright, Dahlia?" Fiona called from somewhere behind me.

"Yes," I answered, unable to manage more than that. A sob of relief escaped me; the sound drowned in the rhythm of the surf. I had seen the Atlantic Ocean on a trip to New York City. It had been flat, static, and gray as steel. It had not commanded my attention; it merely marked the edge of that great city. This was not that. I had come thousands of miles and had lost most everything along the way. I had borne an intractable restlessness for most of my life, the bees that I had always fled. This journey had not lulled the bees, it had set them free. My eyes were seeing the Pacific Ocean for the first time, but something deep inside me recognized this as home.

I squeezed the wet sand between my fingers and came slowly to standing, not bothering to brush off my dress. My bonnet had been blown off my head and hung at my neck as the wind whipped my hair about in the salty air. I knew that I would never again be able to bear living away from the ocean.

"We'd best get to the Land Office before it closes, or we'll be sleeping on this beach tonight," Fiona said, irritation clear in her voice. She began to walk back to the trees and our waiting carriage. I stood there for a moment more, reluctant to take my eyes from the churning beauty before me. I called Kit back from where she was digging furiously in the sand and returned to the carriage.

***

The land agent walked with us to the house that we would let. The house was a storey-and-a-half, the attic one large bedroom. It was built atop a cliff of one hundred feet, the tides crashing at its base. A goat trail wound down from the house to the ocean, where a thin strip of beach appeared at low tide. The house had been built by a sea captain whose wife had wanted to be far away from New England upon his retirement, lest he be drawn back into sailing by the calling of the sea.

No ships docked on these wild shores. All shipping lanes were found in the strait between Vancouver and the eastern shores of this island. The captain had built a widow's walk from the attic balcony. It was a narrow, wooden walkway that jutted out towards the cliff. The view from its heights contained only water and sky, making it seem as if you were standing at the prow of a great ship rather than on a balcony. Perhaps the captain had built the widow's walk on a romantic whim or felt his wife apt to live out her years watching the water for him should he ever return to sea. The land agent told us that the wife had died first, so it was likely that the captain had been the one to stand here and watch the ocean. The house sat vacant for years after the sea captain's death, left in will to his son in New England. It was available for sale or let. We chose to rent it for one month before deciding whether to purchase it.

The house had clapboard siding, grayed from years of salty wind blowing against it. The doorknob was rough, discolored with salt, and difficult to turn. The captain had decorated the inside of his house in the manner of a ship's cabin. The walls were paneled in dark wood, and the floors were of wide planks that were finished to a high sheen. Dust sat everywhere now, but I could imagine how everything would shine when it was cleaned. The rear of the house was composed entirely of windows to provide a continuous view of the ocean and sky. Simple, sheer white curtains hung beside each window, and I could envision them billowing in the wind.

There was a large kitchen, a bright bedroom, a sitting room, a dark study with an impressive desk, and a full bathroom with a clawfoot tub. In the attic there was another bedroom with a settee facing the ocean. The large yard sat neglected, weeds choking many of the native plants.

The land sloped away from the back of the house towards a wood of red cedar that towered high above us. Their trunks seemed to glow orange, the color an exact match for Kit's fur. Tiny saplings had sprung up in the yard, a sign that the forest was reclaiming what had been taken when the site was cleared.

The land agent walked us down a faint trail that was overgrown with ferns and spongy moss, Kit pouncing and crisscrossing our path. The trail led to a river that we would use to fetch water if our rain barrels ever ran dry. He told us that the river ended in a spectacular waterfall a ways down. I vowed silently to see it for myself and could not wait to explore my new home. Fiona and I thanked the man and ran excitedly to our new house. Fiona chose the bedroom on the main floor, leaving me the attic room. I made my way up the narrow staircase, the boards creaking beneath my boots. I walked straight across the room to the French doors that led to a small platform and the widow's walk. At the end of the walk, I leaned against the railing spreading my arms and letting my head fall back.

"I've come," I said softly to the ocean.

Chapter Seventeen

Fiona's restlessness grew each day. Somehow this ocean was not enough for her; she needed more. I spent hours standing on the widow's walk, searching for whatever it was that was calling to me. Fiona paced and sighed and became short with me. She needed companionship, and I was lost in my love affair with the world around me. One Saturday, she returned from the store full of life, her former good cheer shining bright.

"We're going to a dance tonight!" she exclaimed. "I met three men from the logging camp, and they've invited us to meet them tonight. Please say that you'll come; I'll die of boredom if I sit inside of this house for another minute." I considered her offer and decided that meeting some new people might do us both some good.

"I'd love to. Let's go find something to wear!" Fiona squealed with glee and raced to her bedroom to pick out a dress. One hour later we were rushing towards the logging camp that sat just past the store. Fiona's excitement was contagious, and I too was excited for what the night might bring. We came to the tall wooden fence that had been built around the camp; whole logs with spiked tops, pounded right into the ground. We were greeted by whoops and cheers from the men who so rarely had women to spend their Saturday nights with. It was an odd, but pleasant feeling. A large open-air tent was filled with tables and strung with lanterns. Thirty or more men strolled about or played cards at the tables.

The man that Fiona had met at the store was named Lenny Williams, and he greeted us now, leading us towards the tent. He had an easy, loping gait, and seemed to settle into each step before taking the next one. He was tall and thin, with bird-like features and a wide smile. One man began playing his fiddle, and cups of whiskey were thrust into our hands. A man turned as we entered the tent, his eyes locking with mine. He stood and walked my way, never dropping his gaze. A few inches taller than me, he had short, blonde hair. Though average-looking, his smile was self-assured, as if he knew that he would win the prize he sought.

"I'm Hank," he said, taking my hand in his, "and you are the most beautiful woman that I've ever seen." I laughed nervously, never having had a man speak to me this way.

"I'm Dahlia, it's nice to meet you," I said, squirming under his directness. Hank took my arm and led me to a table to sit. Another man approached the table, baring his brown teeth as he smiled at me.

"Hello, Miss. I'm Roy. It's a pleasure to make your acquaintance." He gave a small bow that seemed odd coming from the scruffy man before me.

"I'm Dahlia, pleased to meet you," I answered politely, unsure of how to manage this sudden spate of male attention. Fiona and I were the only women in attendance; the others were all loggers reveling in the freedom of their Saturday night. Hank told me that the crews worked until supper time every Saturday, and then had the rest of the night and all of Sunday off. They worked long hours during the week, leaving before the sun rose and returning to the camp after it had set. They were brought by mule-drawn wagons deep into the forest to fell huge trees. I could smell the forest on him, as if his work had caused the aroma of freshly-hewn wood to emanate from within him.

I declined his offers of a drink over and over, and had put my first cup down at the first opportunity. I had never drunk alcohol, and Mother's behavior at our dinner party had left me scared of losing control as she had. Fiona was dancing with Lenny, joy on her face for the first time since we had left Vancouver. Hank asked me to dance, and I agreed, following him nervously to the spot that had been cleared of tables. He held one of my hands and placed his other hand on the small of my back. His hand was rough and callused from his work. He began leading me around the floor, but I didn't know the dance and stumbled repeatedly.

"I'm sorry, I don't know the steps."

"Just let yourself go; I'll lead you." Smiling, he slowed his steps so that I could catch on. He took two quick steps towards me, and I took two backwards at his pace. These were followed by two slow steps in the same direction. He led me slowly around the floor as I learned, our movements becoming synchronized. He pulled me close to him and then spun me on my heel. I managed a bit of grace and laughed at the feeling of spinning under the lights. We carried on until another man asked if he could have a dance. Hank let me go reluctantly when I agreed, handing me to the other man.

I danced a song with four or five more men, as did Fiona. All of this attention was strange, but welcome. It grew late, and I started to feel that it was time for us to go home. I spotted Fiona in a dark corner on the lap of Lenny, deep in a kiss. I tapped her on the shoulder and told her that we'd best be getting home. Lenny groaned and voiced his protest, and Fiona stood reluctantly to follow me. We bade everyone farewell and promised to return the next Saturday. Hank and Lenny ran after us, insisting on walking us home, and we agreed.

Fiona and Lenny walked ahead of Hank and me. They stumbled and sang, often stopping to kiss. When we reached our house Fiona took Lenny straight into her bedroom. I had wanted to say goodnight to Hank at the door, but now felt that I couldn't turn only him away. We sat on the settee in the sitting area, trying to ignore the yelps and moans that carried from Fiona's bedroom. Hank slid closer to me and leaned in for a kiss. My lips were tightly puckered, my eyes wide open. I had no idea what I was doing. I followed his lead, as I had when we were dancing. I allowed his tongue to explore my mouth, and felt my whole body begin to tingle. He kissed my neck softly, making me shiver. He began to unbutton my dress and I stopped his hand.

"I've only just met you," I said, embarrassed.

"Then get to know me," he replied huskily. I stopped his hand again and we continued kissing. I felt his hand on my knee, pulling my skirts up. I stopped his hand again, annoyed by his persistence.

"I think that you should go now." My throat was dry, my heart pounding, scared of what might happen if I didn't stop him.

"Oh, Dahlia, I'm just trying to have some fun," he said, pouting a little. He composed himself and I walked him to the door. He pinned me to the door with a deep kiss, reigniting the feeling that I'd had on the settee. I returned his kiss, but broke free after a moment.

"I'll come to the tent again next Saturday," I said breathlessly, eager for more of his attention.

"And I'll think of nothing but you until then," he replied smoothly as he pulled away and walked with a skip into the yard. I closed the door behind him, and leaned against it, eyes closed. I went up to my bedroom and straight out onto the widow's walk, my head reeling. I grinned stupidly, heady with the feeling of being desired. I didn't have a sense of whether I liked Hank, or if it was his desire that I craved. I went back inside and undressed, putting on my silky robe over my bare skin. I could hear Fiona calling out in lust, in bed with another man that she had only just met. I hoped for her sake that Lenny was not like the others. I put my pillow over my head and fell into a restless sleep filled with Hank's intense stare and urgent kisses.

***

I was sitting at the kitchen table the next morning having breakfast when Fiona emerged from her room, followed by Lenny. Both wore easy grins and could not keep their hands from one another.

"Where is Hank?" Fiona asked.

"He left last night, shortly after arriving." I shifted in my chair.

"Dahlia, you prude! You couldn't have shown him a good time?" she asked in an accusing tone. I flushed with embarrassment, hurt that Fiona would say those things in front of Lenny.

"I've only just met him. I told him that I would see him again next Saturday."

"If he hasn't lost interest by then," Fiona said, rolling her eyes. I chose not to respond and we sat in silence as Fiona fixed more tea. Once the tea was drunk, the couple went back to Fiona's room, and resumed their raucous lovemaking. I donned Papa's sweater, called Kit, and escaped into the fresh air to avoid the noise. I took the skinny trail down the cliff to the beach. It was impossible to decipher sky from ocean, ocean from sand; all were awash in shades of gray. A fine mist fell, whipped in all directions by the coastal winds. It was low tide, and the sand was littered with a fresh offering of clam shells and bull kelp. Kit sniffed each item as we passed, tasting each long strand of kelp in hopes that one might taste better than the others. I crouched to scratch her neck, laughing at the pep with which she approached everything in this world. Looking up, I saw a tall, broad-shouldered man walking towards me. He raised one hand in greeting.

"Hello, Miss," he said in a deep, confident tone. He bent to pet Kit on the head. I sputtered as I stood.

"Hello. I'm Dahlia Day," I managed, completely rapt by the incredible man standing before me. He stood a full head taller than me, despite my five-foot-eight-inch stature. His skin was a beautiful olive-brown, his cheekbones high and defined, hinting at the lineage of a tribesman. His black hair fell gently onto his forehead, and flipped slightly at the back where it ended at his shoulders. His features were strong and very masculine. Incongruent with the dark man before me were his eyes: a bright, piercing blue just the color of prairie skies.

"I'm Toran. Are you new here?" he asked.

"Yes, my friend Fiona and I have just arrived a week ago. We're renting the gray house on the cliff." I gestured behind me vaguely. "Is Toran an Irish name?"

"No, it's Scottish. It's the name my father gave me. My people call me T'apjuu, which means '*stands tall and straight*'. It's a reference to the red cedar that grow on my island." He looked towards Kit. "Your dog looks an awful lot like a fox." He then whistled to Kit to come. She obeyed, much to my surprise. She was a friendly dog, but very headstrong and usually came only to those she knew.

"Yes, so much so that I've named her Kit. I brought her here from my farm, which sits on the other side of the Rocky Mountains. She's been wonderful company."

"You've come a long way then. What brought you to British Columbia?" He tilted his head, curiosity alight in his eyes.

"I felt that I was looking for something. I was drawn here. It turns out that it was the ocean calling to me," I said, my voice cracking. We both stood looking out over the waves. Fiona's voice rang out from the top of the cliff.

"Dahlia! Dahlia?" she repeated. I waved my arm and shouted back.

"I'm down here!"

"I can see that you have to go. I'll be here for another few weeks. Maybe I'll see you walking again soon?" he asked.

"Yes, I imagine you might," I replied, not wanting to leave Toran in order to deal with whatever crisis Fiona had. He tipped his head in farewell and continued down the beach. I made my way up the steep trail to the house, Kit at my heels. Fiona and Lenny stood impatiently in the yard.

"Who was the man you were talking to?" she asked.

"He's a trader, just passing by," I replied, willing myself not to smile.

"Well, I'm going to the logging camp. Don't wait up," she said over her shoulder, already walking down to the lane.

***

I did not see Toran again that week, despite taking Kit to the beach every day. Instead, I spent my time exploring the tidal pools; I could sit and watch the sea life for hours, getting lost within the little world of each pool. Fat purple and orange sea stars clung to large rocks; their arms bent at awkward angles rather than laid straight. Whole areas of rock were covered with sharp barnacles as well as mussels that would close their shells with a soft hiss when I came near. Crabs sidled with claws raised and legs clicking, angry that I had interrupted their hunting. Sea urchins stood rigidly, their spines daring anything to draw too near. Anemone swayed with each filling of the pools, looking like hair waving gently in the clear water. Kit helped me dig clams on the beach; I would point to the bubbles that indicated something living beneath the sand, and she would dig furiously until she found the clam. If I didn't retrieve the clams quickly enough, Kit would run down the beach, throwing them into the air over and over. Each time that I ventured out into these new wilds I discovered something incredible.

***

Fiona moped around the house during the days and snuck down to the logging camp to be with Lenny every night. The loggers were not allowed to have women in their tents, but neither she nor Lenny cared. She talked incessantly about the upcoming dance and drew me into her excitement. Once I had admitted to asking Hank to leave when he had tried to undress me, Fiona scolded me.

"You don't need to be so buttoned up; you're not in Philadelphia anymore. A little romp would do you some good," she said, a lewd smile on her lips. On Saturday we both took long baths and brushed our hair until it shone. Fiona wore her purple traveling dress and convinced me to wear the only fancy dress I had brought. It was also a traveling dress, beautifully made from emerald green silk. I was no longer used to the stiff collar and corset and felt very restricted. My excitement outweighed my discomfort, and I finished my outfit with a proper hat festooned with feathers. I dabbed some of Fiona's cologne at my wrists and neck, and we set off, giddy as school girls.

Hank and Lenny were waiting for us at the gate, and we were warmly welcomed. I had decided that I would try some whiskey to help me ease my nerves. The first sip burned my throat as I swallowed, and filled my stomach with warmth. I drank slowly at first, sputtering with each sip, and then more quickly as the night wore on. The spirits calmed my nerves, and I soon forgot my fears of feeling awkward. Fiona and I danced with each of the men in turn, our dates scowling all the while. I had become much better at dancing the two-step, and Hank whirled me with ease. We coasted around the floor, my head reeling when we spun. He kissed me often, and I did not care that anyone could see. Pinning me to a tree, he groped my breasts through my dress.

"Let's go to your house," he said as he kissed my neck. We made a hasty exit, not saying goodbye to anyone. Fiona caught my eye as we made our way through the tent, and nodded her approval. We made our way up the lane as Fiona had last week, stumbling, singing, and kissing. We burst into my bedroom, tangled in each other's arms. Hank fumbled with the tiny buttons that ran down the back of my dress, and then tore them apart in frustration. Buttons flew in every direction and my dress fell to the floor. He removed my corset, pulled my shift over my head, and led me to my bed. His hand slipped into the waistband of my bloomers, and his fingers probed me without tenderness. Removing his pants quickly, he laid upon me and thrust into me, sending a shock of pain into my groin. With his head buried in my neck, I could not look into his eyes as I had hoped. I felt like a receptacle rather than a participant. Hank let out a loud groan and then fell still. He pulled himself from me, gave me a small kiss and rolled onto his side away from me.

The excitement and passion that had been running through me all night had no outlet. I laid there unsure of what to say or do, my confusion quickly turning to shame. Hank fell asleep almost immediately, farting and snoring with gusto all night. I spent most of the night on the widow's walk, the salty air causing the effects of the whiskey to fade. I was trying to come to terms with what I had just done, and had no idea what all the fuss was about. Surely there was more to lovemaking than that? The sounds from Fiona's room the previous week had led me to believe so.

Hank rose early, waking me as he did. "I need to help the crew boss plan this week's cut sites. I have to run," he said curtly, not meeting my eyes.

"I can make you some breakfast before you go," I offered.

"I really have to get going," he said as he laid a perfunctory kiss on my forehead. With that he slipped out the door, no backward glance or hint of kindness. Fiona emerged from her bedroom, cheeks pink and eyes bright.

"Did Hank leave? How was it when you came home? Did he send you over the moon?" she asked in rapid succession.

"Yes, he left; he had to do some work today. As for last night, it was over before I could enjoy it," I said flatly.

"Oh, well no matter. The first time is always strange. But then, maybe he's lost interest now that he's gotten what he wanted." Fiona stared at me, her voice dripping with judgment. Her words stung sharply.

"Last week you called me a prude, and now you're implying that I'm a harlot. Which is it?" I demanded.

"Both. You prance around as proper as can be, and then spread your legs to the first man who shows you any interest," Fiona yelled back at me. My eyes widened in disbelief.

"That's rich, coming from you! You've been miserable and cruel since you arrived at the farm. Have I done something to hurt you? I don't think that I deserve to be treated this way."

"You've always had everything, Dahlia; fancy dresses, a grand house, a father that loved you dearly. Yet, you always wanted more."

"What? My family was wealthy, and so I don't deserve your respect? I'm not allowed to seek the company of a man? You don't make any sense. What are you so angry about?"

"You're so used to fancy things, and to having no responsibilities, no work to do. You're life has never been hard, just boring. Lucky me, I get to follow you all over the country in search of more, always more. Poor Dahlia," she finished with mock pity. I closed my eyes to the tears that threatened to fall, and took several deep breaths to slow my racing heart.

"The fancy dresses were simply the costume of a society that I despised. I didn't want to wear them; I was forced to. The grand house was reduced to ash, along with my mother." Fiona winced then, seeing that I'd had losses too. "You can think what you will about my life, Fiona; my time on the farm showed me what I'm made of." I stepped closer, my face inches from hers. "When Papa died and the money and comfort were gone, I was forced to make it on my own, and I did. I will not apologize for trying to find a place that feels like home, we all deserve that," I finished, my voice even, but fury burning hot on my face. Fiona stepped back from me with wide eyes. I stared at her, daring her to challenge me further. I was tired of her sour attitude and unprovoked attacks. Fiona turned and slipped into her room without a word.

I stormed upstairs to dress and then headed out with Kit for a walk. My head was pounding from the whiskey that I drank the night before, and my stomach was turning. The very thought of eating nearly made me vomit. I wore no bonnet, and my hair was whipped every which way by the fresh, salty air. Kit and I wound our way down the trail, and she took off running at full speed as soon as we came to the beach. I followed her with my eyes, and saw Toran. I did not want to see him in my current state but feared that I wouldn't see him again if I turned back.

Toran approached with a wide smile. I feared that he would see my shame and anger plain on my face. If he did, he did not let on. We walked for a while down the beach, and then he asked me if I would like to pick some berries.

"I'd like that. I didn't know which ones were safe to eat here on the coast, so I haven't picked any since arriving."

"I'll show you," he replied with a smile. He led me a short distance into the trees and found a large shrub dotted with clusters of blue berries. "These are elderberries. The blue ones are edible, but red ones are poisonous." As we filled my apron with berries, he told me that they must be cooked, and that their syrup would help fight a cough or relieve pain. I smiled to myself, reminded of Papa and his vast knowledge of many things.

We wandered deeper into the woods as Toran warned me about the cougars that live here. "They are so stealthy that you'd never know they were there until they are upon you. You might want to carry a weapon when walking deep in the forest," he said solemnly. I shuddered at the thought of being stalked by an animal. Spotting a tall bank of bushes then, he pointed out the juicy blackberries. Toran warned me that they may stain my apron, but I assured him that it was fine. He seemed surprised by my disregard for my clothing. We carefully picked the huge berries from their thorny branches, content in each other's company. When my apron was full, we went back to the beach and watched Kit play her games with the shells and sticks that littered the sand. Toran looked up at the sun and announced that he had to meet a fur trader in town.

"I hope to see you before I leave for home in two weeks."

"I'd like that," I replied and walked towards home, my apron full of berries and my head full of that incredible man. I decided not to tell Fiona about him. I didn't want her to ruin the only positive thing in my life at the moment.

Fiona was sitting at the table waiting for me when I returned home. I avoided her eyes and emptied my apron of berries, nearly filling a pot. "I'm sorry for what I said Dahlia," she said flatly. "It wasn't fair of me to be angry with you for your privilege." It was a pitiful excuse for an apology.

"Is that all?" I asked icily. "What about calling me promiscuous? Or selfish for trying to find somewhere that I belong? How about the hundreds of cruel things you've said since we were on the farm? I don't know who hurt you Fiona, but I'm tired of being your whipping post." I felt tired, and past caring about our relationship. I never knew which version of her I would encounter, and could no longer tolerate the uncertainty that defined our friendship.

"Yes, all of that. I'm sorry that I said those things. I was so bored before I met Lenny. I guess I took it out on you."

"That is a pitiful reason to be cruel to your oldest friend."

"I know it is. Please forgive me Dahlia," she said with tears in her eyes.

"I need some time," I said as I walked towards the stairs. We gave each other space all week. Things were civil, but I had lost my blind faith in her. She had attacked me when I was at my most vulnerable, and I would not soon forget it.

I was still confused about what had happened with Hank, and foolishly decided to go to the camp during the week in an attempt to clear the air. I walked down on Wednesday with Fiona, and she asked Lenny to fetch Hank for me. He came back to us alone, saying that Hank was still working and couldn't talk. His eyes would not meet mine, and he wrung his hat nervously in his hands. It was past 11:00, so I saw the lie for what it was. I left Fiona there and walked home alone, hoping not to meet any cougars along the way.

Fiona brought word on Friday that Hank was going out with the crew boss to survey cut sites and would not be at the camp on Saturday night. With no reason to attend a dance if he wasn't there, I stayed home. I felt rejected and ashamed. Wrapping Papa's sweater around me, I wandered down to the beach. As the sun began to set, I stood facing west and roared back at the surf.

"What do you want from me?" I screamed, arms lifted in query. "Why can't I find my way? I came here. I came to you. Now what?" My voice broke, hot tears streamed down my face. No answer came. I hung my head in defeat, feeling lost.

"Dahlia?" I heard Toran say from behind me. I spun to face him, ashamed of what he must have heard. His face held nothing but compassion, and I ran to him. He embraced me and stood there as I cried into his arms. He felt no need to ask anything of me; I felt no need to explain myself. When I finally pulled away, he wiped the tears from my cheeks.

"I'm sorry, I've had a bad few days. Sometimes it feels good to yell into the wind," I said with a shrug and short laugh.

"I do the same," he said. I could not imagine anything that would rattle Toran enough to cause him to yell at the ocean.

"I leave next Sunday." The words sat between us for a while. I silently cursed the Universe for bringing me this man, and then whisking him away. My future stretched out before me, men like Hank and Roy my only options for companionship. I couldn't bear the thought of it and felt the need to roam rising in me. We walked to a log that lay nearby and sat.

"You were wise to wear a sweater. The wind off the water has the bite of winter in it tonight."

"It was my Papa's. It holds many memories for me. It's a pitiful replacement for my him, but it's all that I've got." I looked down at the sweater, a sudden lump in my throat.

"I saw you out on the balcony of your house the other night," he said after a few moments. "You were leaning into the wind and looked very much like the maiden I once saw carved into the prow of a ship." I thought back to my day on the hill at the farm, yelling into the wind and breaking into a million pieces.

"I've felt just like that.; and yet, I cannot guide myself to safe harbor, as a figurehead would do." I swallowed, but the lump would not go away.

"Maybe you're not meant to determine your path. Perhaps it's already laid out and you must only commit to the journey." Toran had a faraway look in his eyes as he spoke. His words were simple, their meaning more profound than anything I had ever heard. I had fought so hard my whole life: against social constructs, feelings of inadequacy, prairie winters, the crushing weight of loss and solitude. Not knowing how to respond, I only nodded. The sun had sunk below the horizon as we talked, full dark upon us now. I stood, telling Toran that I had better be getting home. He walked with Kit and me up the winding trail and to my door.

He did not ask to come in, and was not pushy as Hank had been. It was late, past supper time, and I wondered if Toran had eaten.

"Would you like to come in for a bowl of fish stew?"

"I'd like that, if it's not too much trouble?"

"None at all. I made the stew earlier today. I can warm it while I make biscuits."

"Then I'll stay," he said with a smile. He watched me with interest as I rolled and cut the biscuit dough. I explained that Fiona and I had arrived on the coast too late in the season to plant a garden, but I had happened upon a farmer selling produce outside of the store. I had eagerly bought up a variety of vegetables, missing my large garden on the farm. I ladled stew into two large bowls, and retrieved the biscuits from the woodstove. I set the food on the table, hoping that Toran would enjoy it. He tucked into his stew and I breathed a sigh of relief.

"That was delicious, Dahlia. Thank you."

"There is plenty more if you'd like another bowl."

"I'd love one. I've never had anything quite like that," he said with a smile. I happily filled another bowl and put more buttered biscuits onto a plate. Our conversation was easy and enjoyable. Toran had a very calm, confident air about him, and it made me feel that way as well. After we ate we continued to talk over steaming cups of tea. Toran asked about the Prairies, and I happily told him all about the farm, the landscape, the beauty. It had grown late, and he stood to leave. I walked him to the door, and we stood facing each other for a moment.

"Thank you for the stew, and for the company," he said.

"You're welcome. Fiona is gone most every night, so it was nice to share a meal rather than eating alone." I said with a smile, my eyes dropping for fear that he would see the desire rising in me. Toran stepped closer to me and brought his lips to mine. They were soft but pressing, his kiss deliberate. He slipped one hand to the back of my neck; his hand was rough, but his touch was gentle. He tasted of tea, and smelled faintly of woodsmoke. My hands ran along the muscles of his back and his tongue found mine. When he pulled away I brought my hand to his neck and drew him back to me. I wanted nothing more than to be close to him. After a minute I pulled away with a contented sigh. How easy it would be to get lost in him.

"I should go before my cousins start to worry, they expected me hours ago. You make it very difficult to leave, Dahlia," he said with a pained look and a sigh. "I'll find you on the beach next week." With a small smile he turned to leave. I was left with the taste of him on my lips. I washed up the supper dishes with a wide grin, excited about the next time that I would see him. He kept his promise, meeting me three more times the following week, and I thought of him most every minute of the day. I was dreading saying goodbye when he left on Sunday, as well as the prospect of a future that didn't include him.

On Saturday I dressed in a simple farm dress, no cologne or feathered hat. I walked down to the logging camp with Fiona, determined to talk to Hank. We were greeted by several of the loggers. Lenny wore a clean work shirt and a bow tie. It was an odd combination but held a certain innocent charm. The men's sideways glances upon seeing me told me that something was amiss. I entered the tent to find Hank wrapped around another woman, kissing her. Someone cleared their throat to get Hank's attention, and he lifted his eyes for only a moment, looking completely through me. This was all the confirmation I needed to know that he was a rake, and that I had been fooled by his charm, and then discarded. I told Fiona that I was going home and left, head held high.

I'd had two weeks to digest the hurt that Hank had caused me. He was not worth another moment of thought. My mind went to Toran, and my mood brightened immediately. I heard running behind me and turned to see Fiona and Lenny coming up the road behind me.

"Dahlia! Wait!" Fiona called to me. They caught up to me just as I began climbing the hill to the house. "I have very exciting news!" she said, breathless from running. "Lenny is leaving the logging camp! He's going to join the gold rush, and he's asked me to go with him! We'll head north along the coast; there's a river that's absolutely dripping with gold. We'll be married by the first priest we find. I'm sorry to leave you here by yourself, but life in these small places does not suit me. What do you think? Are you as excited as I am?" she gushed so quickly that I needed a moment to process what she had said. I looked at Lenny, a simple smile upon his face. It occurred to me that I had only heard a handful of words come out of his mouth in the time that I'd known him. Fiona spoke enough for three people, and it seemed that they complemented each other nicely.

"Well, I suppose congratulations are in order. When will you leave?"

"I'm packing up my things right now. We'll leave the camp first thing in the morning!" Fiona ran ahead to the house. It all felt very rushed to me, and I hoped that Fiona was not making a terrible decision. I followed the couple into the house and peeked into Fiona's bedroom. She had pulled all her dresses from the wardrobe and was rolling each one furiously before stuffing it into her travel case. I went up to my bedroom and retrieved my fancy dress and feathered hat. I thought about the money that I had tucked under the floorboards in the shed. I didn't need much to get by, and Fiona was the closest thing that I had to family. I left the dress near the front door and ran to the shed. Lifting the floorboards, I retrieved the velvet bag that had once held Mother's jewelry and now held thousands of dollars in cash. I took half of the stack of bills, put the bag back under the floorboards, and rushed back to the house.

"Fiona? I'd like you to have these things. The dress needs the buttons resewn, but you might be able to remake it into something beautiful. Of course, you'll need the matching hat." I handed her the clothing with a smile.

"Oh, Dahlia! They're beautiful, thank you!" she said, adding them to the pile of clothing on her bed.

"I also ought to give you a wedding gift, since I likely won't see you for a long time." I choked up at the thought. Things had been tense between Fiona and me, but I still wanted her to be happy. I handed her a thick stack of bills, enough to buy a home. Her eyes went wide in disbelief.

"Oh my, Dahlia. I can't accept this, it's way too much."

"You can, and you will. This is half of what I made from selling Mother's jewelry. I have no need for this much money, and I want you to have an easier time from here on out. I'm not great at goodbyes, so I'll go up to my room now." No tears fell as Fiona hugged me.

"Thank you for being a dear friend to me, even though I've acted horribly to you. What will you do now? Will you stay here alone?" The thought of being here alone made me uneasy.

"I'm not sure. Maybe I'll head on down the road too," I said with a small smile. Hugging Fiona once more and bidding Lenny farewell, I climbed the stairs to my bedroom, calling to Kit as I went. I laid face down on my bed, Kit whining at my side. Unable to sleep, I brought her out onto the small platform that led to the widow's walk and stared out over the ocean. It was a still night, lit by a bright moon. I heard Fiona and Lenny leave from the front of the house. I could not make out their words, but the love and excitement in their voices was clear. I was shocked by Fiona's sudden departure, but I had sensed that it was coming long before we reached this island. Fiona was carving her own path, creating the life she had always dreamt of, and I was buoyed by the idea. Would I ever be able to do the same? I felt uncertain at every turn, lamenting all the opportunities that I might be missing due to indecision. I climbed into bed, hoping for the clarity that tomorrows could bring.

Chapter Eighteen

I woke to the muted light of morning sun meeting fog. I buttered my last slice of bread and ate it as I sipped hot tea. I felt listless here, used to the chores and animals of the farm, and I missed the comfort of their sameness. I had no animals, no garden. I would need to find ways to occupy my time, or I'd be as mad as Mother had been before the year was out. I washed my breakfast dishes and laid them on the rack to dry, and then straightened the quilt on Fiona's bed. Looking around the small house, I could see nothing that needed doing. I called to Kit and walked to the beach in hopes of seeing Toran. He was already waiting for me, sitting on a large driftwood log. I sat beside him and watched the tide creep higher onto the sand. The sun burned away the fog that had gathered on the beach in the night, and soon we were bathed in golden light. Toran looked my way and let out a small gasp.

"Your eyes are just the green of the ocean in the shallows. I've never seen anyone with eyes quite like them. They're always a beautiful green, but the sun hitting them like that..." he leaned almost imperceptibly towards me. I met his advance, and he kissed me so softly that I wondered if it had actually happened. It seemed impossible that a man as tall and strong as he could be so gentle. I leaned further in, meeting his lips again. His lips tasted of berries, his skin smelled fresh, like the sea.

"I don't want you to go. I've only just met you, but I scan the beach each day, hoping that I'll see you here." My voice was quiet, my heart racing.

"I don't want to leave you either, but I've already been away too long. I miss my family and my home, and I have obligations there. There's a restlessness I feel when I'm away." Nodding my understanding, I told him about Fiona leaving, and he voiced concern about me being here alone. I assured him that I had lived alone before, and that I would manage.

We sat for a long time, talking very little, but enjoying each other's presence a great deal. He made me feel calm, safe. Toran announced that he had one more meeting at the logging camp, and then he had to leave. I hugged him tightly, not hiding my tears. "I return every autumn, Dahlia. I will look for you then." I shook my head as I walked away, unbelieving that I would need to wait a year to see him again. It was too much to bear. Returning home to splash my tear-streaked face, I retrieved some money to make a trip to the store.

I walked the single aisle of the store, aimless and sad, only buying a small sack of flour to bake bread and some tea for my dinner. After I had paid for my things the bell over the door chimed. Roy entered the store, meeting my eye with a lewd grin on his face.

"Dahlia! You left the tent in such a hurry last night. I was hoping for a dance." He stood much closer to me than I would have liked, his breath heavy with the smell of whiskey, despite it being only lunchtime. His teeth were stained brown by the dip of chewing tobacco that he had tucked into his lower lip.

"I wasn't feeling well, and I'm still not," I answered curtly, trying to walk around him.

"Will you come to the tent next Saturday? Hank may have found someone new, but the rest of us would like some of your attention."

The glint in his eye caused a hot rush of shame to rise in me as the bell on the door signaled someone else entering the store.

"No, I don't believe I will. Now if you'll excuse me," I replied. Roy grabbed my arm painfully as I turned to leave.

"Playing hard to get only makes me want you more," he spat into my ear. Toran suddenly stood beside me, removing Roy's hand from my arm with ease.

"She said she's not interested. Now you let her alone," he said firmly. He stared Roy down until he left the store, and then turned to me.

"Are you alright?" Toran asked kindly. "Those loggers act as if they've never met a woman before." He shook his head.

"I'm fine, just a little shaken. Thank you for stepping in."

"Would you like me to walk you home in case he gives you any more trouble?"

"I can't," I said, tears falling instantly. "I've got Kit outside. She won't let any harm come to me." Unable to bear another goodbye, I hurried out the door, removing Kit's leash from the post and walking quickly down the lane. When I reached the house, I took my purchases inside and climbed the stairs to my bedroom. I wanted to stand out on the widow's walk but decided that I would bathe in the river first, hoping that might wash my shame and sadness away. I doffed my dress and stockings and wrapped myself in my silky robe, leaving Kit in the house so that I might enjoy the water, rather than worrying about where she had run off to.

I grabbed the axe from where it leaned against the door as I had done since Toran had warned me of cougars and took the narrow path to the river. The air was still very warm for late autumn, filled with the scent of damp, fallen leaves and needles, and I walked eagerly towards the cooling water. Finding a tree, I leaned the axe against it and hung my robe from a branch. I entered the water from the grassy banks, and sunk down into its depths, a satisfied sigh escaping me as I did so. Though I scrubbed my hair and skin, the embarrassment of the previous night and the loss of the morning clung to me. As I emerged from the river, and walked towards my robe, I was grabbed clumsily from behind. I froze, feeling Roy's hot, fetid breath against my cheek.

"Hank said you gave it up easy. Now I want mine," he spat, and then ran his filthy tongue up my cheek. I stomped on his feet and kicked at his shins until he finally released me. I fell forward onto the grass and scrambled away. He grabbed my foot, and a hot, searing pain shot through my calf as he bit into the soft flesh. I screamed in pain, stunned.

"I like it even more when you fight," he laughed wickedly. My thoughts of getting my robe were gone, and I scrambled towards the axe. Roy held the back of my thigh tightly with one hand and rammed his fingers inside of me with the other. I howled and kicked at him, connecting with his groin. He groaned in pain, and I escaped his grasp, running towards the axe. By the time I had snatched it up he had scrambled to his feet.

"I like my women fiery, and you're as wild as can be. Now stop playing with the axe; we both know you couldn't swing it hard enough to hurt me." He walked towards me with an awful, rotting sneer as he unbuttoned his pants.

"I can swing it, and I will if you don't get away from me!" I shrieked, terror tearing through me. My heart pounded in my head and chest, and my mouth had gone dry. My arms were shaking, and my head spun. He lunged at me then, full of hatred.

"Hey!" A deep voice boomed from behind me. Roy turned towards the sound just as I swung the axe with all my might. The blunt edge of the axe head connected with his skull just above the ear, ringing out with a sickening crack. He crumpled at the knees and fell to the ground. I looked in the direction from which the call had come, and saw Toran running through the forest towards me. Snatching my robe from the ground, I put it on hastily. Anger and worry were clear in the tightness of his jaw, and the deep furrow of his brow.

"Dahlia!" he yelled as he ran.

"He tried to rape me, and he bit my leg," I said, the trees swimming in my vision as I started to swoon. Toran reached me just as my knees buckled, and scooped me up in his strong arms as if I weighed no more than a child. He held my head to his chest, and I could feel his heart racing through his shirt. I sobbed as he held me, my fear fading slowly. He carried me to a tree and slid his back down it until he was sitting in the long grass, still holding me tight to him.

"I left the store a few minutes after you did, and I saw Roy walking towards your house instead of the logging camp. Thought I'd better follow him to make sure he meant you no harm. I went to your house first, but found it empty, save for Kit. I was in the yard when I heard yelling and came as fast as I could," he said sadly, scanning my face as he shook his head.

"Thank you. It surely would have been me lying there dead if you hadn't have come. I didn't mean to kill him," I sobbed.

"I know. There wasn't much else you could have done." He stroked my hair, reassuring me.

"Let's get you some clothes and then I'll take you to the train station. The station master can send a telegram asking for a law man to be sent out."

"No! They'll think I murdered him. I'll spend the rest of my life in a prison," I said, hysteria creeping into my voice once again.

"I'll tell them that I saw him attack you, and that you swung the axe in defense."

"You know that your word will mean nothing to them. The law men call your people savages. They'll think that you killed Roy!" I said shrilly, hysteria taking over once again. Calmly, Toran came to his feet and extended his hand to me. He pulled me to standing, and we made our way slowly towards the gray house on the cliff. His large hand held mine, calming me as we walked.

"I don't want to stay here, and I don't want you mixed up in this any more than you already are. I've been dreaming of walking into the mountains and making a home among the trees. Maybe it's time," I said wistfully.

"You'd be eaten by a cougar or bear before the sun rose in the morning. The wilds are no place for a woman alone."

"Neither is this, apparently." Steeling myself, I continued, "I will not go back to the station. You can leave me here; I'll find my own way. Thank you for helping me." I walked ahead of Toran before he sighed with exasperation and then trotted to catch up with me.

"I can take you somewhere for the night. You can think things over and make a decision about what to do next in the morning. Best not to take too many of your belongings if you're planning to disappear." We soon broke from the trees into the clearing where the gray house sat. He waited for me outside while I went in to dress. I chose my favorite dress from the wardrobe. It was a simple farm dress of pale green, the exact shade of my eyes, made by a seamstress in Philadelphia, thousands of miles, and a lifetime away from here. I remembered my excitement when it was made, the prospect of a simple life on the farm hanging on the horizon. Putting on two pairs each of bloomers and stockings, I went without the garters and bonnet. I laced my boots, and took one last look around the house. The light here had changed. It no longer poured into the house, lighting even the darkest corner. It was muted, subdued. Papa's sweater was draped over a kitchen chair. I felt Papa alive in me all of the time now; I didn't need the sweater to feel his presence. There was nothing else that I needed. I attached the leash to Kit's neck and walked out of the sea captain's home for the last time.

"I have some money tucked under the floorboards in the shed. Should I get it before we go?" I asked. Toran laughed.

"I think that you need something to eat and a good sleep. I'll bring you back tomorrow when you've decided what you want to do. You can fetch your money then." He took my hand and led me towards the forest. As we padded through the trees on a thick carpet of moss, Toran told me that he lived two days north of here but had been staying at another village for the last month. Two of his cousins had married into the tribe here, and he came once a year to assist them in trading with the logging company, fur traders, and residents. He told me that many of them spoke English, but they'd had unpleasant experiences trading for themselves, and welcomed his help.

We came upon Roy's body at the river, his pants lowered beneath his exposed bottom, his final shameful act captured in eternity. Without hesitation, I grabbed him by the hand and dragged him to the river. Wading into the cool water, I let his hand go, allowing him to float in the current. I watched as he floated downstream, feeling only disgust. He caught on a branch, and I hiked my skirts and calmly walked towards him, pushing his body away from the branch and back into the current. I watched until he floated out of sight, and then retrieved the axe and washed it in the river before pulling the long grass that was covered in blood, and throwing it into the water. Toran stood watching me calmly, sensing that this was something that I needed to do alone. I washed my hands in the river and met his eyes.

"The river will take the body to the ocean, and it'll wash up on a shore far from here, if it isn't eaten before then," I said without emotion. I threw the axe into the woods, and began walking, Toran following me silently. We walked for an hour or more before he suggested stopping for something to eat. He built a fire on the beach, using the shavings from a stick he was carving into a spear as kindling. Once the fire was hot, he removed his boots and waded into the ocean. The sun set behind him, and he appeared to me only as a silhouette. I watched as he speared a large fish, and then splashed water onto his face. He shook his head to clear the water, and the sun caught each of the droplets, turning them to pure gold. An easy, boyish grin played across his face as he waded out of the surf, holding the fish proudly on the spear. I suddenly saw him clearly: his kindness, his poise, his protective nature. I knew in that moment that he was the man who would set my heart on fire. Toran removed the fish from the spear and drew a large knife to gut it.

"Let me," I said, taking the knife from his hand. I slid the knife up the fish's belly, as I had done many times before. Toran watched me as I worked, clearly impressed. I handed the fish to him when I was done and he propped it over the fire to cook. The skin crackled and popped, and my mouth watered in anticipation of the meal. I was not disappointed; the fish was delicious. We ate quietly, the sounds of the fire and surf filling the silence. I stood reluctantly when Toran buried the fire in the sand and said that we had better get to the village before night fell. He took my hand, making my heart race, and led me through the trees for another half hour or so. The forest was much more intimidating in the low light, but I felt safe with Toran at my side. We emerged from the trees into a clearing that sat on a low rise just above the beach. There stood two long, wooden buildings, smoke puffing cheerily from the stacks.

"Oh! I expected to see teepees!" I said in surprise.

"The Plains people live in teepees because they can take them along when they roam to follow their food. My people have lived on these shores for thousands of years and will live here for thousands more. Longhouses are better protection from the rain, and all that hunts in the night," he said with a laugh. I inhaled deeply to calm myself, betraying my apprehension. Sensing my hesitation, he took my hand again and led me towards the nearest longhouse.

Toran had to stoop to enter through the door, and we found ourselves in a long, rectangular room, neat piles of furs and belongings sat at intervals along the perimeter. At the center of the large room was a sunken hearth surrounded by stones stacked a foot high. On the tiered benches around it sat about twenty people, all of their eyes on us. We approached the circle and sat among the people whose voices and songs had fallen silent.

Toran addressed an elderly man and woman, and the room at large, in a mixture of English and their native tongue. I pet Kit as he spoke, avoiding the curious eyes of the tribe. After Toran finished speaking there was silence, and he explained to me that he had told them what had happened at the river. He said that there were no secrets within the tribe, and that all important matters were discussed as a group. He stood and helped me to my feet.

"We'll let them talk while we clean the bite on your leg." Toran led Kit and me from the building. Walking down to the beach, I hiked up my skirts and waded into the surf, the salty water stinging the wound on my calf. We sat on one of the many driftwood logs that lay on the beach.

"I am leaving tomorrow to return to my home. In the morning, I will bring you back to your house if you choose to stay there. I can accompany you to the train station and give my account of what happened. Whether or not they believe my statement is out of my control." He paused then, inhaling deeply before continuing.

"I know that we know very little about each other, but I was drawn to you from the first time I saw you on the beach. You are strong and kind, and it's clear that you are as taken with this land as I am." He looked up at me then, his eyes warm and hopeful. "You can come to my home; my people will welcome you. If you ever become unhappy living there, I will take you to a town with a train station, so that you might find your way back home." I could not speak. I wrapped my arms around his body and buried my head in his neck as relief washed over me. There was nothing more that I wanted than a life on the shores of this ocean, this man by my side.

"I'll go with you. I think that I've been looking for you for a long time," I confessed. Toran took my face tenderly in his hands and brought his lips softly to mine. I was not prepared for what came over me then. I kissed him back hungrily, my hands raking through his hair. He pulled away and looked me in the eyes, and then came at me with a vigor matching mine. We teetered on the log, nearly falling to the sand, causing us to pull apart in laughter. Kit ran down the beach in the direction of the village, signaling someone's approach. We parted reluctantly, painfully. A man about ten years older than me came to where we sat and spoke to Toran.

"We will shelter the girl for the night, and we will not speak of seeing her if anyone should ask. We don't want the trouble that she brings, and fear that you will draw your own trouble if it were known that she fled with you. The women will apply a poultice to her leg so that the wound doesn't fester, and you will leave at first light."

"Thank you," Toran said as we stood to follow the man to the lodge. Kit ran happily at our feet, seeming to sense my newfound ease. It was very late, and the tribespeople were settling into their beds for the night. Toran led me to the spot where he had been sleeping during his stay. A small, hunched, old woman approached with two bowls in her hands and a cloth over her shoulder. She smiled warmly at me, her whole face seeming to disappear into wrinkles, and gestured for me to sit. I lifted my skirts to expose my calf and watched as she gently cleaned the wound with water, and then applied a thick paste to it. She spoke softly in her language, and Toran told me that she was advising me to let the paste dry and leave it there for three days before washing it away. I thanked her for her help, and she waddled slowly off to the far corner of the lodge.

We sat for a few minutes while the paste dried, and I looked around the room. Children were curled up, fast asleep on many of the mats. Some of the adults remained around the fire, speaking softly. There was a deep calm in the lodge, despite the excitement of our arrival. I wondered if it was always this peaceful. Toran removed his shirt and boots and laid down on the furs. He pulled me down beside him and covered us with a rough woolen blanket.

"Sleep, Dahlia. We'll leave for home in the morning," he said, pulling me closely to him. I did not sleep at all, instead listening to his slow, steady breathing as he slept. I was wracked with desire as I lay next to this beautiful, half-dressed man. As the lodge came to life in the morning, I was still gazing upon Toran in awe, wondering if it were possible that I loved this man that I had met only a few weeks ago. He opened his eyes slowly, a wide grin coming over his face.

"I was hoping that you were not a dream," he said as he stretched his arms above his head. "We'll have something to eat, and then it will only take me a few minutes to gather my things. We'll be on the water before you know it." Reaching for me, he kissed my lips again and again.

At the hearth, long strips of bread were being handed out along with dried fish and fresh berries. We ate quickly and thanked the tribespeople for their hospitality. Kit was found hopping about in the ferns, catching her own breakfast. We took her to a stream to drink, and Toran filled four canteens. Back at the lodge he rolled his things into neat bundles and secured them with twine. He bade farewell to the Chief and Elders, and we walked towards the beach, laden with his belongings. We located his canoe among the tall grasses in the sand, removed the blankets that protected it from cracking and loaded it with his things. It was not a simple boat. The canoe was carved from red cedar, and its bow jutted out several feet. There were carvings along the sides of animals with prominent eyes, and smooth, sweeping lines. An eagle graced the front, one wing extending three feet down each side.

"This is so beautiful," I said, running my hands over the carvings. "Who made it?"

"I did. I will start building you one when we return home," Toran replied. "You are always welcome in my canoe, but you will want one of your own." I was shocked at his generous offer. "Would you like to go back to your house to get some things before we go?" he asked as he dragged the canoe near the water of the bay. I shook my head.

"I think you're right about leaving my things there. A clean break and a fresh start sound very appealing to me." I straightened, confident in my decision. "I could fetch the money. Perhaps your people could use it?"

"The land and the water provide everything that we need. Money is of no use where we are going." He ran quickly to have a word with his cousin, while I lifted Kit into the canoe. I could think of nothing that I wanted that could be obtained with money. I imagined the next tenant of the sea captain's house finding it, perhaps years from now. The thought brought a smile to my face.

I helped Toran drag the canoe into the water, and climbed in once the water was at my knees. The poultice on my calf had gotten wet and hoped that it would still be effective. Toran climbed into the canoe with much more grace than a man of his size ought to have possessed. He dipped the paddle smoothly into the water, propelling us gently forward. Falling into a steady rhythm, he paddled a few strokes on each side to keep our path true. I leaned comfortably on the bundled furs with Kit nestled beside me and fell into a deep sleep. When I woke the sun was high in the sky, and Toran was pulling the canoe towards a grassy beach.

"Oh, I must have fallen asleep!" I exclaimed. "I couldn't take my eyes off of you last night and didn't sleep a wink." I smiled sheepishly, making him laugh. His laugh was deep and easy, and I was growing fond of it very quickly.

"I thought that we could have something to eat and refill the canteens. Afterwards I think I'll spend a bit of time looking at *you*," he said playfully. My eyes widened, and my cheeks flushed. I climbed out of the canoe awkwardly, nearly landing in the water.

"It takes some practice." Toran laughed again, dragging the canoe onto the beach. We ate the simple lunch that the women had sent with us.

"I should tell you that I've been with a man," I began in a wavering voice as we ate. "Only once. It was a mistake fueled by my first taste of alcohol, and of being the focus of a man's affections." The food seemed to stick in my throat, but I continued, "I got caught up in the moment, and I regret doing it. It was not how I had imagined. I hope that you don't think me spoiled." I couldn't meet his eyes.

"I've lain with women too. I don't think any less of you. My people do not share the strange, rigid rules of your society," he shrugged. Relief washed over me, and my shame began to fade knowing that his opinion of me had not lessened. We wandered into the trees until we came to a stream from which we filled the canteens. Sunlight found its way through breaks in the trees, giving the space a magical feel. Everywhere I looked there was lush, green growth. Ferns, leaves, and moss merged to create a vibrant, living thing that felt as if it were a part of me. My worries seemed unable to follow me here, and my mood was light.

I had been avoiding Toran's gaze, trying to maintain some semblance of control over myself. I felt lust building in me, consuming my every thought. The bees within me began to swarm, whipping themselves into a fever pitch. Though, there was none of the anxiety that usually brought them. Instead, I felt compelled, near mad with my desire for Toran. He had crossed the stream and walked a short way into the woods. As he returned, I fumbled at the buttons on my dress. I removed my bloomers and stockings and stood waiting. My heart pounded in my chest, sure of its own desire, and hoping to find it mirrored in Toran's. The look upon his face would tell me all that I needed to know.

Toran lifted his eyes from a fern frond that he held in his hand and caught sight of me. His face broke into a look of surprise, but quickly turned to that of a hunter: focused, hungry. He ran at me, crossed the stream, and crashed into me with the power of the ocean into the rocks. He swept me into his arms, his lips finding mine: firm, pressing, frantic. His hands slid down my back, sending shivers down my spine. He grabbed my bottom with both hands and lifted me with ease to settle around his waist. Leaning forward, he brought us to rest in the soft grass.

His lips and tongue found my breasts, my stomach, between my thighs. He made me feel things that I had not even known to dream about. I gave myself to him wholly, not one shred of restraint or hesitation. He freed himself from his pants. I was intimidated by the size of him, and unsure of how to make him feel as good as he'd made me feel. I let instinct take over and used the sounds of his breath and moans to guide me. He flipped me onto my back and entered me, my head spinning from the tandem sensations of sharp pain and pure bliss. We locked eyes, peering deep into the other's very being. I felt as if I had waited a thousand years to meet this man. The struggles and heartbreak of my old life fell away, leaving only this moment.

Toran held me tight to him and rolled onto his back. I moved against him until I felt as if I were somehow both floating and falling. I yelled out, arching my back, and throwing my head back in release. Toran slowed his movements and pulled me down to him. My legs were shaking, and tears ran down my cheeks, as I was completely overwhelmed by everything that I was feeling. He kissed my hair softly and then kissed me deeply, passion still raging within him. When I had recovered and began to move with him again, he lifted me from him and flipped me onto my front, his hot breath in my ear, saying my name again and again. We lost ourselves in each other's bodies, each touch pulling us further into our bliss. Afterwards we laid without speaking, catching our breath and slowing our racing hearts. He laid beside me, looking into my eyes. I now understood the fuss about making love.

"I think that I've fallen in love with you, Dahlia, and I don't want to walk anywhere without you by my side."

"You'll never have to," I replied. We drifted off to sleep in the grass, the creek bubbling happily at our feet.

***

It took us five days to complete a journey that should have taken two. Lost in desire, we were unable to keep our hands from each other's skin. We made love in the ocean with the surf crashing around us, on sandy beaches, in long grass, against the rough bark of a tree. We would sleep in a longhouse when we arrived on the island, with a roomful of Toran's family lying nearby, and we intended to make use of the time that we had alone.

I asked Toran to teach me how to paddle the canoe. He guided me patiently as I moved clumsily at first, becoming deft as I went. We took turns paddling, my path slow and wandering, his fast and direct. Talking as we traveled, we came to know each other in the span of a few days. I told him about Philadelphia and Mother, and the farm and Papa. I told him of Mrs. O'Malley and Fiona, Inga and Willy. It felt at times as if I were telling the story of someone else. The pain and fears that I had carried for so long had been laid to rest somewhere as I had traveled over the mountains.

Toran told me about his mother, who had fallen for a Scottish fur trader during her only trip to the big island. His father had come home with her and had embraced her people's culture and traditions. He had died at sea while fishing when Toran was three, his washed-up canoe the only notice they received of his death. His people had loved his father and spoke fondly of him still. He had taught many of the tribespeople English, and they now spoke fluently in both languages. Toran laughed as told me of his three older sisters, who doted on him as if he were still a small boy instead of a towering man. I could not tear my eyes from his easy smile, or his eyes that lit up when he laughed. It occurred to me that I would soon have three sisters. Loneliness had dominated my life for the last few years, and I could not wait to meet the women who would soon be my family. Toran spoke of his family and tribe with so much love, and it was clear to me that his people valued family above all else.

I grew more excited and curious with each story, eager to see my new home and its people. I had built it up in my mind and hoped that it was as wonderful as I expected it to be. As with the farm years ago, it wasn't. It was much, much better.

Chapter Nineteen

I could feel Toran's excitement growing with every row of his paddle. We made a wide curve around an island, and a much larger island came into view. It had high peaks covered in trees and a clearing behind the beach that held six longhouses. Toran's voice rang out in a long, staccato call. It carried on the still water of the bay and was returned by someone on shore. After a few minutes the beat of drums filled my ears. As we drew closer, I could see people dressed in fringed cloaks dancing, and heard their rhythmic chants. Looking back at Toran, the joy was clear on his face.

"Are they having a ceremony?" I asked, in awe of the performance.

"They are welcoming us home," he said proudly.

"They must have missed you a great deal. I imagine that the King of England would not receive a welcome this wonderful." Toran laughed and paddled onward with renewed energy. We neared the shore and he turned the canoe so that the stern faced the beach. He tied it to a post near the high tide line and covered it with blankets to prevent it from cracking.

"Why have you faced us away from the island?"

"It is the proper way. It shows that we come in peace, and with respect. Leading with the bow is an indication of war."

"But, surely your people know that you've come in peace?"

"Yes, but it is still important to show respect." Toran replied. I admired his dedication to traditions, and felt this was a lovely way to show respect on a daily basis.

I had managed to climb out of the canoe without falling into the water, while Kit jumped into the water and ran to the beach, approaching some children. Toran took my hand and led me towards the people who were drumming and singing. He waited for them to finish, and then walked into the circle with me in tow. A very small, old woman approached Toran slowly and draped a beautiful cloak around his shoulders as he knelt. It was embossed with intricate depictions of fish and animals, the most prominent among them an eagle. I had to restrain myself from reaching out to touch the delicate stitching. Toran kissed the woman on the cheek.

"Thank you, Grandmother," he said as she slowly made her way back to the circle. I looked around and saw adoration on every face.

"I am so glad to be back among my family," Toran began, the crowd hooting in response. "This is Dahlia, and she will be my wife. I know that you will welcome her here with the same spirit that you have welcomed me home." The crowd cheered, and the drums were beaten. Excitement flooded me when I heard Toran's words. I would be his wife. No ridiculous courtship or stuffy proposal; only two people promising to love and stand by one another. Men wearing fringed cloaks similar to Toran's resumed their dancing, and everyone began to sing. The sound vibrated in my chest and my skin broke out in goosebumps. I didn't need to understand the words that were sung; their meaning was clear. They sang of joy, and I had never felt more welcomed than I did in that moment. I smiled up at Toran and he pulled me under his cloak. We walked towards the longhouses, where a towering pole stood. I had been distracted by the ceremony and had not seen it when we arrived. Stopping, my mouth hung open.

"What is this?" I asked, running my hands over the brightly painted carvings. Huge faces of orcas, bears, and other animals looked back at me. The pole was topped with an eagle, its wings folded at its sides.

"It's a gyaaGang, a *house pole*. It represents the clan, as well as the family that lives in the house behind it. It tells the story of our ancestors, through the animals that we live among," he said proudly.

"It's breathtaking." I followed Toran to the longhouse, the crowd splitting to let us through. Downy feathers were being spread at the threshold, and everyone was bowing their heads. A man yelled "Chief!" and a wild call burst from the crowd. I looked to Toran in surprise. He smiled and nodded his head humbly. I was in love with the Chief of this land, these people. I could not imagine a more capable leader, and I was bursting with pride that he had deemed me worthy of his love.

We entered the longhouse, followed by five women. Toran introduced them as his grandmother, mother, and sisters. They all looked at him with pride and love, and it was clear that they had felt his absence deeply. Toran's grandmother held my face in her soft hands and looked deep into my eyes. Her face was solemn at first but softened into a smile.

"You come from away, called by the ocean that you've always carried in your eyes." She nodded, seemingly able to peer into my very soul. My eyes widened and tears began to fall. I looked to Toran and he wrapped his arm proudly around my shoulder.

"I have. I didn't know what I sought until I found it." Pointedly, I looked at Toran. He brought his forehead to mine and closed his eyes for a moment, telling me silently that he felt the same way. His mother approached me next, not bothering with formalities. She pulled me into her arms and hugged me with the love of a mother. I softened in her arms, relishing her warmth.

"I only ask that you love him," she whispered.

"I do," I replied, lost in her embrace. Toran's sisters approached next, all at once. They embraced me in turn, welcoming me home, and into their family. Toran asked his sisters to find the cedar bentwood box that contained the clothing that the women had made over the years, as a gift for his eventual wife. They did, and met us at the head of the longhouse, where Toran and I would sleep. Unlike the longhouse at the other village, this one had an area for the Chief that afforded some privacy by way of hides hung to act as walls.

"We've made these things in hope that T'apjuu would find the woman he loved one day. You can continue to wear your dresses if you prefer, but this is our gift to you. I think we must have known that you would come to us," Toran's mother said, opening the cedar box. Inside were several dresses of soft leather and spun mountain goat's wool, as well as aprons woven from cedar bark. I removed a pair of moccasins lined with rabbit's fur, and a headband that was adorned with beads and porcupine quills.

"Those were acquired through trade, and were made by women whose tribes live on the mainland. They are a reminder that we are all connected," Toran's mother said as I ran my fingers over the beading. "Our people prefer to go barefoot, but you may need to wear something until the rocky beaches toughen your feet," she finished with a gentle laugh. The last item in the trunk was a cloak like the one that Toran wore. I unfolded it and saw that it bore an eagle, and an otter that swam in a sea of soft green. I could not process the beauty that I saw before me, nor the kindness that these strangers were extending to me.

"These are the most beautiful things that I have ever laid eyes on, and it would be an honor to wear them. Thank you all for this gift, and for the warmth with which you have welcomed me." I hugged each woman in turn, tears flowing freely. They left Toran and me alone in the longhouse.

"Your mother called you T'apjuu, but I have been calling you Toran. Which name would you prefer that I call you?"

"Both names were given to me by my parents, with love. My father gave me a name that reminded him of his home far away. My mother named me for the tall, straight cedars that abound here. You can call me whichever name you prefer; they are both a part of me."

"I think that I will call you T'apjuu. It seems more fitting here, among your people." I hurried to remove my dress, eager to wear the beautiful clothes that lay before me. T'apjuu pulled me to him, and we dropped to the soft bed of furs. We lay for a moment after our lovemaking, and I asked T'apjuu why he had not told me that he was the Chief of his people.

I was not the Chief of the place where I met you. It seemed boastful to mention it. Would it have mattered?"

"Of course not. I was yours from the first time we met. Though, it might have been nice to prepare for the royal welcoming that we received," I laughed. I chose one of the simpler dresses to wear, along with the moccasins and a beaded headband to keep my hair from my face. T'apjuu gasped when I turned to face him, fully dressed in his people's traditional clothes. He had also changed out of the trousers and buttoned shirt that he'd worn on the big island. He wore a short-sleeved tunic of leather, and matching pants that laced up at the waist. The hair that had been combed neatly when I met him was now disheveled and fell to a soft curve at his shoulders.

We emerged from the longhouse into the bright sun of midday. The crowd still stood outside of the door, and cheered when we appeared. I flushed with shame at the knowledge that they had waited while we had made love. Every face but one wore a smile. A woman stood off to one side, her striking beauty marred only by the sour look upon her face. I could feel her eyes on me as I walked with T'apjuu through the crowd. Her stare made me uneasy, but I was quickly lost again in the joy of those around me. The group dispersed, resuming the activities that had engaged them before our arrival. I looked about me but could no longer see the woman.

A group of children laughed as they played with Kit on the beach, throwing sticks for her to chase. Others tended cooking fires, scrubbed clothing, or wove long strips of red cedar bark into mats. Before me were what I would come to know as the happiest people that I had ever encountered: purposeful, content, free. I left T'apjuu so that he could meet with the Elders and discuss any issues that had arisen in his absence. Approaching a group of four women who were weaving mats, I asked if I might join them and was given some bark and lessons on how to weave it tightly. We all laughed at my clumsy first attempts, but I quickly learned how to produce a sturdy weave. The conversation was easy, the smiles warm and genuine. Gone were the arbitrary, stifling rules that I had lived under for most of my life, as well as the false people who had imposed them.

The woman that had stared angrily at me on my arrival continued to follow me with her eyes wherever I went. Her looks felt critical and suspicious, but she had never talked to me. After a few days I asked T'apjuu who she was, and if he knew why she might dislike me.

"That's Haana," he said when I pointed her out, a grimace flashing across his face. "She is known to cause trouble and is probably jealous of you. You should try not to worry about her, I don't."

"She might be the most beautiful woman that I have ever seen. Why would she be jealous of me?" I asked, sensing that there was more to her than he was letting on.

"We used to be together, and she wanted to be my wife. Over time her mean spirit revealed itself, and I no longer enjoyed her company. She didn't take my rejection well." Shaking his head, his nostrils flared before he continued. "She became nasty, trying to provoke me into arguing with her so that I would lose the respect of my people. It's best to give her a wide berth and avoid falling into her trap."

"Could you have told her that her behavior was unbecoming, and asked her to leave you alone?"

"I thought that avoiding conflict with her would be best."

"I've encountered very few situations in my life that have been improved by pretending they didn't exist," I said with more sharpness than I intended. I loved T'apjuu's calm nature, but was angry that he had allowed her to act in such ways towards him.

"I had hoped that she would have moved on to someone else by now, but it seems that she hasn't. Pay her no mind, Dahlia. It is you that I love." I tried to do as T'apjuu suggested but continued to feel uneasy anytime that I was in Haana's presence. She became the only thing that I did not enjoy about life on the island.

***

The splitting of firewood was a daily chore on the island. A group of young men would sit near the splitting stump talking and taking turns with the heavy axe. I offered to take a turn one day, but my suggestion was met with polite laughter from the men. I insisted and stepped to the stump. The laughter was silenced with my first swing of the axe; I had split the log cleanly in two. Quickly, I fell into the rhythm I had established long ago when chopping wood was the only thing preventing me from freezing to death. The men sat dumbfounded, mouths agape. T'apjuu walked past and saw me swinging the axe with sharp precision. He shook his head and laughed.

"That'll teach you to challenge Dahlia," he said to the group as he walked on. I split all of the logs that had sat by the stump, and then stacked them into neat piles. Wiping the sweat from my forehead with the back of my hand, I basked in the rush that hard work gave. I regularly helped with splitting wood after that.

My exercise with the axe had reminded me of the last time that I had held one. It weighed on me all day, and later that night I told T'apjuu that I didn't want to live here with secrets, and I wanted to tell the tribe about what had happened at the river. It felt dishonest to enjoy their trust without telling them the truth about my past. T'apjuu called everyone to a large bonfire that night, as all of us could not fit around one of the indoor hearths. I told my story to a hushed crowd, hanging my head when I finished, my tears ineffective at washing my shame away. Our people were shocked, as expected. What I didn't expect was compassion instead of fear, declarations of courage instead of violence. I looked at T'apjuu, unbelieving. He smiled and nodded. An Elder began to speak, and the crowd quieted so that he could be heard.

"There can be no shame in defending a life, and it seems that you did what any of us would have. We are grateful that you are as brave as you are, and that our great Chief was near to help." He paused and met my eyes. "We are happy to have you sitting before us to tell your story and respect your honesty," he finished, to the nods of the others. I thanked them for their understanding and vowed to myself never to keep another secret for as long as I lived. As people left the fire to retire to their homes, I caught the familiar glare of Haana. A smug smile played at her lips, and I feared that eventually she would try to use this new knowledge to her advantage.

***

I fell easily into the rhythm of the island. I welcomed the chores that I performed, and the history that I learned as I spoke with others over a wash basin or cook fire. I began to learn the language of the tribe, a language born of this land. My tongue struggled to learn the shapes of these new words, but my heart knew them instantly. I found their words aptly descriptive of feelings that I'd had my whole life, as well as the beauty that surrounded us here. A lot could be gleaned about a civilization from their language; it was easy to ascertain what they valued, as there were numerous words and phrases that described these things. I learned many words for Elders, family and nature, for courage, honor and love. These were the things that inspired and sustained these people.

A stooped Elder was the tribe's Storyteller, the keeper of their oral history. He spent many afternoons teaching me about his people. He explained the significance of the eagle on my family's house pole and told me fantastic legends that held morals to be applied to our lives. He told me of a great wave that had covered entire islands one hundred years ago, pulling whole tribes out into the ocean as it retreated, and the smallpox brought by Europeans that had nearly decimated their people. He told me the stories that belong to his people, but I will not tell them, as they are not mine to tell. My love for these people and their culture deepened with each tale.

The passion that had ignited T'apjuu and I did not wane or fade; our love did not falter. I loved him more every day as I watched him lead fairly. He exhibited all the qualities of his people, and lived by the same standards that he held them to. We were wed in a grand celebration that lasted nearly two weeks. T'apjuu told me that it was called Potlatch which meant "*to give.*" Guests came from near and far to witness our marriage, and we gave them gifts of carved paddles, copper shields, fine furs and skins, and bentwood boxes. T'apjuu explained that wealth was redistributed in this way. A wealthy couple would give many of their possessions away, resulting in a tribe where no one was extremely rich or poor, and everyone had what they needed. I thought back to Philadelphia, and the people who cared for nothing more than possessions, and assigned value to others based on what they owned. I far preferred this system where wealth was amassed only to be given away.

Eagle down was spread on the ground and the men wore masks that turned them into wolves, birds and bears. They told the story of their people as they whirled and danced, beautiful deep voices singing T'apjuu's praises as Chief, and mine as the woman who stood at his side, the ocean in my eyes. We feasted on salmon and halibut, both dried and smoked; herring roe served on kelp, clams and seal meat, berries and seaweed, and the delectable grease of the candlefish, known as "*oolichan*", from the big island. I began to understand why the people of this tribe stood a full head taller than their European counterparts. Food was so abundant on the island, and eating was seen as a way to bring people together, instead of a mere necessity.

The women danced and sang in their own way. They sang of my appreciation for, and connection to nature. They sang of my eagerness to work and help, and the kindness that I brought to everything that I did. They sang of the fire that I had brought to the heart of their great leader. They sang of the bravery and wisdom, warmth and leadership that our children would inherit. I had always loved a moody, stormy sky, and let myself get lost in the heavy rains of winter as the songs and dance of the Potlatch waged on.

***

T'apjuu took me into the forested hills one day under the guise of picking berries, though it was a chore done by women, and certainly not a Chief. We had made quiet love every night in the longhouse, but we both yearned for a wild romp like the ones we'd had on our journey here, away from the eyes and ears of our family. Chasing each other playfully through the forest, we fell into the grass in a fit of passion and stayed there most of the afternoon. T'apjuu pointed out birds, trees and clouds, teaching me the words for them. My pronunciation was rough, but he said that I was learning quickly.

"Somehow you become more beautiful each day," he said as he ran his hand over the scar on my calf where Roy had bitten me. It was silvery, and shaped like two crescent moons.

"How do you say beautiful?" I asked. He swallowed and looked away briefly.

"Haana."

"Well, that's fitting. I think I'd prefer you use the English word in that case," I said with a laugh. We finally emerged from the woods; our baskets empty of berries. Our people recognized our outing for what it was, and future trips in search of berries were met with winks and knowing smiles.

Grandmother watched me closely that night as we all sat around the hearth, sheltering from the storm that raged outside. I had been telling our people about my life on the farm. Everyone laughed heartily as I told the story of the escaping pig, and carefully tended weeds. I felt nostalgic thinking about my time on the farm, and grateful for all that I had learned there. Someone else began to speak, but Grandmother's eyes remained on me, a thoughtful look upon her face. She approached me as I undressed for bed that night. Her eyes held no scrutiny, rather realization. She put her hand ever so gently on my stomach.

"A child grows from your love. Your face has been lit with the light of two fires. I now know why." T'apjuu rushed to my side.

"Is it true Dahlia?" he asked, his face full of hope.

"I don't know," I stammered, trying to grasp the weight of the prediction. I thought back on my time on the island and realized that I had only bled once, shortly after we had arrived months ago.

"Yes, I think that Grandmother is right." A smile spread across my face. I looked into the face of the man that I loved, and saw my happiness mirrored in him. Our news was celebrated by our people, and everyone treated me with even more tenderness than they already had. I washed my farm dress, bloomers and stockings, and folded them neatly away with my laced boots. T'apjuu had suggested that I keep the clothes in case I wanted to wear them on a visit to the big island. I knew that I would never wear them again.

***

T'apjuu took me on long trips in his canoe, sharing the beauty of the ocean with me. We saw pods of orcas coasting silently, only their tall dorsal fins visible above the water. We saw sea lions sunning themselves on barren stretches of rock. Occasionally a curious seal would lift its head from the water and watch us in the canoe. We saw otters swimming playfully and cracking clamshells on their bellies with rocks.

"It is rare to see otters now; I'm glad that they've shown themselves to us. They were over-hunted for their furs one hundred years ago when the Europeans came. There are very few left." T'apjuu said sadly. I shifted in the canoe, ashamed of the ways that my ancestors' greed had affected his home.

Once we saw a humpback whale; its huge form swam under us, and then glided beside us with an impossible grace. It disappeared for a short while, and then breached the water's surface in a magnificent spray of water. I might not have believed that such a massive animal could lift itself clear out of the water, had I not seen it with my own eyes. T'apjuu pointed out an island in the distance, and told me of the bears with pale fur that lived there. They were known as spirit bears, and legend said that they could lead people to magical places. I could not imagine a place more magical than this. My hand sat almost perpetually at my heart, trying to contain the gratitude that I felt and process the beauty that I saw everywhere that I looked.

I did not have a Farmer's Almanac, but I had something much better: the wisdom of people whose ancestors had lived here for thousands of years. I slowly came to know what the weather would bring by looking at the clouds, or feeling the salt spray and rushing south east winds at my back.

I began to see changes in my body as my pregnancy progressed. T'apjuu and I marveled as my flat stomach grew little by little into a round belly. I was fortunate, and did not experience the nausea, fatigue and discomfort that many women have. I was filled with energy and ravenous at all times. T'apjuu found endless entertainment in watching me make my way around the cooking fires, drawn by the smell of food. I would bring some dried seaweed or *oolichan* grease and trade others for samples of what they had in their pots. I was welcomed at each fire, and in this way I came to know my people.

***

T'apjuu invited me to join him on a two-day trip to the nearest town on the big island to conduct some trade. I did not want to be apart from him but was loath to leave my new home. I had been craving eggs as my belly had grown and asked if it might be alright for me to build a chicken coop, and for him to bring three or four laying hens back for me.

"Dahlia, I'd paddle all the way here with a cow in my canoe if you asked me to. Of course, I can bring you some chickens." He scooped me into his arms laughing. I built the coop with the help of our people while he was away. I was laying some long grass in the coop when Haana approached me, alone as I always was when she spoke to me.

"So, it begins," she said with a sneer.

"What begins?"

"You're trying to erase our culture, turn our home into another white settlement."

"I have no such intentions. I simply wanted some hens. I had hens on my farm and enjoyed caring for them. I also thought that we could use the eggs," I replied, trying to stay calm.

"We eat the eggs of shorebirds. Are those not good enough for you? We use what the land and sea provide for us. We are not farmers; we do not have livestock." Shaking her head, she walked away. Suddenly I regretted asking for hens. Was Haana right? Was I trying to change this land, these people to suit my own tastes?

T'apjuu returned two days later with four chickens in cages, and a roll of chicken wire. I taught the others how to care for the hens, and the children delighted in chasing them around and finding insects to feed them. I made it clear that the chickens belonged to everyone, and that they were all free to use the eggs as they needed. Even still, I would find two eggs in a nest of cloth at the door to our longhouse each morning. I told T'apjuu about Haana's accusations, and my own concerns that she was right.

"Dahlia, they're just hens. I am the Chief of this island, and I allowed it. Haana is trying to create conflict; don't let her affect you. Our people adore you and see you for who you really are. They will not be swayed by Haana's childish attempts to turn others against you." He brought his forehead to mine, and I hoped that he was right.

T'apjuu had brought another gift for me: dahlia bulbs. I had told him about planting them at Papa's grave, and he suggested that I plant some here too. He was eager to see the flower that I had been named for, so I planted them in the full sun in front of our house. I had not stayed on the farm long enough to see the flowers bloom at Papa's grave, but I was able to watch these ones grow. The bag that Tan'tak had bought contained several varieties of bulbs, and we all delighted at the blooms of pink, deep purple and red that appeared.

***

T'apjuu explained the importance of learning to swim, as the water was our only means of transportation. His sister lent me a cloth tunic and short pants to wear for my lessons. At first, I felt very self-conscious dressed so scantily, but the feeling passed as soon as I waded into the water. T'apjuu took me at first to a pond that was small but deep. I learned how to float, dive, and hold my breath under the water. I loved the sensation of being in the water, as I always had. Within a week I was able to swim across the pond with ease. I was taught about the dangers of swimming in the ocean, and how to escape riptides. T'apjuu cautioned me never to swim alone in case I should need help. After each lesson I would spend some time floating on my back, only my face and belly visible above the water. I swam every chance that I got, and people began affectionately referring to me as an otter.

The second thing that I needed was a canoe. Our people were renowned for their superior craftsmanship; they built the only canoes sturdy enough to cross the strait to the big island. The men felled great red cedars on the big island every year and used the rivers to carry the logs to the sea. They were then towed back to our island by war canoes. It took several months to carve and shape the wood into a canoe using water, fire and steam. T'apjuu brought me to the building where they crafted the canoes. Racks of hewn logs lined one wall, canoes in various stages of completion lined another. He asked me to pick the log that he would make my canoe from, advising that I choose a thinner log so that the finished canoe would be narrow and easy to maneuver.

"I'm not sure how to choose. Maybe you should choose for me?"

"I cannot. You feel everything around you, Dahlia. Place your hand on each log until you find one that feels right," he replied patiently. I often struggled to understand the way that things must be done here, but always found deep wisdom in the customs after time. I walked along the racks, touching each log in turn. At first glance they were identical, but I quickly noticed the small variations in color and texture. I came to a narrow log that was the exact shade of reddish orange that I had seen as I crested the hill above the stand of birch on the farm. Closing my eyes, I remembered how I had been overwhelmed by the beauty of the autumn leaves minutes before my world came crashing down.

"This one," I said softly. "This is the one." I sat on the floor amid cedar shavings and cried, remembering Papa and wishing that he were here. He would have loved this island and these people dearly. He had sought the life we had on the farm; if only he had known that this life was a possibility. T'apjuu held me as I cried, and then I told him about the birch tree, the wind in the trembling aspen, the first shovelful of dirt. I told him about the jack pine and the chimney fire, and finally the wind on the hill. I had told him of Papa's death, but not the tiny details that stayed with me still.

"The wind brought your spirit back to you, breathed life into you when you had given up."

"Yes, I suppose it did." I had told him about Papa's sweater when we were at the longhouse in his cousins' village, having since regretted not bringing it when I fled my house, or retrieving it the next morning before we left the big island. I thought of it again now, craving its warm comfort and all of the memories that it held.

I wish that I had taken Papa's sweater. I know it's silly, but it is the only thing that I miss from my old life. It's certainly been taken by the land agent by now; I need to let it go." T'apjuu's eyebrows lifted, and a smile came to his face.

"I can get it for you, Dahlia. I had my cousin go to your house to fetch the money from under the shed, your Papa's sweater, and the blue robe that you were wearing at the river."

"You did?" I said in surprise.

"Yes, I didn't want you to regret leaving them there in your haste to get away. I could tell that the sweater was very dear to you, and that you would come to miss it."

"I have missed it. I looked at it as I left the sea captain's house, and foolishly thought that I no longer needed it."

"I will get your things when I see my cousins in late summer. You can spend the money how you want, or throw it into the surf if you please. I'll admit, the robe was for me. When I saw you wearing it, it seemed as if you had walked out of the ocean, bringing the water with you," he added, laughing. I hugged him to me, marveling at his thoughtfulness.

"I'll start on your canoe today. It will take a few months to complete, but I don't want you to see it until it's done." It was another custom that I did not yet understand but would honor. I had gained a solid respect for the ways of my people. They were kind and fair, generous, and wise; they took only what they needed from the ocean and land and gave thanks for these gifts. Instead of trying to fight against nature's fearsome power as I had done on the Prairies, they lived in harmony with it. They kept the spirits of their ancestors alive through stories and ceremonies, and always strove to uphold their morals. I felt accepted unconditionally, flawed though I was.

Chapter Twenty

1899

I sat on the shore with my sister Skay, my toes dug into the sand and the sun hot on my skin. We had chosen this beach on which to bask, as it was the only one near our home with sand instead of rocks. The sky was as blue as it had always been on the farm, a rarity here. No clouds floated across the sky; no storm brewed to the west. The water of the bay looked like glass, and no distinct line between water and sky could be seen at the horizon. Every few minutes we slid further up the beach to avoid the rising tide. Skay had a temperament much like T'apjuu's: calm and confident. We sat in comfortable silence and listened to the calls of the shorebirds.

"T'apjuu has almost finished your canoe. I can see you in my mind, kneeling in the canoe so that you can paddle across the bay with the speed of an orca and the calm determination of an eagle," she said, her eyes closed to the sun, a small smile on her face.

"He had me choose the log that it would be carved from but hasn't allowed me to watch him build it. I doubt that I will paddle with the speed and calm that you've predicted, but I'm excited all the same," I replied with a chuckle.

"You see the world around you with such clarity, yet you are so blind to your own strength. I hope that you will never need it, but it reassures me to know that it is within you, even if you are unaware of it." Skay's thought was interrupted by a loud call from our watchman. I had not heard this call before. He was not announcing the return of one of our canoes; the call had the distinct ring of alarm. Skay jumped up, pulling me with her.

"Come, Dahlia. We are under attack!" she said urgently. I heard the war drums then, and the frenzied calls of the men approaching in their war canoes. The drums were not beating the steady rhythm used to coordinate the rowing of the men; the pounding was menacing, foreboding. T'apjuu ran to me, worry clear in his drawn brow.

"Dahlia! Go to the longhouse and bar the doors once all of the Elders and children are inside." I looked about me at the calm day that had been transformed so quickly into chaos. People were hurrying the children and Elders into buildings, but the women were not joining them. They were donning armor of reeds and wooden slats and covering those with tunics of seal skin. Their faces were calm, their jaws set with determination.

"I will not! I will fight with my people," I said with a harshness that T'apjuu had never heard from me. "My days of barring the doors and cowering in fear are done."

"You carry my child. Protect our baby if you will not protect yourself," he pleaded, exasperated at my stubbornness.

"By cowering in a longhouse? Find me some armor and a bow. I will fight with the other women." I lifted my chin, making it clear that the matter was settled. T'apjuu pulled me to a group of women and asked them to help me.

"I need to lead our people into the war that is landing on our shores. Go to the cliffs with the other women. I love you." He brought his forehead to mine before turning to call out orders to the men. Quickly, they untied two huge war canoes from where they laid on the beach. Our tribe's Storyteller made his way slowly to a canoe, easily identifiable by the knot of hair atop his head that was dressed with tall eagle feathers. He would protect our men and capture the spirits of our attackers. As I donned armor over my growing belly, I asked the other women how we knew that the men approaching weren't coming to trade or share news.

"Men don't wear armor and carry weapons to trade. Listen to their calls, Dahlia. They are here for war. There is no bad blood between us and their tribe. I don't know why they have come," one woman replied, as she pulled me towards the trees. We climbed to the rocky cliffs to where a fortified wooden platform stood. It should have been difficult in my late stage of pregnancy, but fear had pushed me up the hills as quickly as the others. T'apjuu had taught me to shoot a bow and arrow. I hoped that I would remember my lessons, and that my arrows would land true. I looked out over the ocean, uncaring to the trifles of man as it always was. Large patches of red algae bloom floated in several areas, red as blood.

We watched the battle from high above the beach. Four war canoes approached our shores, though they were smaller and lighter than ours. Two of our canoes pushed out towards the attackers, the calls and drums of our warriors challenging the other men.

"No other tribe can defeat us on the water; their canoes are inferior. They know this and will try to bring the fight to our shores," Skay said. "Ready your bow. When they land, we shoot."

The women began to sing a gentle, haunting song. As the enemy canoes drew nearer to ours the pace of the song quickened, and the volume increased. I watched as the opposing canoes met one another in the bay. Our warriors threw huge stone rings attached to thick rope towards the other canoes. After each crack of splitting wood, the rings would be retrieved and thrown anew. The canoes took on water rapidly after only two or three throws of the stones. The men aboard the two waterlogged canoes began to swim towards the shore, their progress hindered by their armor and weapons. Our warriors brought their canoes around in wide arcs and chased the two remaining canoes with frightening speed. The discrepancy in size between the men of each tribe was remarkable, even from this high vantage point. Our warriors were taller, broader-shouldered, and they propelled their canoes with astonishing speed and accuracy.

The attackers landed on our shores. Fury rose in me; how dare they attack our home? I looked down the shaft of the arrow notched in my bow and loosed it at my enemy. That and the following two landed in the sand. The next arrow lodged in the wooden helmet of a warrior. I notched another and loosed it. This arrow flew true, finding the gap between helmet and tunic, burying itself in the soft flesh of the warrior's neck. He fell forward onto the sand, a raven visible across the shoulders of his tunic. Our singing ceased as we shot. The only sounds from our platform were the faint thrums of our bows and the soft exhales of the women as they loosed arrows. The arrows flew silently, save for a soft whistle as they left the bows. More men fell with each volley from the cliffs.

Our men drew their canoes to the shores among the enemy swimmers. We stilled our bows and watched the battle, lest we hit one of our own men with an arrow. Spears and knives clashed, the men hooting their war cries as they flung themselves at one another. I spotted T'apjuu easily, his tunic emblazoned with the wide wings of an eagle. I felt no fear, no worry. He spun and swung his weapons with impossible grace and fearsome strength. Repelling each attack with ease, he left a path of fallen men in his wake. Our Storyteller danced slowly among the dead, collecting their spirits, and singing to the sky, the target of no attacks.

"They will try to set fire to our homes, killing the old and young inside, erasing our past and future. Our men will die before they allow that to happen," a woman told me solemnly. "We must stay here until the battle is over. It won't be long now." We watched as the enemy grew fewer and fewer, and eventually none were left standing. I rushed from the trees with the other women, each of us searching for our men. They stood in a large group on the shores of our home, chants of victory booming from them. Still our Storyteller danced, collecting spirits. I ran to T'apjuu, full of relief. He embraced me, and then held me at arm's length to look me over.

"Are you alright?" he asked, inspecting my face and body.

"Yes, I'm fine. Are you?" I searched his body in return.

"Yes, those men were brave, but they were not strong." He shook his head. "Go with the women to check on the Elders and children. Gather cloth and fresh water; you will need to help tend to our wounded." Already, he was turning to check on our men. I did as he asked. In our longhouse I found Kit standing at attention just inside the door. The children were playing and dancing, while a circle of Elders surrounded them. Their song was victorious, even sung in the soft, warbling voices of those who had seen many years and many battles. I went to Grandmother's side. Her eyes were closed, her face lost in deep wrinkles that had been laid there by seventy years of smiles. I sat beside her and took her soft hand in mine.

"It is over. We are safe, Grandmother."

"And you've fought to protect our home and our people. Both are now yours. Help me to gather dressings; we'll need to tend to our wounded warriors." She rose slowly from the bench. We went out into the bright sun where the tides continued to creep up the beach, taking the spilled blood of warriors with it. The air was heavy with its metallic smell. Our men were piling the bodies of the dead into their two remaining canoes. T'apjuu stood over the body of the man that I had killed with my arrow.

"I killed this man," I said, my eyes filling with tears.

"He wears the tunic of a Chief. They came to take our homes and our lives. You fought to protect our people." He brought his fingers to the blood pooling from the Chief's neck. Then he stood and faced me, drawing lines across my cheeks in blood. "Wear the blood of your kill with pride, Dahlia. He would have killed anyone here without a second thought."

"What will become of their tribe now?"

"They will be left with only the very young and very old, a whole generation erased. Without men to hunt and protect them they will likely die," he said, a pained look upon his face. "We've had a peace pact with this tribe for over one hundred years. The men were all thin and weak; I think that they were starving and attacked us out of desperation."

"There is no shortage of food here. Surely it is the same where they lived?" "The algae blooms have tainted the shellfish, and tribes that can't fish or find game go hungry. We don't own the ocean; if they had asked to fish these waters I would have allowed it. They chose instead to attack us," he finished, shaking his head trying to understand. I looked towards the two war canoes that were nearly full of the bodies of the dead.

"Will you tow their canoes back to their village so that the families might bury their dead?"

"That is not our way. There is no honor in being brought home by the enemy. We will sing for their spirits to find their way to the sky and then tow the canoes out to sea and set them ablaze." I nodded my understanding. Continuing, he said, "Tonight we will have a great fire. We will sing, dance and give thanks for all that we have." T'apjuu went to help the other men load the dead into canoes. I dropped to my knees and placed my hand on the Chief's back in apology. I had aimed my arrow at him to protect my people, but now felt a deep sadness for ending his life. I thought of his wife and children, scanning the seas as they awaited his return; a return that would never come. Fat tears fell from my eyes, and I struggled to swallow the lump that had formed in my throat.

"I'm so sorry," I whispered to the man.

"Another man slain by the mighty Dahlia." I whipped my head around to find Haana approaching. "You seem proud of your kill, wearing his blood upon your face," she said, her tone biting.

"I was defending our people. I was just apologizing to him," I said softly. Haana snorted in response.

"I'm sure your apology brings him great comfort. How many is that now? This man, the one that you killed with an axe. You seem prone to violence. How many more have there been?" I leapt to my feet at this, my tunic catching awkwardly on my belly, leaving it bare.

"Those are the only two. Two is more than enough," I snapped, pulling my tunic down to cover my swollen belly. Hanna's eyes followed my movements, pain clear on her face. I closed my eyes and inhaled deeply. I thought of T'apjuu's advice to not allow her to rile me, and my own desire to tell her how I felt.

"You think yourself sly, twisting my actions to fit your awful views of me. You are merely a snake in the grass, a coward boiling in your own jealousy."

"A coward?" she asked, incredulous. "I don't fear you."

"Perhaps not, but you fear our people seeing who you really are. Why else would you approach me only when I was alone?" I asked. Haana sputtered at this, her face reddening in frustration.

"You don't belong here," she said as she turned to walk away. "I'll be sure and warn T'apjuu to beware the next time we are alone. Who knows when you'll kill again." I forced a laugh in reply.

"You won't cause uncertainty between us," I said, raising my voice. "The only person that you will hurt is yourself. Leave us alone, Haana. Find another way to occupy your time." I said with a steady voice, though my blood was boiling at her implication that she would be alone with my husband. I watched Haana make her way towards the longhouses, and then turned to watch T'apjuu and the other men. I hoped I had shown her that I would not back down, and that she would grow tired of bothering me. That night we danced around a huge fire in celebration of our victory in battle. I still wore the blood of my kill, not yet with pride, but with acceptance.

***

Near the end of summer T'apjuu announced that he would be accompanying two of our men to his cousins' village on the big island. He would not stay for a month to help them trade as he had done in years past. Instead, the other men would help the tribe to trade. T'apjuu told me that he couldn't bear to be away from me for that long, especially with our child's birth nearing. Before he left, he gave me the canoe that he had built. He had it on the shore facing the bay, next to his own. I gasped as I approached it, and tears fell freely from my eyes. It was narrower and shorter than T'apjuu's, with a small eagle wrapped about the bow. A line of animals led from the bow, beginning in the sea, and ending on high peaks at the stern. There were orcas and otters, seals, and salmon. Backed by red cedar in profile were foxes, wolves and bears atop rocky peaks. Tiny flowers and ferns ran the length of the gunwale. As I drew nearer, I saw a single dahlia carved into the center seat. My hand covered my mouth, which hung agape. Stammering, I was unable to find words to express my appreciation for the beautiful gift. I ran my hand along each carving as I inhaled the heady scent of cedar.

"I couldn't settle on a single animal to carve. You are so connected to everything around you, so I decided to include them all on the canoe that will carry you across these waters. I hope that you like it." He wore a gentle smile, and his eyebrows were raised hopefully.

"Oh, T'apjuu! It is so beautiful, and I can see how much time and effort have gone into making it for me. How have I been so lucky to have you for my own? Will you take it out with me?" I said quickly, already dragging it to the water.

"Yes, of course I will," he laughed, racing to catch up with me. "Your balance might feel off because of the baby, but you'll find it in time." I hopped in without tipping the canoe, loud laughter escaping me. I knelt instead of sitting on the seat, bracing my knees against the sides before dipping the paddle that T'apjuu had carved to fit my height and hands. It cut silently into the water and sent me forward smoothly. I paddled faster, leaning into the wind. My hair flew behind me as I found my rhythm. I cut a clean line across the bay, exhilaration thrumming through every fiber of my being. I was free. T'apjuu knew better than to try and rein me in. He followed with a smile that took over his whole face. When my arms grew tired, I slowed and turned to face my husband.

"This is the most incredible thing that anyone has ever done for me. I will use it every single day." I grinned through my tears.

"I'm glad that you like it. Seeing you paddle it is worth every second that I spent making it. I'll race you to that island up ahead. We've got a bit of time before I have to leave for the big island," he said playfully as he began to paddle faster. I followed close behind and maneuvered my canoe easily to the shore. T'apjuu pulled my canoe onto the beach, and I followed him into the trees, eager for some time alone with this man whose tenderness somehow equaled his strength.

***

I spent the week that T'apjuu was away helping our people prepare for winter. Back on the farm, I had made similar preparations, but these were on a much grander scale. Every member of the tribe helped to collect berries and roots for drying, harvest potatoes, clean and hang fish, seal and deer meat, and pack oily candlefish into barrels. The food supply was not as seasonal on our island as it was in places that saw snow, but preparation was still completed every year. I wove fresh mats of cedar bark for our sleeping area, and a small bassinet with the help of my sisters. I lined it with the softest fur, my excitement about our baby growing each day. We were nearly done with preparations, and I had just packed my first barrel of candlefish one afternoon when Haana stalked towards me.

"That isn't how we do it. Those fish will spoil, and you will be responsible," she sneered.

"Our way is to teach, not to ridicule, Haana," Grandmother said as she approached slowly from behind. "I was coming to show Dahlia a better way, but you have chosen to criticize. You have caused shame for Dahlia, and still the fish will rot." Tilting her head, she said gently, "Can you see that this is not the best way?"

"She doesn't understand our culture," Haana snapped.

"Then teach her."

"It should have been me," she said, gesturing to my belly. "I was supposed to marry T'apjuu, and you stole him away." Haana brushed back angry tears.

"You drove T'apjuu away with your behavior long before he ever met Dahlia," Grandmother said, more strongly now, straightening her spine. Haana's fists were balled at her sides, and a deep groan escaped her lips before she lunged at me. Others had been drawn by the commotion and stopped her from attacking me. She continued to struggle against the arms that held her, tears of anger running down her cheeks.

"Can't you see what she is doing?" she screamed. "She took our Chief and is trying to change everything about our way of life!"

Stepping forward, our Storyteller said calmly, "I see a woman who has embraced our culture and our people and has made every attempt to belong. When I look at you, Haana, I see a woman filled with hatred."

Shaking his head, he continued, "Our people have faced many outside threats from missionaries and explorers, but Dahlia is not one of these threats. You cannot assume that every stranger that lands on our shores is an enemy." Grandmother had come to my side and smoothed my hair, her arms now wrapped protectively around my middle. I nodded my thanks to the Storyteller, took a deep breath to calm myself, and began to speak.

"My whole life I have sought the comfort of a society that shares my values and beliefs. While some of your beliefs are new to me, I have never felt more that I belonged somewhere than I have among your people." I paused to look Haana in the eyes, to make her understand me. "I have no desire to change the ways of your people, and I am comforted by the knowledge, Haana, that you will always fight fiercely to protect the people and lands that I have come to know as my family, my home." I was still shaking from the conflict, but my voice had remained even, confident. I walked towards Haana, and took her into my arms. At first, she resisted, but then she slumped into my embrace, sobbing. Those surrounding us were hushed, stealing glances at one another, but not speaking.

"I'm so sorry, Dahlia. I have treated you horribly since you arrived. I've lost myself; I need to call my spirits, find my way," Haana said in a strained voice, her head hung in shame. She walked away slowly, our Storyteller following behind to offer guidance.

"It takes a strong woman to remain calm when being attacked, and a gentle spirit to offer kindness in return. You have shown us all why T'apjuu chose you, Dahlia, and I am proud to call you my granddaughter," Grandmother said, beaming up at me. "Let's get back to your barrel of fish." I was shaking from the argument, but felt at peace with Haana. Something had shifted between us, and I knew that she would not bother me again.

***

I had promised T'apjuu that I would not go out in my canoe alone, and so I found someone to accompany me into the bay each day. Kit always hopped happily into my canoe and took her place at the bow. I paddled until my hair flew straight out behind me, the wind breathing more life into my body, though it already felt as if it were full to bursting. I met T'apjuu on the beach when he returned. He swept me into his arms and buried his face in my hair.

"You smell like the sea, Dahlia. I've missed you terribly; seven days is far too long to be away," he said softly.

"Yes, I've missed you too. I've been in my canoe every day. You should see how fast I can go now!" I pulled back, smiling at him. T'apjuu's smile faded when he saw me drop my eyes.

"Has something happened?" he asked.

"I'm fine. Haana's anger with me finally boiled over, but we've worked things out. We now understand each other a little better, and I think you'll find that she has a new outlook on things." Soothing him, I continued, "It's over as far as I'm concerned, and all is forgiven. I'm sure that you'll hear the story from someone else, but I won't be the one to tell it to you. Now, let's get your things inside."

Eager to move on, I helped T'apjuu carry his rolled bundles into the longhouse. He unrolled a fur, revealing Papa's sweater, my silky blue robe, and the large velvet bag containing the money from selling Mother's jewelry. He held Papa's sweater out to me, and I put it on. I felt the familiar warmth of the knit against my skin and felt Papa there with me. The sweater smelled of cedar, as it had likely been stored in a chest since it was retrieved from the sea captain's house. T'apjuu held up the blue robe.

"I've seen you wear this in my dreams. I can't wait to see it on you again," he smiled slyly. I picked up the velvet bag of money and buried it under my farm dress and boots in my large cedar chest. There was nothing that I needed, but I would keep it to buy supplies for our tribe if needed.

"Thank you for bringing my things, and for arranging for your cousin to fetch them all those months ago. Sometimes I think that you know me better than I know myself. And for that, I'll wear the robe every night," I said, pulling T'apjuu to me. After I had welcomed him home, he went off to find the Elders so that he might get caught up on what had happened in his absence. He found me an hour later, a pained look on his face.

"I've heard what Haana has done. I've also heard the kindness with which you met her attack. You have impressed the Elders, and me."

"As I said, all is forgiven. I saw a woman who was hurting. I could have met her aggression, but what she needed was love."

"You may have forgiven Haana, but amends need to be made. She will hold a shame Potlatch, and give you her belongings as well as gifts of service." T'apjuu paused and took my hands in his. "I must also make amends. I did not see how Haana was causing you pain and worry. I did not protect you, and advised you to ignore her. I shouldn't have avoided confronting her because it was uncomfortable for me. I'm sorry, Dahlia."

"I think we have both learned something, and I accept your apology. I don't want Haana to give me her things, I already have all that I need. I don't want to shame her."

"It is our way. She will do these things in order to be rid of her shame. To refuse her gifts would deny her that chance," T'apjuu finished.

A few weeks later Haana held her Potlatch. She gave me buttery soft hides, beautifully woven baskets, carved wooden bowls, and my own seal skin tunic and slatted armor to wear in battle. In addition to these gifts she would share her seaweed and clam harvests with me for one year. It was uncomfortable for me to accept her gifts, but I saw the importance of the tradition. I sat near the fire, warming my hands when Haana approached.

"I hope that we can begin again, on better footing."

"We can. Thank you for all of the beautiful gifts that you have given me."

"It was an honor to give them. I hope that you will not need the battle armor, I intended it to be a reminder. Every time that you put it on I want you to know that you *do* belong here," Haana said with conviction. We sat and watched the fire, content in the knowledge that debts had been repaid, and we had been given the chance to start anew.

***

I had buried Papa two years ago under October's full Hunter's moon. We welcomed our first son under the same moon. The women of my family had tended to me during my labor and had shooed T'apjuu away once my waters had broken. He paced nervously outside of the longhouse as the moon made its way across the night sky. Inside, the women rubbed my back, gave me sips of tea and broth, wiped sweat from my brow, and sang over me. They had allowed T'apjuu to come to my side when I began pushing, on his insistence. I saw fear and worry on his face for the first time as I labored to bring our child into the world. He confessed later that it was very hard for him to watch me suffer, and not be able to ease my pain.

A beautiful boy emerged with my final push, his lusty cry music to my ears. Grandmother laid him on my belly and rubbed him vigorously with a cloth. I brought him to my breast, and he suckled as he stared up at me with eyes of blue-green hazel. T'apjuu cried without shame, overjoyed by the precious boy that I held tight to me. We named him Arlo James, for Papa. In the language of our people, we named him GaysiiGas, which means "*calm water between rough waves.*" We would have three more sons, followed by a daughter, just like Inga had. All were loved beyond measure.

We would live mostly in peace, for a time at least. After some years new enemies would land on our shores. They did not wear armor and carry weapons, and they did not announce their intentions with drums and war cries. Instead, robes were their armor, and they were armed with Bibles and a deep-seated intolerance for anything not found in those pages. They were determined to erase the culture and traditions practiced here for thousands of years, but that is a story for another day. Today I have a large, healthy family. I have the love and devotion of the most incredible man that I have ever known. I want for nothing and no longer feel compelled to roam. I am home.

Epilogue

Couple Strikes It Rich In Goldrush, Builds Grandest Home In Vancouver

Mr. and Mrs. Leonard and Fiona Williams did what thousands of others have dreamt of: they amassed a large fortune panning for gold. Mr. and Mrs. Williams, originally of Toronto and Philadelphia, respectively, found no gold in eight months on their first claim on the Klondike River. Their second claim was much more fruitful, producing the largest nugget ever found, weighing 4.8 lbs. They found many more over the next three months and have returned to Vancouver to build a grand home with some of their considerable fortune. When asked what they plan to do once their home is completed, Mrs. Williams emphatically replied, "We'll fill it with children, of course!"

Master tilers are slated to lay the Italian marble floors this week, and the landscapers have already begun planting the gardens. Mrs. Williams reports that they will be "bursting with dahlias, in honor of the best friend that I've ever had…" (story continued on page 4).

***

Dearest Inga,

I've disappeared, as I once dreamt that I might. I did not climb straight up a mountain, rather sailed into the ocean. I am wed to the kindest man, a great leader who is gentle with my heart. To use Papa's words: he is the one who sets my heart on fire. We are expecting our first child in the autumn, and I am happy beyond anything that I dared to hope for. I am home.

I hope that you and your family are healthy and happy. I think of you often and miss you always. Please send word to Willy that I am well.

With love,

Dahlia

The End

Acknowledgments

Writing may be a solitary pursuit, but writing well is most certainly not. I was fortunate to have several early readers that followed along as I wrote. My mom (Jill McCaughey), mother-in-law (Eileen Bothner), sisters (Meg and Molly Lowe), dear friend (Cynthia Miadonye), and lifelong family friend (Dean Romfo VanCamp) were all invaluable throughout the writing process. Their keen eyes, thoughtful responses to each chapter and excitement for the next one kept me going when I felt like I was in over my head. My dad (Jeff Lowe) inspired Papa's character. Dad, thank you for instilling in me a deep love of nature, a reverence for Indigenous culture and a fondness for cozy sweaters. My deepest thanks to each of you for the care with which you approached my first draft, and the kindness with which you delivered your suggestions.

Hawaa *thank you* to the people of Haida Gwaii First Nation, whose land, culture, and incredible history inspired me. Hawaa *thank you* to SGaana Gaahlandaay *Alix Goetzinger* for your thorough and thoughtful responses to my many questions, and for sharing your love of Haida history with me. I am certain that you brought a depth to the last few chapters that I could not have created on my own.

And finally, my deepest thanks to my husband (Eric Bothner) for the gentle push in the direction of my dreams, for being gentle with my heart, and steady when I am not. For my sons (Chase and Cameron): the grace and perseverance with which you face your own struggles have inspired me more than you know.

Author's Note

This story had been running around in my head for five years when I finally sat down to write it. I wrote scenes as they came to me, jotting down descriptions of characters and landscapes when I felt inspired. I live on the Alberta Prairies at the foot of the Rocky Mountains, so inspiration is never far away. As my notebook filled up, I realized that I might have the makings of a novel. I was compelled to write about things like scarcity, the appalling treatment of Indigenous Peoples, arbitrary social rules, and the struggles of mental illness. These issues are as relevant today as they were in the 1890's, and I hope that they resonated with you.

This is a work of fiction, but I made every effort to remain true to the period in which my story occurred. In some instances, I chose to keep aspects that were not entirely accurate. For example, rapeseed (now called canola) was not planted in Alberta until the 1950's, but Dahlia describes seeing fields of it from atop a mountain. I cannot think of the Prairies without seeing vast fields of shocking yellow canola, and I wanted you to see it too. I did not name the town near Dahlia's farm, as I wanted each reader to imagine a rural setting near to them, a haven within reach. Cathedral Grove on Vancouver Island did not carry that name in the 1890's, but I used it because it perfectly describes the hush and suggestion of something Divine that strikes you when you enter those woods.

I took many liberties in my creation of the islands and culture that Dahlia makes her home among. T'apjuu's tribe was heavily inspired by the great Haida People. By 1898 Haida Gwaii had been deeply impacted by colonization, but unlike the Haida, I had the luxury of keeping the culture and traditions intact for the purpose of my story. I was truly fortunate to have the help of SGaana Gaahlandaay *Alix Goetzinger,* a Haida writer. She helped me to describe the land and seascape, and gave me details about Potlatch, house poles, traditional foods, as well as fitting names for my characters.

I hope that I have piqued your interest in Haida Gwaii, and that you will spend some time getting lost in its incredible history, as I did. You will not be disappointed; looking at photos of the beautiful art and war canoes was enough to reduce me to tears. Thank you, dear reader, for allowing me to lead you on this journey. I hope that you enjoyed reading it as much as I enjoyed writing it.

Manufactured by Amazon.ca
Bolton, ON